"A gripping, haunting exploration of the lengths to which we'll go to belong, *Half Past* will hold you in its thrall until the very last page. Stone's expert storytelling, vivid characterizations, and tantalizing dropping of clues left me utterly breathless, longing for more—and a newly minted Victoria Helen Stone fan!"

—Emily Carpenter, bestselling author of *Burying the Honeysuckle Girls* and *The Weight of Lies*

"A captivating, suspenseful tale of love and lies, mystery and self-discovery, *Half Past* kept me flipping the pages through the final, startling twist."

—A. J. Banner, #1 Kindle and *USA Today* bestselling author of *The Good Neighbor* and *The Twilight Wife*

"What would you do if you found out that your mother wasn't your biological mother? Would you go looking for the answer to how that happened if she couldn't provide an explanation? That's the intriguing question at the heart of *Half Past*, Stone's strong follow-up to *Evelyn, After*. [It's] both a mystery and an exploration of what family really means. Fans of Jodi Picoult will race through this."

—Catherine McKenzie, bestselling author of *Hidden* and *The Good Liar*

"Stone does a masterful job of creating in Jane a complex character, making her both scary and more than a little appealing . . . This beautifully balanced thriller will keep readers tense, surprised, pleased, and surprised again as a master manipulator unfolds her plan of revenge."

—*Kirkus Reviews* (starred review)

"Revenge drives this fascinating thriller . . . Stone keeps the suspense high throughout. Readers will relish Jane's Machiavellian maneuvers to even the score with the unlikable Steven."

—*Publishers Weekly*

"Crafty, interesting, and vengeful."

—NovelGossip

"Crazy great book!"

—*Good Life Family* magazine

"Stone skillfully, deviously and gleefully leads the reader down a garden path to a knockout WHAM-O of an ending. *Jane Doe* will not disappoint."

—New York Journal of Books

"*Jane Doe* is a riveting, engrossing story about a man who screws over the wrong woman, with a picture-perfect ending that's the equivalent of a big red bow on a shiny new car. It's that good. Ladies, we finally have the revenge story we've always deserved."

—Criminal Element

"Jane, the self-described sociopath at the center of Victoria Helen Stone's novel, [is] filling a hole in storytelling that we've long been waiting for."

—Bitch Media

"We loved being propelled into the complicated mind of Jane, intrigued as she bobbed and weaved her way through life with the knowledge she's just a little bit different. You'll be debating whether to make Jane your new best friend or lock your door and hide from her in fear. Both incredibly insightful and tautly suspenseful, *Jane Doe* is a must-read!"

—Liz Fenton and Lisa Steinke, bestselling authors of *The Good Widow*

"With biting wit and a complete disregard for societal double standards, Victoria Helen Stone's antihero will slice a path through your expectations and leave you begging for more. Make room in the darkest corner of your heart for Jane Doe."

—Eliza Maxwell, bestselling author of *The Unremembered Girl*

"If revenge is a dish best served cold, Jane Doe is Julia Child. Though Jane's a heroine who claims to be a sociopath, Jane's heart and soul shine through in this addicting, suspenseful tale of love, loss, and justice."

—Wendy Webb, bestselling author of *The End of Temperance Dare*

"One word: wow. This novel is compelling from the first sentence. An emotional ride with a deliciously vengeful narrator, Jane's tale keeps readers on the edge without the security of knowing who the good guy really is. Honest, cutting, and at times even humorous, this is one powerhouse of a read!"

—Brandi Reeds, bestselling author of *Trespassing*

FALSE STEP

"[A] cleverly plotted thriller . . . Danger and savage emotions surface as [Veronica] discovers that she's not the only one whose life is built on secrets and lies. Stone keeps the reader guessing to the end."

—*Publishers Weekly*

"Intense and chilling, *False Step* wickedly rewards thriller fans with a compulsive read that'll leave readers wondering how well they know their loved ones. I was riveted!"

—Kerry Lonsdale, Amazon Charts and *Wall Street Journal* bestselling author

PROBLEM CHILD

ALSO BY VICTORIA HELEN STONE

Evelyn, After
Half Past
Jane Doe
False Step

PROBLEM CHILD

A JANE DOE THRILLER

VICTORIA HELEN STONE

LAKE UNION
PUBLISHING

Text copyright © 2020 by Victoria Helen Stone
All rights reserved.

No part of this book may be reproduced, or stored in a retrieval system, or transmitted in any form or by any means, electronic, mechanical, photocopying, recording, or otherwise, without express written permission of the publisher.

Published by Lake Union Publishing, Seattle

www.apub.com

Amazon, the Amazon logo, and Lake Union Publishing are trademarks of Amazon.com, Inc., or its affiliates.

ISBN-13: 9781542014397
ISBN-10: 1542014395

Cover design by Faceout Studios, Derek Thornton

Printed in the United States of America

PROBLEM CHILD

CHAPTER 1

He's in my office again, bothering me. It bothers me just to look at him, but it particularly bothers me when he speaks, and Rob speaks a lot, plumped up on mediocre male confidence and throbbing, virile ego. He's the partners' favorite, so until I take care of him, I have to play it as nicely as I can. But when we're alone, I don't pretend. I turn dead eyes on him and stare as he prattles.

"Regardless of all that," he says, continuing whatever train of thought I've blocked out, "you did a pretty good job with this one, Jane."

"I did a great job," I counter.

"Like I said, pretty good. I'll turn over the final numbers to—"

"I already sent the final numbers to the partners, with appropriate credit where it was due. It's all taken care of. Thanks, Robert. You can go."

He blinks, spun into confusion by being casually dismissed. "Excuse me?"

"I took care of the details. Wasn't that what you told me to do, Robert? 'Take care of the details'? I sent the wrap-up email to the partners so you wouldn't have to bother with it. You're welcome."

He shakes his head. "What? *When?*"

"Oh no, did I forget to cc you? I guess I was tired from all those late hours last week. I'll be sure to forward it right now." I smile and hit a few keys on my laptop. The original email wings its way to his account. I also forward the praise-filled responses from two of the founding partners of the law firm, along with my enthusiastic and upbeat thank-yous. Rob can respond now, of course, but he'll still be the guy who stumbled up an hour after all the action, trying to get a leftover piece. A mere postscript. Poor Rob.

He's staring at me. I cut my narrowed eyes toward him. "Is there something else you need?"

Rob has been outmaneuvered and he knows it, but he can't reasonably assume it was anything but helpful gumption on my part. His stupid little lipless hole of a mouth bubbles open and closed like he's a goldfish. *Pop, pop.*

The trill of my phone cuts off his shocked bubbling. "Oh, I'd better get this. Thank you so much for coming by, Robert. And hey, good job."

His eyes widen at the indignity of being praised by someone lower on the ladder, as if I've snuck up the rungs and peed on his head in passing. "I'll see you at the meeting later." I wink as I say hello into the receiver.

"There's a woman calling for you," the receptionist intones in a voice that's a strange combination of chirpy and depressed. She's an odd, forlorn bird. "She says it's about your niece."

My niece? Luke has a niece, but I don't. Well, I do, actually. Three of them. Could be four by now if my brother got even one moment out of jail between sentences last year, but I don't know any of them.

"Send her to voice mail."

"She says it's important."

"Voice mail is fine." I hang up and find I am blessedly alone. A new email arrives. It's Rob responding at long last to the partners' praise. Tsk, tsk, Robert. Not very responsible.

Mid-grin, I realize it's almost lunchtime, and I'm instantly famished. I woke up this morning craving the lobster ravioli at a restaurant two blocks from my downtown law office, and I hop up from my seat with a watering mouth and a simply fantastic idea.

"Robert!" I call across the hallway. His office faces mine, but we don't face each other. He has his desk angled for privacy so he can look like he's hard at work even when he's trolling Tinder. I have mine near the door so I can watch every move in the hallway and eavesdrop on office gossip.

When I pop into his doorway, he's scowling, still irritated with me. "Let me take you to lunch!" I exclaim, making bright eyes at him.

His gaze narrows at this shift. I smile wider. "As a thank-you for guiding me through this negotiation. What a bear, huh?"

The truth is this contract was nothing I haven't managed before, and negotiations were made more difficult by Rob's brotastic style. But now he's blinking and off-balance. I lean back and wave at the receptionist, who's glancing over her shoulder toward me. She waves in return.

"Come on," I urge, sticking my head back into Rob's office like we're co-conspirators. "A celebration!"

"Uh, yeah," he finally answers. "Yeah, sure."

"I've been craving Camille's all day. That time of month, you know." He winces a little at the hint of bodily functions. I wink in return, which seems to help him recover. It's a lie, of course. I control my body with ruthless efficiency with nonstop birth control pills.

"Camille's sounds great," he says tentatively. "Thanks for the offer."

"Are you ready? We'd better not dawdle. We've got that meeting at two."

"Let's go." He grabs a slim-cut peacoat and a tastefully masculine cashmere scarf to ward off the slight chill of the cool September afternoon, but then he just drapes the scarf over the lapels, which won't ward off anything except dandruff. I snag my purse and a new red raincoat from my office and bounce happily toward the door. The receptionist, Amy, looks woefully cheerful at this scene of camaraderie.

I'm so hungry.

As we step into the elevator, I ask Rob about another case, and that flips the switch to get him talking again. So much talking. An embarrassment of talking, because he knows so much, our Rob. So much, and all I can do is soak it in and learn. I've been at the firm for a year now and I've become a crucial member of the team, the point man, so to speak, on international contract negotiations. But I'm a woman, so I will always still have so much to learn.

He begins to explain a complicated contract between an American car parts company and a Vietnamese manufacturer, because he's forgotten that I helped the firm hammer out the details during my first month on the job. "These guys were unbelievable," he says. "They were hoping the trade war meant they could—"

But I'm thinking about lobster ravioli and the restaurant's famous warm bread, which they serve with salted butter. Mmm.

The day is colder than it looks; an early arctic front has dipped down from Canada to bring a shiver to the sunny day, and I love it. No more buzzing mosquitoes. And no buzzing lithe-limbed girls wearing tiny shorts as they try to flirt with my boyfriend. Try and fail.

I have the sex drive of a woman who's unable to process shame or self-consciousness, so their buzzing is a mere annoyance. I keep him very busy. But I've never had a real boyfriend before, so I sometimes find it hard to control my temper when I see them trying to steal what's mine. *Mine.* Those little girls are easy to scare off with an icy-eyed hiss, and if that doesn't work, there's always a well-timed foot to trip them up on their way past the table. Still, I'm satisfied that they'll have to put their ass cheeks away for a few months now. Buttocks are a summer accessory this far north in the world.

We're walking toward my condo—the restaurant is halfway between my office and the home I share with my cat—so I'm on familiar turf as Rob continues explaining shit I already know.

My place of work is biased toward men, as most law firms are. If I were still in my twenties, I'd have already slept with one of the married partners and leveraged that into a fast track, because why not? There's only one female partner out of eight at this firm, and I've heard several of the men make secret, snide comments about her "time off." Her time off was to have a baby and then recover from massive hemorrhaging during the birth, and that was three full years ago. They can't seem to understand why she wasn't smart enough to simply marry a woman and get that female to stay home and whelp progeny the way they did.

That's why Rob is their current favorite for becoming partner. No maternity leave, and no paternity leave for that broseph either. He's only been married for two years, and even though they have no children, his wife still stays home. "She's an amazing girl," he says reverently. Also, he's screwing the mournful receptionist on the side. I wonder if she sounds sad when she comes.

Just kidding. I'm sure he never bothers to get her off.

When we arrive at the restaurant, I grab the door and hold it open for Rob. "After you," I offer cheerfully.

"Why, thank you, sir," he responds.

"Would you get a table? I need to run to the restroom." I leave him behind, no doubt horrified at my menstrual needs, and I saunter to the bathroom to reapply my favorite red lipstick and make kissy faces at myself in the mirror. When I emerge, I head straight for the nearly empty bar.

"One white wine spritzer, please. And a double of High West Bourye on the rocks."

The bartender looks gray and tired despite the fact that he's only about forty. If I had to guess, I'd say he has a little pill problem and he'd rather be anywhere but here on a Thursday afternoon. He doesn't even raise an eyebrow at my twenty-five-dollar order of whiskey; he just pours it out and slides it over, along with my spritzer. "Put a couple of cherries in the spritzer," I suggest, which finally prompts a reaction, a disgusted wince as he drops two cherries into my glass. He throws in an orange slice too, so I add an extra dollar to the tip. My drink is practically health food now.

"Cheers!" I exclaim as I slide into the booth Rob has chosen at the front window.

"Whoa." His mouth crooks down a little when he sees the drinks in my hands, but I push his toward him and pretend not to notice.

"The High West," I drawl, and the downturn of his mouth changes into a smile.

"Wow, that's quite a treat!"

"I remembered that you like it."

Rob has never looked at me as a sexual conquest before. I'm assertive and nearly plain, and as far as I can tell, he likes his girls superhot and pliable. But my admission that I've paid attention to his wants and needs softens his face a little. His eyelids dip in a lazy blink. "Thank you very much, Jane. I didn't expect this."

I clink my ostentatiously girly drink against his glass and we each take a sip. I hum with pleasure as the bubbles touch my tongue. Wine spritzers are fucking delicious, and I have no idea why they ever fell out of fashion. I fish a cherry out of the glass and beam. "Let's order. I'm starving!"

We place our orders with a cheerful young man with an Ethiopian accent, and when the bread arrives, I'm ecstatic. "Another round!" I insist, gesturing at our drinks.

"That's a terrible idea," Rob protests, but when his twenty-five-dollar drink arrives, he can't just let it sit there, can he? Eyes slightly wide, he gamely finishes the last sip from his first tumbler and moves it toward the edge of the table.

"This is really nice," I say.

He cocks his head as if he's trying to puzzle something out. "Yeah, it *is* nice, isn't it?" Do I want to get in his pants? Have I wanted that all along and that's why I've been so prickly and difficult? I can see him reasoning it out and relaxing into the explanation. It's really the only thing that makes sense, after all. He's *Rob*. Everyone loves Rob, and a plain Jane like me must be more susceptible to his charms than most would be.

Cheeks flushed, he lounges back into the high cushions of the leather booth, a knowing smile on his face as the waiter delivers our meals. Rob has ordered a sensible lunch of baked sole and steamed veggies. I ordered the dinner portion of lobster ravioli, and it's even bigger than I remember.

"Oh God," I sigh as I take my first bite. "That's so good." I groan as the taste sinks in.

Rob chuckles. "Looks like it's very exciting."

"Oh, it is. Have you ever had this?"

He shakes his head, and I lean into the table in excitement. "You have to taste it. It's better than sex." I cut a ravioli in half—no way am I losing a whole ravioli to Rob—and spear it. As I hold it toward his mouth, I imitate what I've seen other people do, parting my lips and darting out my tongue as if I'm reaching for a bite too.

He doesn't really care about sex with me. I'm not his type. But he understands this interaction. I can see his confidence grow as he chews, his eyes warming with the knowledge that he can finally get me in line. He grins and nods. He is in his element and he's no longer thinking that he really shouldn't have this much whiskey at a pre-meeting lunch.

"Isn't it amazing?" I whisper.

"It's very, very nice," he concedes, smiling indulgently as he chews. "I like it."

"Me too." I leave the rest of my spritzer until half my dish is gone, but Rob is tipsy enough that he's forgetting how to pace himself, and the man hasn't ordered nearly enough fat and calories.

7

By the time I order one last round of drinks for dessert, he's drunk and he's lost all sight of vulnerability and any hint of wisdom. Why shouldn't he have another drink? He's a goddamn successful lawyer on his way to making partner, and he's a man, damn it. A big man with a wife at home and a piece on the side, and one more ballbuster making eyes at him over lunch too. He's a king among men, and he's never lost at anything.

He accepts the final drink and raises it high. "To another great deal."

"Thank you," I respond, taking full credit. I deserve it.

Rob is a showboat, and he reflects the light of better lawyers off his shiny facade, recycling their knowledge and taking all the praise. The first few times we worked together, I kept my mouth shut, because I was still learning the delicate intricacies that make up the web of politics in this office. But I know them now. It will take me a couple of years to even be considered for partner, but they won't notice me at all with Rob glinting into their eyes all the damn time.

"I've got this," I say when the bill comes. I've spent almost eighty bucks on whiskey this afternoon and I don't regret one penny. "I owe you for everything you've taught me this year, Robert. What a ride it's been."

"Anything you need, Jane," he drawls with a wink. "Your work is really coming along."

I worked on the legal team of an international conglomerate in Kuala Lumpur for five years. Rob worked for a furniture manufacturing group in St. Paul before he started here. He can kiss my ass and thank me for the privilege as far as I'm concerned.

"I've got those final numbers you asked for on the North Unlimited proposal," I say, reminding him of the meeting we're heading into.

"Good. Good job. I'll stop by and grab them when we get back."

"Yeah. That'll give you half an hour to learn what I know so you can steal the show."

His flushed face crumples for a brief moment. "What?"

I giggle as if I've just made a silly joke. "I get so nervous before these big client meetings."

His lizard brain prompts a slow blink, sensing the danger of what I said a moment ago, but his ego wins out and he grins at my tipsy giggling. I dare to reach out and touch his hand as if I'm feeling naughty after the spritzers.

I *am* feeling naughty, but it's not the spritzers. It's the power. His defenses are down and his confidence is up, and I could make anything happen right now. I could tell him my condo is right around the corner, confess that I've thought about him while I touch myself in bed at night. That idea is practically lesbian porn for this future business leader of America. I could get him back to my place and compromised within a few minutes.

Or I could hit RECORD on my phone as we walk and ask him whether the mournful receptionist is a good lay and whether her breasts are as nice as they look under sweaters. He's drunk enough to brag about it, and then I'd have him under my thumb, his job and his marriage in danger.

Really, I don't understand why people don't record more conversations in life. Is there any downside?

But I don't need to work that hard this time around, risking animosity and accusation. And I don't need to put my current relationship on the line by letting this boy wonder touch me. He deserves a much lazier approach.

Rob doesn't sway or stumble as we walk back toward the office, but he looks confused whenever he stops talking. Not that he stops talking much. He carries on loudly, talking about his wife, of all things. How great she is. How beautiful. The trip she took to India to learn advanced yoga and meditation. How much she loves cooking. He brags about the blog she hosts on positivity.

She sounds like a goddamn nightmare, but she does have a great ass, I'll give her that. I've been to her Instagram, and she's definitely positive about how she looks in pink Lululemon pants.

"Can I tell you a secret?" Rob practically shouts.

"Oh, please do," I prompt.

"Savannah might be pregnant. She's taking a test tonight. She's been taking the vitamins for months, laying off wine. Just in case."

"Wow. That's cool. But you have to get sperm involved too. The vitamins alone won't do it."

"Yeah," he answers, his eyes bright with some far-off vision. Then he shakes off his joy and frowns. "What?"

"Nothing. Congrats. Sounds like everything is really lining up for you. And you definitely deserve it all."

"Thanks, Jane."

"My pleasure, Robert."

"It's Rob," he corrects absentmindedly for about the fiftieth time this year.

"I know."

When we reach our building, he pushes the glass doors open with way too much force, and one of them clangs against the discreet rubber stopper with a gong that echoes through the atrium. Faces turn. He doesn't notice.

"I'm going to run to the bathroom," I say as he moves toward the elevators. "I need to piss like crazy."

He wrinkles his nose at the crude words. Savannah would never say anything that gross. She'll make such a great mom.

I give Rob a little wave and head toward the lobby bathrooms. "See you in a few!"

I take my time. I pee and wash my hands. Check my teeth for lunch remnants. Reapply the crimson lipstick. Smooth down my dark-brown bob. Then I dab a little moisturizer on my hands and slowly rub it in.

The meeting starts in thirty minutes, but I've already prepared, so there's no rush. In fact, I pop back outside to grab a coffee.

I've worn my power suit today, not that Rob noticed. It's dark charcoal gray, nearly black, with a subtle red pinstripe that matches my mouth. The skirt is knee length and tight, hugging my hips and pointing the eye down to my scarlet heels. I feel like the queen of the world as I ride the elevator back up with my mocha latte and all the notes I memorized last night so I wouldn't need to write them down.

The meeting starts in five minutes. I log into Google Docs using Rob's name and password. All that teamwork we put in together means I know all of his passwords. Well. There's only one. He uses the same one to access his laptop and unlock documents and log into Google. It's *Rob#1in2017.*

I'm not kidding. He could at least update the year every once in a while.

"Jane." Rob is leaning against the doorjamb of my office, a coffee cup in hand, his eyes bleary. "Did you get those last numbers on district budgets?"

"Yeah, I'll just chime in when you get to that part, no problem."

"Great."

He dips back into his office to grab his laptop. I leave the first page of notes for the meeting intact so everything will look normal for Rob when he opens the document; then I handwrite a few critical details on my notepad before deleting pages two to four of the shared document. Rob is heading down the hall when I log him off Google and stand up to join the fun.

Here we go!

We met the client before, but this time there's a whole team of people in attendance, faces open with possibility. I shine as bright as I can, shaking hands all around as I'm introduced as one of the lawyers helping with this project. I glow with friendliness.

Rob, on the other hand, is glowing with whiskey fumes. It's not a subtle alcohol, and I can see eyes dart toward him as he weaves in and out of the gathering. Jesus Christ, Rob, it's 2:00 p.m. on a Thursday! Control yourself!

He shakes every hand in the room before taking a seat near the two partners in attendance. I fade into the background at a far corner of the conference table. I'm dressed to impress, sure, but no one likes a woman who shows off. So I become modesty incarnate, zipping my lips and smiling benignly at everyone and no one. I fade the way I used to watch my best friend fade, making myself smaller and easier to swallow.

But Rob's glow intensifies, blooming from his pink, flushed cheeks. "I guess I'll start things off," he booms, his too-loud words shaking my eardrums as they settle over the table. "It's great to finally meet everyone in person after all those email exchanges."

The two partners glance at each other before turning to stare at Rob. Why is he taking control of the meeting?

One of them clears his throat. "Yes, welcome, everyone," he says, his words half the volume of Rob's as he steps in. "Let's get down to business. As you know, you asked us to put out some feelers about additional buyers for your imported supply of premium chicken products after your success with the state prison system. What we've found is that the contract possibilities are incredibly promising . . ."

The partner continues his spiel, but I'm focused on Rob. He dabs a drop of sweat from his temple as he stares at his open laptop. Frowning, his eyes creased with concentration, he keeps trying to scroll down on something on his screen, but it doesn't seem to work.

I watch him click a couple of things and then click and click again. Another sweat drop forms and a wave of shivery pleasure laps at my gut, easing higher until my nipples tighten.

"Rob?" I hear someone say, and he and I both realize at the same moment that he's been asked a question.

"Uh," he replies. "Yes?"

"Rob, the numbers." It's no longer a question but a demand. The partner nearest Rob, Jeremy Browning, who's distinguishable from the other silverbacks by his retro black-rimmed glasses, is turning nearly as pink as Rob now. He must be breathing in Rob's whiskey fumes. A vein in his temple begins to throb, slowly but surely. Approachable glasses aside, Jeremy is known for his quick temper.

"Right," Rob finally says. "The numbers. As you know . . ." That's all he says, *As you know . . .* , instinctively repeating a phrase used moments before by one of his bosses. That's his whole shtick. Mirror the partners and make junior associates do the real work.

It's not hard for him to fit in with the senior guys. He's so easy to get along with, and there's none of the tiptoeing you have to do with the female or minority employees. God, they're all so prickly. But not good old Rob. He's just more . . . *comfortable* to be around.

"As you know," he repeats; then he clears his throat and tries to get it together with a fierce glance in my direction. I smile.

"As you know, our calculations show there are a shit-ton of fantastic opportunities for you right now."

Jeremy Browning blinks. Several times.

"Quite a few of the entities we approached were very interested in the high value and low cost that you're offering." He frowns again. "All three of the largest school systems in the state . . ."

The client clears his throat.

"Sorry," Rob says, "I do have the numbers right here."

Others in the room are beginning to shift and squirm. The whole client team looks toward the partners. They look toward each other. I wait a few more seconds. Then a few more.

"Pardon the interruption," I say, just as Mr. Browning is tensing to open his mouth. "Robert and I ran the numbers, and we're predicting district cost savings of over fifteen percent just on frozen processed chicken alone. Frozen raw chicken? Well, that gets even better, and, believe me, the school districts we approached were *very* excited."

I flash a smile at the table and dip my head toward Rob. "I apologize, I don't have Robert's notes, but let me sum up the numbers for you on the board." I stand and spin to the whiteboard behind me, snatching up a pen to immediately start jotting down the costs I've memorized along with the offers we've predicted we could pitch for years one through three.

"These are just rough estimates, of course. We can move forward with a deep dive before negotiations begin, but we all agree that North Unlimited is offering an ideal arrangement, and of course everyone is looking to cut costs, especially in non–education-related expenses. Reduced school funding only works toward your advantage in this environment. I even got a hint of interest from the state college system."

"Whoa," the president of North Unlimited breathes. "That would be unbelievable."

It *is* unbelievable, because this is absolutely untrue, but who could know that? Four weeks from now, if anyone asks, I'll glumly inform them that it didn't work out.

"Obviously, the laws governing raw chicken imports create quite a complication, but that's why you've hired us. So . . . do you think your supplier in Brazil could handle an order increase of three hundred percent? Because those are the kind of numbers we're looking at."

"Absolutely." His supplier isn't really in Brazil and the owner of North Unlimited is a goddamn scammer, but what do I care?

"So this should be our starting point with the first school districts," I finish, poking the marker hard into the board. "You've indicated that we can afford to budge quite a bit from here, but I'm not sure we'll have to. They're excited by your assurances about the product being all-natural and minimally processed at that price point." I swing back to smile at the clients. "We can definitely open with a two-year contract. What do you think?"

I don't care what they think, of course, just like I'm not actually sorry for interrupting good old Rob. But I need to be likable as well as capable and confident. What a tightrope.

The room has relaxed, thrilled that someone stepped in to avert disaster. Rob is slumped into a loose lump of puzzlement on the other side of the table, thinking, *What just happened?*

The clients jump in with questions. I answer most of them, though I bite my tongue occasionally to let others at the table share in the triumph. We've got ourselves a plan now, and there's profit to be had by all.

Half an hour later, I'm the one shaking hands with everyone in the room as they file out, though Rob has rallied enough to make a game effort of it. Still, quite a few people manage to slip by him with eyes locked on the doorway and hands occupied. The partners don't bother avoiding his eyes. They clap my shoulder and say good job, and then they walk past him with lips curled.

"Thanks, Robert," I say as I breeze through the door, the last to leave him standing there. "I'll type up a summary of the details we covered and cc you on it. Don't worry."

"Oh," I hear him murmur behind me. "Yeah, great."

He won't be fired, though once I start dropping hints about him and the mournful receptionist, he might become too much of a liability to keep around. But for now his job is safe; he's just lost his golden-boy shine, and I've stolen it to rub all over myself.

Jane really saved the day, stepping in like that. Did you see her pull those numbers out of the air? What an asset she is in times like these.

Good old unflappable Jane.

I leave the door of my office open so I can catch snatches of conversation from the hallway as people buzz by. Rob closes his door with a hollow *thunk* that shivers over my excited nerves.

Grinning, I get out my phone to send a text. Meet me for a drink at The Train Car? 5:30?

Yes, he responds immediately.

They have individual bathrooms there. We can go in together and lock the door. ☺

Luke is a nice, quiet guy. Modest and kind. But I can get him to do anything. I make him nervous, but he feels alive, and isn't that what really matters?

I hope it is, because that's all I've got.

CHAPTER 2

The problem with having sex early in the evening is that it frees up too many hours for things like talking. This is my first committed relationship, and it's the thing I hate most about it, that moment when he says "Jane . . ." in that serious tone.

"Nope," I respond.

Luke looks startled by that and twists on the couch to face me more fully. "Pardon?"

"Nope," I repeat.

"But I didn't ask anything."

"Well, I'm reading."

"Oh." He pauses for only a moment before trying again. "I just wanted to talk about something with you while we have the time."

I don't have the time. I'm in the middle of a book, and I just said that. But if I push him off now, he'll bring it up later when I'm trying to fall asleep, and that will be even worse. I'll say something that hurts his feelings because I'm tired and not being careful.

Then again, even if he brings it up later, I could distract him with sex because he'll be fully recovered.

But I've hesitated too long, and Luke takes that as acceptance. "We've been dating for a year now, and it's been great."

Well, here it is. This is why I hate talking. It never leads to anything good, like food or sex or action movies. It leads to this: Luke is breaking up with me.

I've known it would come eventually. I'm not the marrying type. I'm not even the girlfriend type, because I have a kind of . . . disability. I'm not capable of experiencing a full range of emotion, and most emotions I can't pull off at all, but that's not my fault.

That's the thing no one wants to acknowledge about sociopaths. It's not my fault. I didn't choose this.

But whether or not I can feel sympathy or tenderness or true, genuine love, I can pretend. It's not difficult even for normal people to manipulate their way into a longer relationship, after all. I just have to tell him what he wants to hear. Easy as pie.

He might want to break it off now, but I can keep it going for months longer. Maybe even years. Guilt is a powerful drug for people like Luke. But I now know this is the beginning of the end, at least.

"I think it's been great?" Luke ventures. That means he is expecting me to chime in with something.

I stare at him and wait. Does he think I'll actually help him along? Make it easier for him to toss me out of his life? If so, he doesn't know me at all, and that means I'm not responsible for this breakdown in our relationship. He is.

Luke finally swallows and soldiers on without my encouragement. "For the past few months, I've been thinking of making some changes."

I can't let him go easily. I can't, and I certainly *won't*. He's my one person. My connection. My only entrée into the flow and pulse of humanity.

I had an enjoyable life with men before Luke, of course, but it was cool and distant. The only moments of connection were manipulations at work and meaningless sex. I never had this before. His hand warm around my ankle the way it always is when we sit and read together.

Thoughtful texts to make sure I'm happy. Cozy heat at night that I actually want to snuggle close to.

The common belief is that people like me don't feel love at all, but I do feel *something*. We're not robots. We crave the connections we can't make.

The silence between us swells, ticking like a clock as he waits for me to blink or cry or gasp in panic. I don't.

"I think we should move in together," he finally blurts out.

That shocks me into yelling, "What the hell?"

Luke nods. "I told you I've been thinking of a bigger place."

"Yes?"

"Maybe something a little closer to Holly."

"Yeah, I know."

"And I'd like to share that place with you."

"Me," I say dully, briefly confused by the shift. I've read him incorrectly, and I like that almost as little as I like this surprise he's presenting.

"You," Luke confirms, his hand now clutching nervously at my ankle instead of caressing. "Absolutely. I think we should get a place together. A little house. White picket fence."

I pull my foot away and set my book down. "You're kidding."

"No. Well, the white picket fence part was a joke."

"I don't want a husband, Luke."

"I know that. I respect that you don't want to get married."

"It's weird!" I say too loudly. "All it does is mix up your finances without giving any kind of security, because you can just get divorced at any time. It doesn't even make any sense! What's wrong with people?"

Luke's mouth twitches into a nervous smile. "I get what you're saying, but that's not what I'm asking. We've been dating a year. One of us is usually at the other's house, which gets a little inconvenient. We don't even have to buy a place together if that's not what you want. I'd like to be closer to my niece, and I'd love it if you moved in with me."

19

I'm just staring at him again. I really wasn't expecting this. Though now that he's asked, I see that there were hints I ignored. Clues he's been dropping that I just stepped over because I didn't want to acknowledge them.

Luke's brother got married a couple of years ago, and last year he and his husband adopted a newborn girl. Luke fell head over heels in love with his baby niece, and he lights up like the sun when he spends time with her. Even I can see the pink hearts floating over his head.

And now he imagines a white picket fence of his own. Of course.

He wants that, and I don't. I like my solitary space. I like my condo and my cat and my views of the city. But I like Luke too.

I shake my head. "I don't know about any of this."

"You need to think about it. That's only fair. I've been thinking about it for months, so you need time."

I study him for a long moment. "You want kids," I say flatly.

His eyes widen. He blinks. He doesn't say no. Goddamn it.

"Luke!" I snap in horror.

"I've never wanted kids," he says carefully.

"You know, I'm an attorney, and I can tell pretty easily when someone isn't addressing the implied question at hand. You never wanted kids before. I know that. We've talked about it plenty of times. But *now*? After Holly?"

Another blink and he finally looks away, guilt tightening his face. Something frantic rises in my chest, confusing me. It's unpleasant and I don't like it at all, and Luke is the one doing this to me. *My* Luke. "I don't like this," I mutter, pushing out of his clingy, cushiony leather couch to look for my shoes. "I'm going home."

I should be the one to break up with him. I should be the one to leave, and this may be the right moment to end this so I don't have to endure any more unpleasant surprises in the future.

"Jane, come on. Let's talk."

"No, I need to feed my cat. And you want to change everything."

"Not everything. It'll be just like this, every night. Just the same, but in a bigger place, together."

"No, it won't. The same won't be enough."

"Enough of what?"

"Enough of what you want. You want"—I wave a hand—"something else. *Someone* else. I'm not going to stick around and watch you yearn for a wife and a baby when what you have is *me*. That's stupid."

I stalk off and he follows me to the table where I left my purse. "I want *you*, Jane. You know that."

"I know you want me, but you want more than me too. I won't give you that. I'm not . . ." I growl, unable to find the right word. I don't even want to find the right word. None of this is fair. "You know I'm not!" I yell as I yank open the door.

"Not what?"

That scratching, swelling mess of anger inside me gets bigger and climbs into my throat as I lurch through the door. *"I'm not a real person!"* I scream.

My voice echoes off the ten-foot ceilings of his hallway, banging around on the doors of the other five loft condos up here. I don't care. I'll yell it in their faces if they stick their heads out. He doesn't know I'm a sociopath, but he knows I'm different. He said he liked that, so what the hell does he think he's pulling here?

"Jane," Luke calls from behind me as I rush for the stairwell.

"Don't follow me," I warn. And he doesn't. He never pushes me. Or he never did before today.

I race down the metal stairs, clanking my fury out in rapid steps. It doesn't help.

Why would he do this? Everything has been going fine. Luke and I had a routine, a relationship, and for the first time in my life I've been . . . *comfortable*.

No, that isn't the right word. I've always been satisfied with the life I lead. I've always made myself happy, doing exactly what I want to do. Every creature comfort I've ever wanted as an adult, I've given myself.

But Luke *loves* me, which is different. And in my own way I love him back. I try, anyway. I give him sex and gifts and attention, because that's what I have to give. But he needs more. Of course he does. He needs real love to bask in, not this strange mirrored heat I throw.

I knew this day would come, just not like this. I thought I'd be in charge of it. Now Luke is asking more of me when he's already scraped the shallowest depths of my soul. "Fuck!"

Still cursing, I slam through the stairwell door into the sparse hallway that serves as a lobby to his building. One of his neighbors is getting mail, and she squeaks with alarm and drops everything on the floor as I storm past and out into the night.

If I were a real girl, I'd be excited by Luke's sudden proposal to cohabitate. My man wants to take it to the next level! He's ready to settle down!

I'd be looking up real estate websites and planning my dream kitchen. That's what my best friend, Meg, would have done. But those kinds of dreams destroyed her like they've destroyed so many others, so I'm better off. She's dead. She's dead because those dreams fell apart and she killed herself, and I'm glad I've never felt anything that deeply.

I know I can't have it all, so I won't bother trying to fool myself into thinking I can make Luke's dreams come true.

"Shit," I growl as I beep my car door open and drop into the seat. My phone buzzes.

Please come back. Let's talk.

He may as well have typed, Come back so we can feed your fingers to a rabid wolverine, because that sounds like just as much fun.

I thought you'd be at least a little happy??? he tries.

Well, there's the problem. Luke doesn't see me for what I am. When we started dating, he guessed that I was on the autism spectrum, and I let him believe that. He accepted me and my quirks, so I could let my guard down with him. Stop constantly masquerading as normal. It was nice.

But I haven't told him the real truth, and I won't; so as fun as this relationship has been, it's over now. The end.

"The fucking end," I growl past clenched teeth.

I ignore the phone and peel out onto the quiet downtown street, desperate to get home. Four blocks away from his building I have to slow for a small bar district. People walk past, young and happy and buzzing. They all seem to be in groups, connected by companionship and looped arms. Their faces flash beneath streetlamps that light up their joy in the dark.

I want some of that. I'm too empty. Always too empty.

Impulsive is my favorite speed, so when I see an open parking spot at the end of the block, I drop my desperate run for home and swing toward the curb to park. As I shove my phone and wallet into my coat pocket, the unfamiliar claws of that bad feeling—anxiety? fear? I'm not experienced enough to identify it—begin to retreat, and by the time I reach the door of the closest bar, the pain is gone entirely.

The biggest sign on the window reads TAPAS in fancy letters. Below that is a promise of CURATED COCKTAILS, whatever the hell that means. Most important, the music shaking through the glass is far too loud, and laughing people crowd the tables, even on a Thursday night.

I open the door and walk into the friendly chaos, and that's all it takes. I'm instantly myself again. No scratchy, strange pain. No doubt about anything.

Fifteen minutes later I have a seat at the bar, a delicious dish of melted cheese and toast points in front of me, and one perfectly curated cocktail in my hand. There's a man next to me, working hard to get into the good graces of the woman next to him, and I eavesdrop with delight.

"Yeah, I broke up with her last month," he shouts over the music. "Didn't she tell you?"

"No, but we're not really that close," the woman responds. "I mean, we're friends, I guess, but she seems really high-maintenance, and I'm not into that kind of thing. Too much drama." She laughs coyly as she throws her friend under the bus.

"Yeah, I don't know. I mean, she seemed down-to-earth at first, but then shit got really demanding, you know?"

Way to set up this new woman to lower her expectations. *Don't expect things from me—that's unreasonable—and if you do, I'll leave.* I love it. So does the skinny brunette, who tosses her hair and laughs, desperate to be cooler than her friend.

Ah, the cool chick. We've all been there. Pretending to love sports and unsatisfying booty calls just so he'll pay attention to you. Even I've walked that line in four-inch heels, though I never did it in the pursuit of love. I had other motivations.

Mr. Low Expectations waves a hand and orders two shots of tequila. The bartender, who has a styled mustache and probably calls himself a barkeep, flinches a little but sets two shot glasses down with an elegant spin. I raise my eyebrows in acknowledgment of his craft and he winks as he pours.

Low Expectations is utterly focused on his prey and hasn't noticed me at all. Why would he? I'm ten years older than the brunette and I'm still dressed like the badass bitch I am in my pin-striped suit. He doesn't need that kind of trouble. Still, plenty of other men are willing to screw a girl like me, even if I'm nothing close to a ten. Theoretically, a few extra pounds and a lack of striking beauty make someone like me more desperate and therefore better in bed. Or so I've heard. It's amazing what you can pick up on the dating scene if you pay close enough attention.

The flirting pair down their tequila and giggle together as if they've done something particularly naughty.

"I probably shouldn't have skipped dinner!" the brunette declares.

Instead of offering to order some delicious tapas, the guy calls for another round of tequila, then mentions something about how he has all the ingredients for a late-night grilled cheese at his house. She laughs at his obvious plan to get her to drink way too much and come home with him. "You're so bad," she squeaks.

Already bored with this tired scene, I make eye contact with a forty-something guy at the end of the bar wearing a too-tight shirt, but it's just habit on my part. I don't need that kind of energy tonight. I already had sex with Luke, and it was hotter than anything I can get with a stranger. Even during a frantic quickie in a bar bathroom, Luke took the time and effort to make me come. Half these guys couldn't even do that if they were trying, and—let's be honest—they wouldn't be trying.

I sigh and sip my spicy ginger highball before digging into the cheese.

I haven't cheated on Luke once. It's not that I'd feel guilty. I don't feel guilt. I don't understand it. If you don't get caught doing something, nothing terrible happens to anyone, so why would you bother feeling bad about it? I could have sex with any one of these guys right now, and my boyfriend would never find out. But I don't want to. I'm physically satisfied, so there's no need to risk a wasted thirty minutes with Bad Sex Bob. That's just common sense.

But this relationship is drawing to a close, and I'll have to get back in the game. It'll be fine. I haven't lost my edge. I can glance right down the line of men at this bar and immediately tell which guys might make a woman come and which of these jokers have never given it a thought. Still, caring isn't doing. There are no guarantees for us humans born with clits. It's a crapshoot but without all the fun crowds and shouting. Usually.

When we first dated in college, Luke was fine in bed, but during our years apart he became downright delightful. I ran into him unexpectedly when I was visiting Minneapolis, and I took him home for old times' sake. That gamble really paid off.

Since then our time together has amped up his kinkiness. He was a pretty vanilla guy, but a little time with a horny monster like me can inspire a man to live out his secret fantasies. Anal? Yes. Spanking? Yes. Rough role play? Heck yes, miss, I'll try anything.

But they'll all try anything. I can find someone else.

I'm scowling into my delicious cheese dish, and that won't do. I get the bartender's attention with a lingering glance, then I order a gin drink made with blood orange essence and pink peppercorn, of course. When I hear Mr. Low Expectations trying to talk the drunk girl into a third shot, I tap him gently on the shoulder. He turns and raises his eyebrows in friendly question.

"Don't you work at Sebastian and Fields?" I ask, naming the big accounting firm whose logo I see on a key card clipped to his coat pocket.

He brightens a little. "Yeah!"

"Hi, I'm Jane." I offer my hand.

"Kyle," he says as he shakes. "I don't think we've met."

"I'm pretty sure I've seen you on the elevator recently. I work in Human Resources."

"Oh, nice to meet you," he says, just as a little twinge of uncertainty dances over his face. His eyes dart toward the four empty shot glasses and the pretty woman who's trying to wait patiently. She likely doesn't realize she's frowning over his diverted attention, and that makes her eyes look small and slightly crossed.

"Long week already, huh?" I offer Kyle with a hint of kind amusement in my voice.

"Ha. I guess."

"I get it. You're not on the clock or anything, so please don't worry. Have fun!"

"Right. Sure. Thanks."

I hold up my hands in assurance. "I'll close my eyes and ears, Kyle, I promise! Do your worst."

His uncertainty is blooming into fear now. I watch as the fear twitches momentarily into panic. And then, finally, the delicious slow slide of his face into the sad-dog curves of disappointment. He can't take a drunk woman home for sex with a witness from the HR department looking on. He's an upstanding young man on the rise at Sebastian and Fields, and people in a corporate environment suddenly care about harassment and sexism. Damn it.

"This manchego is amazing," I gush. "You two should try it." I grin past him to the woman, whose pinched scowl has gotten a little blearier since I last looked.

"Right. Yeah." Kyle smiles tightly and nods. "Good idea. Can I get one of these?" he calls to the bartender, pointing at my half-eaten cheese. "And then I'll wrap up that tab."

People have never called me a hero, but ten minutes later the drunk brunette is happily eating her crock of manchego cheese and Kyle is heading out to catch an Uber. The woman has totally lost her irritation with me, and if she registered my conversation with Kyle about work, she's forgotten it now.

She's regaling me with the story of Kyle and High-Maintenance Girl's abrupt end. I order some bacon-wrapped shrimp and dig for all the deepest secrets as if I'm part of this woman's world.

"Let me ask you something serious," I say.

"Okay!" She claps her hands onto her thighs and sits up straight as if she's ready for a quiz.

"Is your friend really high-maintenance, or is Kyle just a fuckboy?"

27

The brunette—Laura, I think—squints hard, wrinkling her nose. "I don't know. Genevieve is kind of demanding. She gets very touchy when you don't return her texts."

"But Kyle is also clearly a fuckboy."

"Yeah. Yeah, I guess he is."

"So it won't be worth it if Genevieve decides to slash your tires and shit-talk you to all your mutual friends. There are a sea of fuckboys here tonight. Choose one that didn't date in your friend group. It's just smarter."

Her eyes widen. She pops some toast into her mouth and nods. "Oh my God, you're so right. What am I doing? Oh my God, you're my new best friend!"

I'm finally having fun, and when I accidentally catch the eye of the guy in the too-tight shirt at the end of the bar, I realize he's still watching for another signal from me. Before I can shake my head, he vanishes, then reappears next to me and begins to slide into the seat I vacated when I moved closer to my new friend, Laura.

"No," I say, and turn my back to him. You have to be cruel or they won't believe you. Even then it's pretty dodgy. I can feel him hovering, the possibility of sex too buoyant a lifesaver to let go of easily. But a few minutes of staring at my back finally begins to sink him. "Fucking bitch," he mutters.

"Good food is one hundred times better than random dick," I say as I pop my last toast point into my mouth and chew. "Every time." My new friend collapses with laughter. A nice evening, all in all. By the time I finally head home to feed my cat, I'm not worrying about Luke at all.

CHAPTER 3

Good times always come to an end, and I'm restless now that I'm clean, well rested, and back at work. Rob's door is closed when I get in. It stays closed all day, though I can hear him furiously typing away, likely producing the best work he's ever done for the firm in an attempt to claw his way back into the partners' good graces.

All I have to work on is boring prep stuff and contract research, so when my phone rings, I snatch it up quickly out of desperation.

"I have another call about your niece," I hear in mournful tones. What the hell? My family is pure trouble, and I cut contact with my parents a year ago. They're the only family that would ever get in touch. My grandma is long dead, and my brother and I haven't spoken since I left Oklahoma ten years ago. Truth be told, he wouldn't bother reaching out even if Mom and Dad were struck dead in an entertaining freak accident. So what's up?

I open my mouth to tell the receptionist to put the call through to voice mail again, but I hesitate. My parents are overstepping by tracking me down at my new place of employment, but I'm also really bored, and my family is great for providing eye-rolling stories. I always feel superior after our interactions, and that's an additional plus.

"I'll take it," I finally answer, and the line clicks open. "Yes, this is Jane," I say, a warning in the words.

"Jane? Jane, oh my gosh!" Not Mom or Dad. So maybe they *are* both dead. The unfamiliar female voice keeps gushing. "I'm so glad I got through to you! This is Joylene. Did you get my message?"

"No."

"Oh." She takes a breath and blows it out for long seconds. "Okay, I'd better start from the top, then. I found your name and office number online, so I thought I'd reach out. I hope that's okay."

"I don't know you."

"You're right. I'm sorry. I'm your brother's ex. Joylene?"

I roll my eyes and wait to hear how much money she wants and for what. Does this woman really think I give a shit what happens to my shiftless, asshole big brother? I care exactly as much about his well-being as he cared about mine when we were growing up: not one good goddamn tiny little bit. And I care even less about his exes and children.

Finally giving up on any gracious forgiveness on my part, Joylene takes another deep breath. "I think we met once at Christmas a long time ago. When your brother and I were together."

"I'm sorry," I offer, and she actually laughs like she gets it.

"Yeah, well. I was young, and times were desperate. Regardless, we have a son together, so I stay in touch, and I've been involved with his other kids, because they are Wesley's siblings and I feel like he should have a relationship with his own family."

Wesley. I remember them now. Joylene was a short, curvy black woman who'd seemed far smarter and more responsible than Ricky or any of the other women he'd ever dated or impregnated. He complained bitterly that she was no fun after he knocked her up. Apparently she'd been quite a drunk, which explains her long-ago attraction to my brother. Once she got pregnant, she went cold turkey and turned her life around. Ricky was outraged at her sobriety. Her naming the boy Wesley was the last straw. "Fucking nerd name," he'd grunted out right in front of the child.

"The reason I'm calling is," Joylene ventures, "well . . . you're an attorney."

"I don't practice criminal law, so whatever he's done, I can't help." And I *won't* help. My brother has been in and out of the court system since the age of seventeen for various felonies. Breaking and entering, grand larceny, aggravated assault. That kind of thing. He impregnates a woman during each brief furlough, like a salmon returning home to spawn.

"I wouldn't ask for him," Joylene says. "This is about his daughter. I really don't care what happens to Ricky. If he violates probation again, he'll be back in for three years and out just in time for Wesley's graduation, and that's all I care about. A boy needs his father." She said that last part hard and fast, as if she'd been trying to convince her son and everyone else of that for many years.

"But this isn't about him," she continues. "His daughter Kayla is missing and no one gives a damn."

"She's missing?"

"Yes. The girl just turned sixteen and no one has heard from her in a month. The officials don't care because everyone involved is considered trash. I don't know who else to call. No one is doing anything. Not the police. Not her mother. Nobody."

I roll my eyes. "She's *missing* or she ran off?"

"I don't know. She's missing or kidnapped or dead. Anything could have happened to her, and no one even *cares*? How is that right? She's Wesley's sister! And if he disappeared, I'd want someone to look for him. If I weren't here . . . Good Lord, I shudder to think what could happen to my son."

"Look, Joylene, I don't even know this girl. I'm in Minnesota. I'm not a criminal attorney or a detective, and I'm certainly not a children's advocate. I couldn't help if I wanted to."

"She's been in a little trouble," she says, as if I haven't spoken, "but nothing real bad. And she's just a tiny little thing. She can't look out for herself."

"Sorry."

"It's not right. Everyone has just thrown her away. I'm not a blood relation, so no one will even return my phone calls!"

"You should call an attorney in your area. Get help there."

Joylene sighs, and I'm moving the phone away from my ear, ready to hang up, when she speaks again. "Everyone always says she's just like you, so I hoped maybe you two had a connection or something."

Frowning, I pause in mid-motion, the phone three inches from my ear. What does she mean, "just like" me?

I slide the phone another inch toward the receiver, but I'm a cat when it comes to curiosity, so I impulsively change my mind and put it back to my ear. "What do you mean?"

"I thought maybe you'd been involved with her when she was young."

"No. Why do people say she's just like me?" I'm also a cat when it comes to narcissism. Joylene hesitates, so I press harder. "She looks like me? Or she's mouthy or something?"

"Yes, she's definitely mouthy."

"Good for her. She sounds like a teenager."

"Yeah, but . . ."

I groan at her hesitation. "Joylene, I don't have time for this. It's the middle of a workday. Spit it out."

"Okay." Her voice is harder now, sick of my shit. "Everyone says she's a cold-blooded little bitch just like you always were."

I freeze, but my heart beats faster, harder. Just like *me*. Is it possible? My condition does run in families, especially if you throw in hardship and a healthy dose of instability. "Cold-blooded how?"

"She's a little . . . I don't know. I guess she's a little spooky. But that's no reason to throw a child away! Wesley loves her. Or he used to, anyway. We moved to Moore, and he hasn't seen her in a good three years, maybe four. But when she was little, she was more wild than spooky."

Spooky. Her chatter fades in my ears as my pulse fills my head. Ricky has a daughter who's a spooky, cold-blooded bitch *just like I am.* Is it possible? A little Baby Jane out in the world?

I settle back in my chair and cross my legs. "All right, Joylene, let's start from the beginning. Tell me everything you know."

CHAPTER 4

She doesn't appear sixteen in her picture. Not even close. She's a weak-looking thing, scrawny and pale, and my first instinct when I find her photo online is to dismiss the whole story entirely. She's nothing like me. Look at her.

But her eyes stop me. It's a school photo, the cheap blue-gray background a dead giveaway, and she doesn't seem pleased to be sitting for a forced portrait. Kayla's dark-blond hair is parted in the middle and falls in a flat line a couple of inches past her shoulders. Her white skin is dotted with freckles and her thin mouth is set in a stubborn line, nostrils flared, as if she's refusing the command to smile.

Everything about her is unremarkable, maybe even pitiful. Everything except the eyes. A dull green, they're fixed on the camera, and if they were sad or scared, she'd look every inch the neglected child she likely is. But there's no fear there. No sorrow. There's nothing. Just a slight sheen of moisture and the cold emptiness of deep space.

"Hello, hello, hello," I whisper to my missing niece. She does look a little like me after all.

I turn on my laptop camera and pose for a humorless full-face shot, just as Kayla did. We don't resemble each other in any other way. I have dark-brown hair cut in a fringed bob, and my face is a nice, full oval without the bony angles of hers. But the spooky eyes? Yeah. Those are the same.

I can cover it up by smiling, crinkling my eyes into little half-moons of happiness. But that takes effort to pull off, and Kayla clearly doesn't give a shit.

Is my niece a sociopath?

Joylene said the girl had been in a little trouble before but nothing huge. A couple of fights at school. A few items shoplifted from the grocery store. Or maybe more than a few.

"What kind of society calls the police on a child for stealing *food*?" Joylene huffed. But we all know what kind of society does that. *Our* kind. And Kayla had known it too, and she hadn't been afraid to try it. Maybe she wasn't as weak as she looked.

There are no details about her disappearance online. Just her birth date and description and the day she was seen last, on a website about missing and endangered children. Kayla was last seen four weeks ago, just as Joylene explained. She didn't know too much beyond that. "Your mama says she must have run off. I called the police, and they said they've filed a missing-person report but had no reason to believe she was at risk. They sounded bored about the whole thing."

"And Kayla's mother?"

Joylene snorted. "She won't even call me back. Your brother says no one has heard from Kayla, and he can't do shit from jail, so to leave him alone. The end. No one cares, Jane. I can't get any information from CPS or the county or the police because we're not related."

Joylene came to the wrong place looking for concern, but I still find myself fascinated as I google my niece's name. Did she just run away? God knows, I considered it a hundred times, knowing I'd be better off without my shitty family weighing me down. But in the end I decided the free room and board was worth it. I wanted to finish high school so I could get to college and show them all how much better I was than them.

And I did it. But maybe Kayla came up with a different plan. Leave these losers in the dust and hope for the best.

Or maybe she was raped and killed and left on the side of the road.

"It's none of my business," I tell myself aloud. But I still spend most of my afternoon looking up information on missing teens in Oklahoma. No bodies have been found that look like hers. No random feet washed up in rivers. Maybe she's just being sex trafficked.

This time when Luke texts me, I don't ignore him. Jane, come on. Can we talk?

Yes, I write. Come by my place tonight.

Sounds like a setup for murder??? he responds.

I laugh at that. Maybe he knows me better than I think. Perhaps you can appease me with calzones and save yourself.

Done.

There's an Italian take-out place a block from his condo that I love. He already knows my order. There are good things about being in a relationship.

I'm not ready to give him up. I know that. But I refuse to hang around until he dumps me. That's not an acceptable outcome, and I might lose my shit and do something dangerous to the next girl he sleeps with.

A conundrum. Give him up now or later? Or . . . maybe there's a third choice. String him along forever, promising children we'll never have. That's an option to consider. I can distract him with good sex for years, and then I'll surely get tired of him and walk away before he has a chance to realize I've been voluntarily infertile this whole time. I will get sick of him. Nothing lasts forever. The sex has to get boring at some point, and there's not much more to me.

When I leave work at six, Rob is still typing away in his office, hard at work, and I've never seen that before. This experience is going to be so great for his personal growth.

Half an hour later, Luke knocks on the door of my condo. When I open it and see him, I feel strange inside: a tight, vibrating sensation high in my belly that makes me nervous. He sets the bag of food on the counter along with a bottle of wine and turns to face me. "I'm sorry I freaked you out yesterday. That wasn't my intention."

"I know," I respond, and then I add, "I'm sorry too," because I understand that I'm supposed to, but I don't know what to add after that. I don't have anything else to say except *Stop it, stop it, stop it, I don't like this.* But that would cause another conversation, and who can live like that? So instead of telling him to stop, I *make* him stop by sliding into his arms and squeezing him tight. He squeezes back and within seconds we're kissing.

The fight has triggered something rough and desperate in him, and I like rough and desperate, so I'm thrilled when he backs me up to the countertop of my galley kitchen and lifts me onto it. He doesn't have to move carefully or ask if I'm in the mood. I've trained him not to. I'll lash out if he does. I know my own bad habits.

I groan when he shoves my skirt up, then hiss with pleasure when he slides his hand into my underwear to touch me.

"Christ, I can't get enough of you," he whispers, and I'm suddenly filled up and overflowing with power and delight. I'm not a soft and caring person. I'm not nurturing. But I have this, damn it. And he loves it. He still loves it.

"Show me," I beg. "Fuck me." He does.

I don't have a soul, but in this moment I feel as if I do. I feel beautiful and full and glowing with the kind of life that other people take for granted. Luke *needs* this, and I'm human for a few minutes, his soul filling me up as he thrusts. This is love. This is emotion.

Is it real?

I expand, my heart swelling until it pops wide-open with my climax. Then I'm myself again, my insides cooling as the sweat evaporates on my skin.

And there are still the calzones to look forward to.

"I missed you," he murmurs against my neck.

"It's only been twenty hours."

He grins like an embarrassed little boy, and he's so cute that I laugh and kiss him on the cheek. "Tell me you love me," I demand.

"I love you," he says, and I know he means it, which is strange and wonderful and sad.

"Me too," I say solemnly, hoping it's close to the truth. If it's not love, it's as near as I've ever gotten. "Now let's eat."

"I brought your favorite wine."

"I saw that. How do you think we ended up on the counter?"

"My boundless charm?"

I slide off the cold granite, pull my underwear back on, and open the bag of food. What a great reunion.

By the time I pop the last bite of calzone into my mouth, Luke and I are sprawled on the couch, my legs draped over his lap, and half the bottle of wine is gone. I lick my greasy fingers and watch him watch my tongue.

"Something weird happened today," I say. "My niece is missing."

His reaction is delayed, because I suck a finger into my mouth and he finds that distracting.

"What?" he asks.

"My niece is missing."

He frowns, his head cocked, then he pushes himself upright on the couch. "Your niece? Jane, are you joking?"

"No."

"What niece? Where? What happened?"

"One of my brother's many children, of course. His first one, I think. Down in Oklahoma. I don't know her."

He only looks more alarmed. "How old is she?"

"Sixteen."

"But . . ." He shakes his head hard, as if he's trying to clear it. "How did you find out?"

"Someone called." He raises his eyebrows at my words and gestures impatiently for more information.

Tipping my head back in weariness, I call on my best storytelling capabilities and find little to nothing to tap into. "One of my brother's baby mamas tracked me down online and called the office. A couple of times. I finally took her call this afternoon. She explained the situation."

"And that situation is . . . ?"

"You're a regular Curious George tonight."

"Jane, come on! This is awful. Tell me everything."

"She's sixteen. She's been in a little trouble. She vanished four weeks ago. Maybe she just ran away. No one seems to know or care."

"But the woman who called you cares."

"Yeah." I wiggle my legs against his thighs, looking for attention, and he obliges by settling his hands on my skin. "I guess Joylene cares. But the state doesn't care, and the cops don't care, and neither do her parents."

"Jesus, they sound just like *your* parents."

"Well, the apple doesn't fall far from the tree and all that. And that place is a whole goddamn orchard."

"Do you think she ran away?" he presses.

I shrug. "I don't know. If I ever met her, she was a baby at the time. I guess I did meet her, but I don't remember. Still . . ." I glance at him under my lashes, studying his open face. "Apparently she's a lot like me. That's what Joylene said. Everyone says she's like me."

"Oh. How so?"

"You know. She acts like me. And if that part is true, she's logical and straightforward, so she's probably fine."

He squeezes my calf, his hand a warm anchor for my body. "That's not true at all. Didn't you need help when you were a little girl?"

I shrug.

"You did. Someone should have helped you, Jane."

No. Not really. I didn't need help by the time I was sixteen. I needed help when I was a neglected, needy seven-year-old, and I didn't get it, so I learned to help myself. No one can go back in time and rescue Baby Kayla any more than they can rescue stupid Baby Jane. What's done is done.

"Anyway, she asked me to help."

"You should!" he says immediately.

"How? I'd have to go down there. There's nothing I can do from here." As soon as I say it, I realize I want to. I want to get out of my office and stir up trouble and track down this girl who might be like me. I'm bored. And let's face it, I don't want to deal with Luke and his ridiculous fantasies about what our life could be like together. I want to get away from here.

"You can get some time off, can't you? This is an emergency."

"Yes," I answer. It's almost inevitable now. This is how I make decisions. I think of something, and if I like the idea, I do it. Trying to deny myself just makes me cranky and delays the outcome. "God. If only my family were from Southern California. I really don't want to waste vacation days in the middle of nowhere."

"Family leave?"

Hmm. I don't know the ins and outs, as I don't have that kind of family, and I'm certainly not any kind of caretaker at all. "I'll check into it. But maybe they'll be sympathetic."

"Your niece is missing! Of course they'll be sympathetic."

That's news to me. Girls are thrown away all the time in our world. The only thing going for her is that she's a white girl, but even that advantage was pretty much lost once she started shoplifting. And if she's not a virgin, forget it. She's worthless trash at this point! Not that I'll let the firm know that.

"You really think I should go?" I ask, not to reassure myself but because I want him to think he helped decide to give me a break from relationship talk for a while.

"Definitely. You're smart as hell and you're an attorney. At the very least, you can light a fire under someone's ass and see what's really going on. And, at best, maybe you'll find this girl."

"Perhaps. But there's a better-than-even chance she's just staying with some inappropriately aged boyfriend."

"Still not good."

I shrug and pick up the book I'm almost done with. My cat bounces up from the floor and lands silently on the coffee table before stepping onto the couch. She considers me a moment, then climbs between my calves to settle onto Luke's lap. I roll my eyes at her betrayal, but I'd pick Luke for warmth too. She's rewarded for her superior choice when he absentmindedly strokes between her ears, and I watch her eyes narrow in satisfaction. Those are *my* moments of affection she's stealing, but I'll let her have him for a little while.

"And . . . ," he ventures quietly. I hear what I don't want to hear in his voice and I tense. "Maybe this could be a good time for you to think about us."

"'Us'?" I snap.

"Whether you want this to evolve or not."

"What does 'or not' mean? You're presenting this as some kind of choice, but it reads more like an ultimatum."

Luke rolls his shoulders before slumping into the couch. "It's really not. But if I buy a house, we might not see each other as often. Right now you're only ten minutes away from my place and my job. I don't want to spring this change on you. I'm trying to involve you in the decision."

"This hardly seems like the time." I pull my legs back, hoping to stop this now. "My niece is missing."

He's a good guy. A genuinely good guy, so I know mentioning my niece will make him feel guilty. I see his mouth twist with it. But he still doesn't stop talking. "I know, but this might be just the break we need to think it through."

"Now it's a break. I see. You need to come right out and say it. You're breaking up with me."

"No, I'm not. Not at all. I love you. I want a future with you. I'm just not sure *you're* determined to have a future with *me*." He snags my hand and looks me straight in the face. "Are you?"

No, I'm definitely not determined, because it's not possible. I'm not normal. I'm not a wife and mother and soft place to fall. There are new studies that claim sociopaths *can* feel something like love, but it's our own kind of attachment, shallow and selfish. Or even more shallow and selfish than most people's claims of love are.

I loved Meg. I know I did. But that wasn't the same as romantic love. It wasn't commitment and fidelity and promises. It was friendship. This is something tighter. Something strangling.

Every once in a while, like right here in this moment, I want to be what other people are and I hate who I am. I hate what my parents made me with their terrible combination of emotional abuse and their genetic predisposition.

I wanted to kill them many times when I was Kayla's age. I wanted to burn down that trailer with them in it, blame it on a cigarette or a space heater or nothing at all. But luckily my own self-interest won out against raging teen hormones. I wanted to punish my family, but I did not want to go to prison and struggle for money and social standing for the rest of my life. I wanted more and better. So I let them be.

And most days I truly like what I am. It makes me strong. I saw how the world destroyed my best friend, using her own feelings to grind her into nothing. She killed herself to escape from that. To finally make it stop. She died and left me alone, and now Luke is all I have, and that can't last forever. It can't. I don't have enough emotion inside me to cloud out the stark reality of our chances.

"This obviously isn't going to work out," I mutter.

"Why would you say that? Jane, come on. We get along great. We get along so damn well, I want to spend *more* time with you. Why does that scare you?"

"It doesn't scare me!" I shove his hand away and stand up. "I'm not good at relationships, and I've told you that. I've been very clear about it. You said that was what you liked about me, and now you're asking me to"—I wave a frantic hand in the air—"do *this*?"

"Yes. I'm asking you to do this. Move in with me, Jane. It'll just get better."

"Who says it will get better? That's ridiculous. We both agreed that we have issues, thanks to our shitty families, but everything has been working really well, and now you've screwed it up. I can't do this. I can't be that."

"Be *what*?" Now he's standing too, his voice rising along with his body.

"Some kind of . . ." I growl in frustration and pace to the fridge to pour more wine. "I don't know. Some kind of constant fucking companion. A stupid, nurturing idiot."

"Jane, listen to yourself. There's nothing stupid about loving someone."

I laugh. I can't help it. "Really? Tell that to Meg."

I loved her. I didn't recognize it at the time, but I loved her, and she left. Loving her brought me pain, and I don't accept pain. I put it behind me and I won't ever accept it again. I have to get out of this.

"Jane—" he starts, but I shake my head.

"You should go. I need to make travel arrangements."

"I get it, okay? I know what your family was like. And I know it hurt you so much when Meg died. But can't we just try?"

"Try what? Settling down? Fuck up a little family together, just like both our parents did? What's the point, Luke?"

He knows better than this. His own mother focused so much manic, destructive energy on him in childhood that he didn't speak to her for most of his adult years and has always sworn he doesn't want a traditional life. That was why he liked me.

"The point is that I love you," Luke says, "and I've never wanted to live with anyone before either. Never. But I want to live with you, so you take that however you want. Just . . ." He throws up his hands in exasperation. "Go on your trip. Think about it. Really think about it. And decide what you want to do when you get back."

He dons his jacket in quick tugs, telegraphing his anger, wanting me to feel it and respond. But I *can't* feel it, just like I can't feel much of anything. He grabs his wallet and keys and jerks the door open, wanting some words from me that I don't know; but just as he's stepping out and closing the door behind him, he stops.

I stand there staring. I have techniques for making people like me, but I have no tools for smoothing things like this over, because I usually don't care. This time I do care, but all I can feel is outrage that he's doing this to me. Making me hurt when he's supposed to love me.

The tight expectation in his face sags to disappointment. "Call me, okay? Let me know what's going on with your niece?"

"Sure," I say, "whatever."

Luke waits for another heartbeat before closing the door. He's finally done talking, at least. I take the bottle of wine to the couch and sulk, waiting for my cat to pay attention to me. I'll look into plane tickets tomorrow. I'm too exhausted to bother tonight.

CHAPTER 5

The Oklahoma City airport has changed. It's beautiful now, buffed to a shine by energy-industry money into a very modern facility. I rent a car and tell Siri to find me a good barbecue restaurant on my way out of town. Home is still two hours away.

Home. It doesn't mean to me what it means to other people. I scowl at the very idea of nostalgia. Even if someone had a great childhood, it was still childhood, full of powerlessness and dependency. Why would anyone want that back?

I don't understand that any more than I understand why I would want tiny people depending on me. The idea of children feels cloying and gross. Just being loved by Luke is sometimes too much. It feels like he needs me, and I want to hurt him for that. And lately, very occasionally, it feels like I need him, and that's a violent crack of lightning inside me. Another good reason to end this.

I'm free now. Glad that I left. The sticky, niggling hints of fear and commitment are washed away with the distance.

Sighing, I turn my mind toward planning my lunch. I'll definitely have brisket and maybe a few ribs with extra-spicy sauce. Corn bread with honey butter. Pudding for dessert. Sweet tea.

"Mmm. Sweet tea." I smile as my phone tells me to exit the freeway and turn onto Freedom Street.

Freedom Street. Jesus Christ. There's a fucking Indian reservation five miles from this spot. And I'm the screwed-up psycho in this world?

The barbecue place is tiny and run-down, and there's a Route 66 sign in the corner of the window even though Route 66 is half an hour south of here. But Siri was looking out for me. The food is almost as good as I want it to be, and the young Hispanic guy named Felix who serves me is very pleasant to look at and quite flirtatious. All in all, a good afternoon.

I didn't have any trouble getting time off work, because I didn't give them an opportunity to imagine they should be upset. I emailed my bosses over the weekend and presented the issue as an emergency, assuring them I knew I could count on their support. They wouldn't have dared to contradict me, especially when I mentioned that Kayla is my firstborn niece. I was only sixteen years old when she was born. The first grandchild in the family!

That's all true, though I barely remember anything but the scorn I felt for my stupid brother, who was turning twenty-one and on his way to his first state prison stint when the baby arrived.

Regardless, now I'm on paid short-term leave. I suppose I shouldn't have abandoned Rob to his own devices at this delicate juncture. If I'm gone more than a week, he might be the golden boy again by the time I get back. But Jesus, he was boring, and, hard work or not, he'll never live down his drunken fuckup. I can pick up my campaign when I get back and continue slowly destroying his reputation. And if I find my wayward niece? I'll make sure they all know I'm a goddamn hero.

I grin at the idea and set off toward home sweet home.

The land is flat and ugly, drying out with the dying sun of fall, and the suburbs go on forever now, broken up by tiny old towns that have been shriveling since they got bypassed by the interstate. There is no freeway to my old stomping grounds. Not enough people want to go there. It's all two-lane highways and stop signs at every main street. But the highways are built wide enough for trucks. Lots of trucks.

It's been so long since I've driven here that I'm startled by the red of the dirt. I'd forgotten it. I'd never even noticed it growing up, to be honest. But now I see the huge wounds in the earth leaching iron into puddles like spreading blood. Construction on a new house has opened a huge, pretty gash filled with reddened rainwater. It's a startling change. The soil of Minnesota is black as pitch.

When I was young these scrubby lands were dotted with pumpjacks bobbing up and down. They pulled crude oil from the ground and provided nice points of interests in the landscape, like lolling cattle. I don't see any bobbing pumpjacks now. No big oil derricks either. They've all been replaced with boring pipes that bring the natural gas out of the rock. The few pumps I do spy are stubby and misshapen, working to press wastewater and earthquakes into the ground.

Ah well. Maybe I'm nostalgic after all. I want things to be what I expect them to be, and this all looks stupid to me.

An hour into the drive, I crest a rare rolling hill and see something brand-new, and this time it's something so delightful, it makes me gasp with delight. Windmills! Huge white windmills!

They seem a mile high as their blades turn slowly in the wind. I squeal in wonder at the beautiful scene laid out before me. A dozen of these giants are scattered over ranchland, and as I keep driving, more peek over the horizon to reveal themselves. They look like colossal robots marching toward an invasion, determined to defeat all the things I hate about this place.

So perfectly beautiful. I can't believe Oklahoma found yet another energy to farm. It's quite an accomplishment since that Silkwood scandal put the kibosh on the nuclear industry here decades ago.

I'm impressed. I'm also a little giddy. This is exciting.

I was bored before this trip, and that's a dangerous state for a girl like me. Something cool and unexpected suddenly becomes catnip, and I want to roll around in it. When I was younger, that meant a dangerous affair or a high-risk scheme, but now I'm feeling a strange rush of endorphins over these inanimate objects. Maturity, I guess.

A mile down the road I see that one of the towers is relatively close to the highway, and I slow to roll down my window. I'm surprised at the silence of this great beast. I'd expected a *whomp-whomp* sound, but the blades turn too slowly for that. They are masters of disguise, actually seeming larger from a distance than they are up close. Something about the proportion makes this illusion possible. I clap my hands in wonder.

What pure delight to find that the stolid metal soldiers follow me through my whole drive. I feel like their general, in charge and taking stock.

Though I lose sight of them occasionally as they stick to a faint rise in the land, looking for the highest points, they soon return toward me in a wave like they can't resist my draw. When I near another that looks close to the road, I pull into a narrow dirt lane that ends abruptly at a metal gate just thirty feet into the scrub pasture.

After turning off the car, I put my shoes to the red dust. I can see a door at the base of the metal tower, and it's only about a hundred feet past the gate. I want to be up close in the worst way. And there's a chance there won't be a lock, or a bigger chance that someone could have forgotten to lock it.

It's a long shot, but I still ignore the "Private Property" sign and climb over the metal gate to pick my way through rows of crop stubble. I can't tell what it was from the few inches that stick from the ground, but a small herd of cattle graze on the leftovers a quarter mile away. People think cows are so docile, but these beef cattle are half-wild and mean as hell. Take it from my misspent youth: you do not want them riled up and freaked out. At least all the calves have been weaned and separated and de-balled, so the group seems comparatively laid-back with no babies to protect. They're far enough away that I'm not worried, but bovine trampling in rural Oklahoma is not the way I plan to go down.

When I get to the huge base of the tower, I hop up eight metal stairs and try to twist the door handle. It's definitely locked. "Damn it," I growl, tugging and twisting and cursing. The mechanism doesn't budge, and I can clearly see the keyhole in the lock. Why oh why didn't I summon the patience to learn lock picking when I was younger? I watched videos and everything, but the practice wasn't enough fun to stick with.

Away from the traffic noise, I can hear the blades now, whooshing above me. I put my hand to the tower wall and I *feel* the whooshing now, along with a mechanical hum.

God. This is so cool. I wonder if there's a big spiral staircase inside, like a lighthouse. After tugging at the door one last time, I give up and stomp down the stairs.

Bastards.

I loudly mutter curse words as I pick my way back through the stubbly field and beep my vehicle open again. I wanted one little fun thing, but now there's nothing to keep me from driving straight to my boring destination. I'm thirty minutes away at most.

But I'm not going home. Not really. My parents have nothing to do with Kayla's disappearance as far as I can tell, and the run-down roadside motel in my hometown isn't suitable to my tastes. I'll be staying in the county seat instead, and that would be my first stop anyway. Joylene confirmed that Ricky is currently in the county jail for a six-month stint for parole violations. The penitentiaries are too full for that kind of shit, so he gets to stay in lockup with nine other men and one toilet. What a life, my darling brother. What a life.

When I reach the city limits, I check into the nicest hotel in town. It has an indoor pool and an attached bar, and all the kids I knew who got married right out of high school had their wedding receptions here. I came to each one I found out about. I wasn't invited or anything. I didn't have any actual friends. But there was always booze and free cake, so why not help them celebrate?

49

Sometimes there was a hot young uncle in the parking lot with weed, the kind who would say, "You're eighteen, right?" with a little wink. I wanted access to the Jacuzzi and their cooler full of beer, so I was more than willing to flirt.

Anyway, this place is filled with memories.

"Inside room," I tell the scrawny old woman checking me in. "First floor, overlooking the pool."

"No problem, sweetie. Get to the buffet before five thirty tonight if you want to avoid the rush."

The rush? I glance around at the empty lobby and shrug. Then I take three of the fresh cookies laid out on a plate next to the American Express sign and roll my bag to my room. It's a perfect location. I can sit on a chair with my lights off and watch the people in the pool area, and they'll never even notice me. Unless I want to be noticed. I often do.

But no time for fun now. Visiting hours at the jail end in ninety minutes, and I may as well get this over with.

I grab one more cookie on my way out, eating it as I slide my driver's license into my jeans and lock my phone and wallet in the glove compartment of my rental. It's not my first time visiting this asshole, though it is my first time not being dragged along by my parents. Another moment of maturity.

I inform the officer at the front who I'm visiting, then start the half-hour process of getting examined and quizzed and patted.

"You can leave your phone and valuables here," a guard says, sliding over a numbered plastic bin, as if I'd trust him with my shit.

"I didn't bring anything. Just my ID."

"Done this before, have you?" he asks, finally looking up from his paperwork to run his eyes over my breasts before he looks at my face. I'm obviously a desperate bitch and probably a lonely one if I'm visiting a man in jail.

"Sure, I've made the rounds," I volunteer, just to confuse him.

"What?"

"You can have your bin back, sir," I say, sliding it toward him slowly as if it's a treasured possession. "I'm all taken care of. Are we done?"

After a blank stare, he finally jerks his chin toward a platoon of dirty plastic chairs. "Wait there." All my amusement falls away at the sight of the cheap chairs, the stackable kind you can buy for eight dollars outside the grocery store during the summer. They're meant to be hosed off in the yard every once in a while. These chairs have not been hosed off in a very long time. I stare at the gray grime of layers of skin cells and body oil that's worked deep into the texture on the plastic and I decide to stand.

There are no pictures or even upbeat slogans on the walls, only tattered paper signs repeating rules and cautions to visitors.

No foul language.

No suggestive clothing or conversation.

No food or drink allowed.

No cameras or phones.

Stay seated during the visit.

No touching of any kind.

Aw, no hugs for Ricky, I guess. What will I do with all this sisterly affection coursing through my veins?

Ricky was always a terrible brother. Always. If he'd been loving and protective, I might not have turned out this way. Though I know my shitty genes helped the process along, I remember feeling scared as a child. Hurt. Vulnerable.

Some people are born sociopaths, but some are created in childhood. I think I felt too much at one point. Those memories are a strange recurring nightmare now. I can remember them existing, but they make no sense in the daylight of my current life. Someone else felt those emotions. Not me.

My lip lifts in scorn at that memory of weakness. I was pitiful, left at the mercy of my neglectful, narcissist parents and my heartless older brother. Abandoned for days to fend for myself and stifle my tears into a blanket at night. I scrounged for food and begged for attention.

Sometimes my parents provided both. Sometimes they took off for days at a time. I was left in the care of a brother who considered me a worthless nuisance. Or I was left with someone worse.

After years of bouncing back and forth between need and fear, my brain learned a better way. A stronger way. And now that it's stopped developing, I'm permanently wired to look out for myself and only myself. Some people aren't so lucky.

Eventually I'm led through a steel door into a cement-block hallway. Our footsteps echo above the distant, droning rumble of men's voices. A door slams somewhere, and then we turn left into a room dotted with school cafeteria–style tables, round with little stools attached for sitting. No loose chairs around that someone might throw.

A female guard in the room points to a table and I sit there. She watches me impassively for a moment before sliding her eyes away.

When Ricky enters, I barely recognize him. Ten years ago he looked bulky and mean, a literal redneck, his nape already leathered and wrinkled from the Oklahoma sun. Now he's thin and mean, a bushy beard covering most of his pale face. He's on pills, no doubt. Everyone is these days. It's a lot easier to get high when you can pick up your drugs from a legal clinic instead of hoping something makes it across the border.

My brother looks around the room blankly, trying to figure out who's come to visit. "Good afternoon, Ricky," I drawl.

He turns a frown on me and glares. "Jane?" he finally barks out too loudly.

"Yes! It is I, the prodigal sister!"

He's not happy to see me. He's not disgruntled either. I never meant anything to him, and I'm a break in his long day, so he shuffles over. "What the fuck," he huffs as he sits down on one of the round seats, the words half question and half philosophy.

"I've come to visit my big brother!"

"What the *fuck*?" he ponders more loudly.

The female guard takes a step forward, but I hold up an apologetic hand and scrunch my face into a sheepish smile before turning back to my brother. "Keep your voice down, idiot. I got a call from someone that your daughter is missing."

Ricky shrugs one shoulder. "I guess. Whatever. She took off."

"That's not what your ex thinks."

"Joylene? That fucking nosy drama queen. She came by here last week. Jesus."

"So you're utterly unconcerned that your sixteen-year-old daughter has fallen off the face of the earth."

"That bitch can take care of herself, believe me. She's like a vicious goddamn cat." He smiles, seeming triumphant that he managed a simile; then his lips widen into a grin, revealing that his upper teeth on the right side are dark brown and dying. He probably got punched there and damaged the roots. Or maybe it was a purposeful injury, a good source for a pain pill prescription. "She's a hateful bitch," he says, "just like you always were."

"You still mad about that time I kicked you in the balls in front of your friends, Ricky?"

His grin snaps to an ugly thin line in his ugly thick beard.

"Fuck you, you whore."

"You were the one commenting on your own sister's ass. Who exactly is the whore in this situation, you goddamn felon?"

He rolls his eyes and crosses his arms. "What are you doing here? You don't live here no more. And don't give me any shit that you care what happens to Kayla."

"No more than you do, certainly."

He's unmoved by the criticism of his parenting. His eyes don't even narrow. "She's been thinking she's grown since she was eleven. If she wants to be grown, she can take care of herself. All I know is I'm not paying any more child support."

"So you were really keeping up with those payments until now, huh?"

"Fuck off."

"I just came here for her address. I don't actually assume you'd know anything about your daughter. I'm going to guess there weren't any Saturday guilt trips to the arcade whenever you were briefly out of prison."

"You want her address so much, you'll have to pay for it. Put twenty bucks in my commissary account."

I almost laugh in his face at the lowball demand, but better to save that until after I get the address. "Did Dad die yet?" I ask instead.

"Nah. He's scamming for all the help he can get. Seems fine to me."

"Of course." My mother called a year before, demanding help for my father after a stroke. She got a little too sassy for her own good, though, so I simply changed my number and left her behind. Apparently dear old Dad had pulled through without my help. A cozy country miracle.

"Give me Kayla's address and I'll put twenty in your account."

"Go do it now."

"So they can take you back to your cell and leave me high and dry? No way."

"That's the deal."

"Jesus Christ, Ricky, I'm pretty sure I can find her mom's address without your help. This is just my first stop. Give me the information or I'll drive straight to Mom and Dad's to ask them and you'll be out twenty dollars. Those pills are rotting your brain, and you didn't even start off smart."

Ricky grunts at the insult, but he finally gives in and recites an address I recognize as a block of two-story apartments a couple of towns over. "Great. I'll go see if I can track down your missing daughter for you. Cheers, Ricky."

"You're a bitch," he grumbles as I signal to the guard that the visit is done.

I walk out of the room without any trouble or any parting hug. There are no searches on the way out, and I have nothing to collect, so I breeze past the checkpoints and stop to sign out at the front window. There's a plaque there with instructions on depositing into an inmate's commissary account.

I walk out to my rental car and get in. It's dinnertime and I hope my favorite restaurant isn't closed. I want chicken-fried steak and mashed potatoes and coconut cream pie for dinner.

I imagine Ricky's fury when he goes to buy a bag of Doritos and discovers his balance is still at zero. He can kiss my sisterly ass.

CHAPTER 6

My favorite diner has closed. I have to settle for my second choice, a steak joint that was far too pricey for me when I was young.

I pass a brand-new Walmart with a sign that reads "Visit our new Garden Center!" in excited letters. It probably felt promising in the spring, but summers here really beat dreams of a green garden out of you. The sun and wind suck the life out of everything, be it plant or human.

I loved coming into town as a kid, especially in the winter, when it was dark by six and all the buildings glowed with light. They always put up Christmas lights on the telephone poles that ran through town, and I loved the sparkly angels blowing horns and even the twinkling golden crosses. I thought it looked like the Disneyland parade I'd seen commercials for on TV.

But this county seat is a boomtown, and being a boomtown means being a bust town too. Everyone's fortunes—everyone's power bills and car repairs and groceries—depend upon the whims of the oil market and the decisions of billionaires in DC and Houston and Saudi Arabia.

Natural gas came to town to shake things up, but it's no more stable a market than oil. You can watch fortunes rise and fall in real time here. Shiny new trucks pack the streets one month, only to be taken over by tow trucks repossessing them the next. Right now things look prosperous, but I passed two piping companies with "For Sale" signs on the fences. Trouble is coming. Trouble is always coming here.

The steak house has a light in the window that says OPEN when I pull up, thank God. I breeze into the restaurant, which seemed impossibly fancy when I was young.

It isn't impossibly fancy. It's not even kind of fancy. This place is just a salad bar and a hostess station and red stained glass over the lighting fixtures.

I order a giant margarita on the rocks as an appetizer, then ask my waitress about the other restaurant that closed. "What happened to it?"

"Old Mr. Handelson died and left it to his son, Brad. He tried to keep it going for a little while, but . . . you know." She raises her blond eyebrows at me.

I shake my head. "I know what?"

She glances around to reassure herself that I'm the only one in hearing distance. "Opioids."

"Ah. I get it."

The woman sighs deeply. "Frankly, I'm glad I never had kids now." She looks about fifty, but it's hard to say out here. No one I knew ever used sunscreen when we were kids. We just burned and peeled and built up an amazing base tan as we weathered away in the wind.

"My sister lost a girl to it already," she continues. "And one of her three sons is heading down that road too." She clucks her tongue. "We've got to do something about that border."

I snort and mutter, "Yeah, right," before raising my menu to study it.

I'm unsure what the border has to do with it. When I was young, the drugs around here were made in trailers by our neighbors, which was why they kept the Sudafed behind the counter and put up bulletproof glass in the pharmacy window. Now the drugs are made by giant corporations in the US and overseas, or ordered on the dark web and shipped in by international mail. No poor brown people are needed to make that shiny pipeline work. There are probably more people at my law office involved in making these drugs happen. Import-export, baby. We know how to work those laws.

I sip my margarita and try to plan the perfect meal. Cowgirl steak? No. Cowboy steak? Yes. Asparagus? No way. I'll take a loaded baked potato instead. Or would I rather have onion rings? No, onion rings I can get at Sonic Drive-In anytime I want. Definitely baked potato. That's not a good to-go item.

When the waitress returns to take my order, she's colder than before. Polite but not warm. I guess I didn't react correctly to her passing the drug blame to the Others. Oh well.

I can manage empathy. I work hard at figuring out what people are feeling at any given moment. How else would I manipulate them? But it *is* work, and I'm trying to relax here, damn it, and it's not my job to regurgitate propaganda for my server.

I place my order and request another margarita too. Traveling makes me tense.

A family comes in, calling out hellos to my waitress. The old man is wearing a tan cowboy hat and battered old boots, and the thirty-something woman with him is dressed the same. Local ranchers, no doubt.

In my imagination, I assume this woman is a second or third wife, but that's not the norm out here in the heartland. It happens, but you'd better be prepared for people to talk for decades, until you finally keel over in your young wife's bed and give them even more to talk about at the funeral.

No, out here on the plains it's more likely the woman is his daughter and the three kids are his grandchildren. But just in case, I eavesdrop to see if I catch anything scandalous.

Nope, no such luck. One of the kids calls out a loud "Grandpa?" before they're even settled. The woman wears a wedding ring, and I wonder where her husband is. Working? Dead? Or did he run off with his coworker and force her to move back in with Dad to make ends meet? There could be any kind of story there.

God, I wish I could read minds. Life would be so much more fascinating.

Or maybe it would be just as boring. People are all the same. Everyone wants what they don't have and shouldn't need. Even me.

I check my work emails, but they're all standard fare. Smiling to myself, I send a quick email to Rob asking how things are going with the North Unlimited account in the hopes of making him feel terrible.

I don't doubt that he's suspicious of me at this point, but in my experience that suspicion will quickly fade. Most people are blessed with a lot of benefit of the doubt, and his belief in his own superiority gives him a cozy layer of comfort and protection. He'd never be bested by me. He's Rob! And I'm just a girl, after all. Not even a beautiful girl. Just . . . Jane. All I need to do is present myself as harmless to him once again, and he'll eventually forget his mistrust.

When I was younger I wanted to be the most beautiful woman in the world. I kept waiting for my outside to match the perfect cool surface beneath. I was every lady villain in every 007 movie, and I wanted that to be seen and acknowledged.

God, I was so angry that others were blind to how absolutely stunning I was: *Look at me, you unseeing idiots!*

But I've grown wiser, and I now recognize how much easier it is to triumph when people barely notice you. My looks are my chameleon skin, and I can hide my superpowers under a perfect camouflage of averageness.

My dinner arrives, and I'm so glad I got the loaded baked potato. I pride myself on making the best possible food choices in every situation. It's a gift, but I've worked hard to hone it.

My phone dings with a text as I'm chewing my first bite of delicious steak. It's slightly more than the medium doneness I've ordered, but the seasoning is delicious, so I'm happy.

I'm even happier when I see that Luke has reached out. Even if I'm going to break up with him, I still want him thinking about me. I'll always want him thinking about me. Did you make it safely? he asks. Any information yet?

I set down my fork and take another sip of margarita, rolling my eyes in exasperation when I realize I'm already slurping the last of it. I'm in town, I type back. Saw my brother. That's it so far.

Is he out?

No, I went to the jail.

Sounds dangerous, Luke writes with a frowny face. Stay safe out there.

It's not dangerous here, but it's not as safe as you might expect. Boomtowns never are. Too many people coming through every day, the highways full of workers moving from job to job. It was no place for a young girl to be running wild when I was young any more than it is now. I certainly found my share of mischief, and none of these hardworking, salt-of-the-earth, economically anxious men were looking out for my well-being, as far as I ever saw.

They wanted to use me. Use me up until nothing was left. Instead I used them every chance I got.

My phone dings again. Let me know what you find out, ok?

Sure, if you're still interested, I text back.

Of course I'm interested, Jane. I love you.

Whatever. If he loved me, he wouldn't be pushing me for something he knows I don't want.

Bleh. I'm not good at melodrama because I'm too logical, and I know love rarely means shit when it comes down to it. Luke actually

60

does love me—or, to be clear, Luke loves the parts of me I let him know. But what has that ever mattered in the world?

The ranch family two tables over has been utterly circumspect and polite, and even the children are well behaved. Everyone is kind to each other, not a hint of scandal about them. The kids' clothes are worn but neatly pressed, their hair clean and combed. This is the kind of family I envied, even in my teenage years.

What would it have been like to grow up in a calm, supportive household with food in the fridge and the lights always on? What would life have been like with a hardworking father figure and a mom who never once called you a sneaky little cunt? What if there had even been siblings who wanted to play games and share secrets?

I roll my eyes at the lovely scene before me as the two kids squeal, "Thank you, Grandpa!" when he orders them ice cream. There's bad here just the same as there is in the city. And there's good here too, just like everywhere else. It's all the luck of the parental draw no matter where you're born.

By the time I get back to the hotel, it's 7:00 p.m. and the previously deserted lot is crammed full of trucks and SUVs. I guess I know what the front desk clerk meant by "rush" now. The place is packed. Men in coveralls stand outside smoking cigarettes, and I follow footprints of red mud through the doors.

A couple of guys are checking in at the front desk, several are gathered in a little laundry room, and two more are working out in the tiny gym near the pool. It's a weekday, and none of the guests seem like they're here for a wedding, but I'll keep my fingers crossed. I'd love to crash a reception for old times' sake, and I do so love cake.

The margaritas have loosened me up nicely, so I freshen up and head right back out the way I came. Instead of going to my car, I turn left toward the entrance of the bar. When I get there, I laugh with delight.

I can't remember what this place was called when I was young, but now the letters S-E-C-R-E-T-S are spelled out in big wooden squares on the first wall I see when I walk in. Secrets! In a small-town bar!

I giggle at the false promise of it, as if a certain amount of drinking will shield you from the prying eyes of your neighbors. Delightful. So many secrets here, and everyone knows them. I'm clapping my hands as I waltz through a set of open doors into the main bar area.

I freeze mid-clap.

I used to sneak in here on a Saturday night, but on a Monday it's dead as hell. The big wooden dance floor is empty, and only three tables are occupied. It's going to be a long night for me and for the bored bartender, who rushes over as soon as I grab an empty table. "Hello!" she coos as she sets down a Coors coaster, her pitch-black ponytail bobbing. "I'm Maria! What can I get for you?"

"I'll take a screwdriver with a splash of soda." I glance past her toward the bar. "Slim Jims?" I ask, glimpsing the familiar giant canister stuffed with plastic-wrapped meat snacks.

"They're a dollar each," she says.

What the hell. "Just one."

"I'll be right back, hon," she says cheerfully, her round face glowing. She moves fast to make my drink, her enormous butt bouncing under a tiny waist in her stretchy pants. She likely needs an electric fence to keep the cowboys' drunken hands off her cheeks. She either tolerates their groping with a smile or she stabs any man who gets close. I doubt there's a workable middle ground with an ass like that.

I imagine I'll find out if anyone else shows up, but it could be a while. There are two old guys playing darts, a younger couple with pool cues leaning against their table while they flirt, and one big group of older ladies sharing pitchers of beer. None of them look like they have grabby hands. I'm probably the most likely candidate here, if only because I'm so impulsive.

Some upbeat music begins playing, and the old ladies hop up with shouts of delight and head to the empty floor for a line dance. The bartender returns with my drink and a Slim Jim. "You want to start a tab, honey?"

I sure do.

My first bite of Slim Jim floods my tongue with salt. I haven't had one of these since I left Oklahoma, and my mouth waters like crazy at the familiar taste. The perfect bar snack to keep me drinking.

I suppose I should be running over to the address Ricky gave me to see if his daughter has been found. Or maybe I could solve the whole mystery tonight with just a few questions around town. But I'm tired and melting into my seat as an old country ballad begins playing and the group of women return to their long table to wet their whistles. An ancient cowboy I hadn't noticed before suddenly appears to ask one of them to waltz. She happily agrees and heads back out to the floor.

"You can join us if you like!" one of the women at the table calls out. When I realize she's talking to me, I point to myself in surprise. "It's Friends and Fun Night!" she yells back, as if that explains everything.

"Oh. Okay. Sure."

Always looking for more emotion and energy than I can generate on my own, I gather my purse and drink and half-eaten Slim Jim and slide over to an empty chair. My kind really likes company. When it's too quiet we can hear the hollowness inside us. When things get loud, the echoes fill us up.

The women, five in all, not counting the lady with the cowboy, introduce themselves, but their names flit away from me as they're spoken. "I'm Jane," I offer in return.

"You here visiting?" the skinny one with the no-nonsense gray buzz cut asks.

"Yep."

"You have family here, then?"

"Yeah, my brother is over in the county jail."

"Oh," she says flatly, but another woman bursts into laughter.

"My husband was in that jail a few times."

"I'm sorry," I say without being sorry at all.

"Nah. Good riddance to bad rubbish, I say. He finally died five years ago, and look at me now!" She jiggles her shoulders, showing off her cleavage and the hot-pink lace bra peeking out from her V-neck sweater.

"Go, girl!" I raise my drink, and they all hoot and raise their drinks as well, and just like that, I'm one of the girls! They push a bowl of tortilla chips toward me and fall back into their gossip.

"That's Clarence," the woman with the cleavage says as she leans closer. She tips her head toward the waltzing cowboy. "He's harmless. Comes down from a ranch an hour north of here to keep us company on Mondays."

"Harmless, huh? You sure about that?"

She giggles when I wink, but he really does look harmless, thin and gentlemanly with deep layers of wrinkles on his leathery face. Before I know it, I'm on my second drink and being pulled out onto the dance floor for the Electric Slide. I've done it a million times, but I'm still terrible at it. I'm no good at music or art, but I also don't have any shame, so I throw my hands in the air and slide and spin, making the ladies laugh when I bump into them. They're my new best friends. We're having so much fun together.

By the time we exit the dance floor, the place is finally starting to fill up. I survey the men—and they're all men—but I'm disappointed by the findings.

Cowboys wear tight jeans no matter how old they are or how big their gut is. You can still fit a size 34 waist under a huge beer belly if you wear those jeans low enough, and I admire that kind of persistence. But these traveling oil field workers? Good Lord, I've never seen such a baggy, sloppy mess of men. Worn-out, oversize jeans, canvas cargo pants with pockets stuffed full of who knows what . . . There are even a few guys here still in coveralls, their boots half laced and muddy as hell.

That really doesn't give me much hope for the state of their groins.

Would picking up one of these men—one of the few recently washed ones—be cheating on Luke? I'm not sure if we're still together. We're on some sort of a break, but which sort?

Sex with Luke is of a far higher quality than anything I can find in a bar. He knows right where my clitoris is and worships it with the lavish attention it deserves. Given my own personal studies, I'd guess that none of the guys here would even try to find it.

But I definitely miss the mystery of it all. The strange fun of strange bodies. Big men with little dicks. Little men with big dicks. Short, fat guys with skinny dicks. Tall guys with . . . You get the picture. With penises you just never know. It's a surprise package and you can unwrap a new one every night if that's what you want!

Same goes for women's parts, of course, but I'm only rarely interested in those. Still, everyone likes a little variety. Would it be cheating if I went home with one of my new line-dancing buddies? Cleavage lady went to a lot of effort with her lingerie tonight.

I mean, I guess it would be cheating if Luke and I are still together. If.

I get out my phone. What are you doing? I text to Luke as another slow song starts. Are you out? If he's at a bar, taking advantage of our "break," then that will be a clear answer.

Just finished a jog, he texts back a minute later. About to get in the shower.

Ooo. Send a pic.

How about I send one later when you're in bed too.

You filthy boy. Absolutely.

He sends back a smiley face. He's still mine if I want him. I think I still do.

My friend Meg was my only connection in this world. She felt emotions so deeply and so frequently that I could absorb her experiences and pretend they were mine. But they weren't mine, and when she died, I thought I would never feel attached to anything again.

But then I found Luke.

He's a real person, with a real life. He has a family: a brother and brother-in-law and their adorable baby daughter. He accepts me as I am and gives me space. Or he did until now. The now part is the problem.

I suddenly wish I were home. His hand around my ankle as I read. My cat snuggled between us, with her soft fur and deadly claws. Warmth and happiness and the illusion that I'm a real girl.

What a dumb thing to wish for. Any guy here would be happy to wrap his hand around my ankle. Still, I look over the growing crowd and feel my lip curl.

Yeah. I'd rather have cookies and some phone sex tonight. What the hell do I want with muddy shoes and sweaty balls?

I bid farewell to my new friends and approach the bar to settle my tab. Eyes follow me. So many eyes. These men are on the road tending to wells and lines for weeks at a time, and they're *hungry*. They want to play with me. Eat me up. Some of them want me to enjoy it. And some of them prefer that I don't. I've had enough of them over the years to detect the different kinds pretty easily.

For example, the handsome blue-eyed fellow who smiles when I sidle up to the bar is trying for charming, but I see the cruelty beneath, shining through like greasy skin through matte makeup.

"Hey, beautiful," he says, as if I'd believe a gorgeous twenty-something like him thinks I'm beautiful. He doesn't think I'm gorgeous. He thinks I'm plain, and plain means desperate and easy for a boy with sparkling blue eyes. He thinks I'm the type who'll be so grateful for his attention that I'll let him use my mouth in a dirty bathroom stall. I'm not beautiful but I'm right here.

Silly boy doesn't know I already got laid in a bathroom this week, and my exquisite mouth is reserved for better men than him.

"Buy you a drink?" he purrs.

"No thanks!" I chirp. "I'm heading back to my room."

"Oh yeah? Want some company?"

I turn to him and giggle nervously at his wide, white grin. "You're funny."

"Nah, I'm serious as a heart attack, darlin'. I haven't seen you here before, and I love making new friends."

I shrug one shoulder and duck my head, pretending to blush. "I'm just visiting."

"Well, I wouldn't want you to be lonely while you're visiting. Why don't you sit down and keep me company?"

"Stop it! You're so silly!"

"At least let me buy you one more drink. I'm James."

"James," I repeat, not offering my own name. He doesn't notice or care. "Okay, James. Sure. I'll have another drink. Thank you."

When Maria brings over my tab, I sign off on it and James tells her he'll get me another of whatever I'm drinking. Her friendly smile falls away and her gaze goes sharp and ugly, first on him and then on me. "Great," she says, with none of her earlier enthusiasm.

Poor thing. She obviously fell for his false charm at some point or another. He probably convinced her that he was mad for her, wild for her big ass, and she believed it. Plenty of men are, after all.

But not James. One look at him and I can see exactly who he is: a big fish in a tiny pond. He wants the petite blond rodeo queen on his arm while he screws his way through the county. After that relationship falls apart, he'll marry some rich daddy's girl from Oklahoma City and get a job with her old man, then screw his way through that county while her daddy pays their mortgage and keeps him employed.

But Maria doesn't see that. She probably crushed on him for a while; maybe he was an older boy in school, and then he finally turned those eyes on her and she fell hard. But that's not my fault, Maria. I don't deserve the icy stare that comes as she delivers my drink.

It's definitely a little more watered-down than the first ones. That's fine. I'll be drinking it quickly. I take two big gulps and watch James flash a sly smile at the man next to him.

"Thanks again for the drink," I say. "You're sweet."

"Sit down," he suggests.

I hold up a hand and gulp the rest of the drink. His cocky grin tips down into a cocky scowl.

"Sorry. I'd love to but I can't. I have to call Mama before she goes to bed or she'll worry."

"All right. Go make your call and come back. I'll be right here waiting for you."

Who the hell does James think he is, telling me how to make his night easier? I'm tired of playing with him, and I have to pee, so I drop my faux shyness and set my empty glass down. "Nah."

"All right, then," he says tightly. "Tell me your room number and I'll bring you another drink. We can talk and get to know each other. Must be lonely being in a strange town alone."

"Room 205. Fifteen minutes?"

"Sure. I think I can do that." Even his assent is a little condescending, meant to make me thankful he'll waste a quarter hour waiting to use me.

I'm only ten feet away before James and his friend are laughing, loud ugly chuckles at my expense. *This dumb bitch thinks I like her. What a pitiful little slut she'll be for me.* There are so many small monsters in this world.

After hurrying back to my room, I jump in the shower and wash off the travel grime. Then I pull on sexy undies and soft socks and my favorite ancient T-shirt to wait. The mattress is a little soft, but the room is warm and cozy and I settle in with a sigh. A few breathless minutes later his knock raps through the pool atrium, so I bounce up with a laugh. He's not patient, of course, so a second knock follows close behind. "Open up, baby," he calls.

I crack open my door to better hear him, and, right on time, loud bootsteps echo through the ceiling above me. The door swings open. "What the hell do you want?" a man upstairs growls in a deep, phlegmy voice.

"What the shit?" yelps James.

I clap a hand over my mouth to stifle giggles. I'd clearly heard the boots of two men above my head when I dropped by earlier, and James is making the acquaintance of at least one of them.

"Is . . . uh . . ." He's realizing he never bothered getting my name. "I was supposed to meet someone here?"

"Well, fuck off. Looks like you'll be meeting Rosie Palm tonight, you dickwad." The man's guffaw bounces around the high metal ceiling of the atrium before being cut in half by his slamming door. I giggle harder, my laughter trying to leak out and join in the fun.

James seems to stand silently for a long moment before he lets out a string of curses beneath his breath.

"Better luck next time!" some asshole calls from farther down the row of rooms, and I have to close my door to hide my snorting.

"Fuck you straight to hell!" James snarls out before I hear his boots stomping down the nearest set of stairs. When I peek out the open curtains of my window, I see him charging toward the front entry, a beer and a tumbler still clutched in his fists. If I'd stayed dressed, I could have followed him back to spy on his ignominious return to the bar, but, oh well. I've chosen comfort over entertainment this time.

Utterly pleased with myself, I retrieve my cookies and grab my book before turning off the lights and climbing into bed. The curtains are still parted. I love to watch people going by, especially when they're unaware. It's like watching TV, their little lives playing out for me to see.

I like this place.

Send me that pic when you're in bed, I text to Luke. Then I tuck myself in for a great drunk evening of dessert, reading, and masturbation. What more could a girl ask for on a chilly autumn night?

CHAPTER 7

My hometown is about ten minutes outside of the county seat. It isn't much. There are no government offices here. No retail shops. It's big enough for a pitifully small school, but not big enough for a McDonald's. There's no Dairy Queen either. No Sonic. The only thing the population can support is a knockoff drive-in called Taste 'n Freeze that's only open during the summer.

Taste 'n Freeze. What the fuck does that even mean?

But even the Taste 'n Freeze looks permanently boarded up as I approach the edge of town. And I was wrong about the retail. There's a brand-new dollar store that cropped up next to the ancient gas station.

Beyond the new store, there are other changes. The one run-down motel has been converted into a cheap studio apartment complex by the looks of the hand-painted sign propped on the roof. Half the doors are open to let out cigarette smoke and welcome in fresh air.

A ragged old coffee joint has been turned into a high-interest loan company decked out in shiny yellows and blues to make signing your meager earnings away seem more fun. The used-car lot next door is now just empty asphalt and destroyed light poles. Otherwise, things look pretty much the same. I pass the street that leads to my parents' home and drive toward the narrow steam cloud that climbs into the sky like the grasping, greedy arm of some lowly god.

The smoke is attached to the huge white tower that looms above the power plant. I hate that damn plant with a passion. I scowl as I drive by, because I know that passing it won't leave it behind. It'll be there in my rearview mirror for the next ten miles.

You can't ever forget where you come from when the land is so mercilessly flat. On a clear, cold day that steam follows you forever, calling you back.

"Assholes," I say to no one in particular, then I focus my eyes on the one windmill I can see peeking over the road ahead.

No, not windmills. Wind *turbines*. I looked them up last night. Wind turbines. I keep my eyes on my big robot friend and drive on toward the next town over to dig up dirt on Little Miss Kayla. I smile at the first sign that warns me not to pick up any hitchhikers because they could be escaped convicts.

The area I'm heading to is mostly populated by prison guards and their families. On the far side of the town limits is a small Oklahoma state prison. Ricky has never been housed there, because they try to keep inmates out of their own stomping grounds for fear that escape would be too tempting. Plus they don't want your troubled buddies gathering around the exterior fences to wave and hoot at you during yard time.

Let's be honest: I probably would have done that to Ricky, given such easy opportunity. A little payback for all those years of making fun of me every time I walked anywhere near him in the house.

Of course, the best revenge is living well, but really the *best* best revenge is living well while mocking him to his face. Why not have it all?

The apartment complex I'm looking for is at the closest edge of town, a big semicircle of two-story buildings constructed sometime in the early nineties. Most of the patios are empty but for rusting charcoal grills and a chair here and there. The one I park in front of is screened in, and two cats sit on a couch looking out scornfully at me. The sight of them makes me wonder what my own cat is doing and whether she misses me.

She doesn't. I dropped her off at Luke's, and she's far too busy enjoying new, strange environs and getting into all the high hiding places and fun shadows to be found in his converted loft. She probably won't even want to come home with me, but that's too bad for her, because I'm not leaving her there.

Would she like a little house in the suburbs with a white picket fence? Yeah. She would.

But then there's me.

Maybe I should just try it. I can leave anytime I want. Maybe I can even secretly keep my place in the city and escape there when I need to get away from my loving, supportive boyfriend.

Damn it. I hate him so much.

I get out of my car and head toward the building number Ricky gave me. As I approach apartment B, I'm surprised to see a tidy little patio overflowing with potted plants, including a few that are still flowering, the old buds neatly nipped off. Between the pots nestle colorful ceramics of bejeweled fish and animals with big eyes. Several bouncy balls and a plastic trike take up the rest of the cement space. Not what I was expecting from a family that doesn't care that a daughter has gone missing.

The faint sounds of cartoons dance through the door as I knock. Just a few seconds later the door opens to reveal a tall Native American woman I'm sure I've never seen before. She has a brown-haired young boy on her hip and a spatula in her hand, and she's still wearing her state prison guard uniform. "Yes?" she prompts.

"I'm looking for Kayla."

"Kayla?"

I don't really need her answer to know I have the wrong place. The apartment behind her is clean and neat, and I smell something delicious cooking in the kitchen. "She's a teenage girl who went missing a few weeks ago. I was told her mother lives here."

She shrugs her free shoulder as the boy lays his head on the other. "Maybe try the next building?" She points with the spatula. "I've seen cops over there once or twice."

"Yeah, that sounds about right."

I walk around to apartment B of the building she indicated, and I find a moldy old love seat on the porch, the cement beneath it strewn with dead leaves and dried-out cigarette butts, and my Spidey senses tingle. This place feels like home.

The patio door is cracked open, and the sound of a raucous talk show spills loudly out, but the noise fades to a dull roar as I approach the front door and knock, giving it an extra-hard rap so I sound official.

"What?" a woman yells from inside. I ignore the question and knock again, which prompts muttered cursing from the other side of the door. Finally it opens, revealing a painfully thin blonde in a tank top that's so worn and loose, it's nearly exposing one of her nipples. It's Wanda Stringer.

"I'm with the county," I lie. "I'm looking for Kayla Stringer." I'm taking a chance that Wanda might recognize me, but why would she? The last time I saw her I was eighteen or so, and if I introduce myself as Ricky's sister, I'll have to listen to a long tirade about what an asshole my brother is. I could supply that tirade myself, so I'm not interested.

Kayla's mother shrugs. "I don't know. She doesn't live here."

"Your sixteen-year-old daughter doesn't live here?"

Wanda rolls her eyes. "Don't give me that shit. She's been staying with her dad's parents." Oh, great. Of course. Because my parents were so capable with kids the first time around that they produced at least one sociopath and probably two.

"But she is missing," I prompt.

"She hasn't come around asking for money or stealing my shit in the past month, so if you want to call that missing, then sure."

"Ma'am"—I try on my most snippy tone, the one I remember from so many school meetings as a child—"you're telling me that you have lost track of your girl, you haven't seen her in a month, but you don't know if she's *missing*. Is that correct?"

"Check in with her pimp; maybe he's got that little bitch on a tight leash."

She swings the door closed, but I catch it with a slap of my hand just in time. "Your teenage daughter is being prostituted?"

"Kayla is a little truck-stop whore and she loves it. Does that clear it up for you? Do you think you can still save her? She's a lazy slut who didn't want to get a real job and decided to run wild in the streets instead. She's the one who wanted to go stay with her grandparents. If they lost her, is that my fault?"

Well, technically I'd put responsibility for her child right in her lap, but who am I to judge? "Who's her pimp?" I ask. "Does he live around here?"

"We don't sit around and braid each other's hair and discuss her pimp, lady. How should I know where he lives?"

"You must have a name."

"Sure," she spits. "His name is Little Dog. Does that help? *Little Dog?* Think you can find him? Maybe he's in the fucking phone book! If you find that piece of shit, tell him he owes me two hundred bucks for that iPad. I know damn well he's the one who stole it."

"What's he look like?" I ask, but I've relaxed too much, and she sees her chance to escape and shoves the door closed in my face.

"Bitch," I say to the door. The TV volume rises on the other side. I pause for a moment to think of a way to get revenge for her disrespect, but she's not worth the time. Kayla clearly isn't here and hasn't been here for a while.

My cold heart sinks a little. If Kayla was turned out by some small-town pimp, then she's nothing at all like me. She's just a poor abused girl like all the other poor abused girls out there.

In a nice suburban neighborhood, if a girl disappears, it's city news. Maybe even national news. Posters everywhere. Manhunts. Strangers weeping for this vulnerable child. If a grown man is having sex with a teenage neighbor who lives in a McMansion in the good part of town, the police will be notified. Consequences will be swift.

But if that girl is poor trash when she goes missing, or if she's being *paid* for the sex, then all law and sympathy gets thrown out the window. She's a whore and she deserves whatever she gets, even if she's only sixteen. She's all used up and worthless now. She probably was from the moment she was born.

Hell, if she's a brown child, she might not even be called missing at all. Just another girl who hardly deserved to live. What did she expect?

I stroll slowly back to my car, frowning at this lifestyle news about Kayla. She's obviously a very troubled young woman. "Troubled," I say aloud to myself with a smile, because I've always loved that description.

Troubled means that she very likely walked away from her family and hooked up with Little Dog or some other award-winning loser, because choosing your own bad path is better than following someone else's. At best, she's a runaway headed for a long, hard life that will never get better. At worst, this pitiful, pimped-out girl has been killed or kidnapped or loaned out to work for someone else in some big city.

She might be in deep trouble, she might be dead, or she could be nodding off in someone's heroin basement, having the time of her life on the fast track to an overdose.

I'm not a social worker, and there's nothing I can do about any of those situations. I was hoping to find someone kick-ass, and that prospect is looking less and less likely. Kayla is just another sad girl who wasn't ever going to have a chance in this world. There are millions of them. Junkie mom, dad in prison, too many men watching and waiting . . . Come on.

I should just go home. But the kind of trouble I hate is waiting at home. Emotional trouble, the one kind I have no aptitude for, and I hate being bad at things.

And there are more benefits to staying in Oklahoma. There's road food, of course, always the best part of any trip. And there are strangers to interact with, which is always exciting. And there's one last benefit to this trip that I wasn't expecting: each of the partners at my firm has emailed to express their support for what I'm doing. One even mentioned my "heroism."

Me! A hero!

If I go home with no results and no resolution, I'll give up this newfound glory and all the bragging rights of returning triumphant. So onward I slog.

As I round the edge of Kayla's building I see the same pitiful swing set that exists in every apartment complex of this kind. Two swings, one of them broken and wound tight around the supporting pole, the other one hanging at a slight angle. The swings are flanked by the kind of metal slide that causes second-degree burns on a hot summer day. That's a particularly sadistic touch when it's one hundred degrees in Oklahoma for the entire season that kids are out of school. Even I could plan a better park, and I'm a goddamn sociopath.

Past the swing set is an ancient picnic table, and gathered around that are several teenagers who decided not to bother with school today. Or this year. Hard to say.

"Hey!" I bark out. They glance up without any alarm at all. Punks. "You guys know Kayla?" I've been in Minnesota too long, and now I've identified myself as an outsider, but maybe that's okay. They know I'm not a local cop, certainly.

Two of the kids shrug, but the youngest, a boy, tips up his chin in a nod.

"She been around?" I ask.

"What'd she do?" the boy calls as I walk closer.

"She won the lottery. I'm just trying to deliver her prize money."

All three of them collapse into drug-induced giggles at that. I smile as if I'm friendly and hand the young white boy a twenty. "A clue, a clue," I sing, echoing an old kids' show I used to watch when I was alone in our trailer for days. The three kids giggle again at the hilarity.

Maybe I'm better with children than I thought I was. At least when they're high. I could start an outreach program for high teens. I'll suggest it at our annual five-minute-long meeting about how the firm can have a beneficial presence in our community. Now I'm giggling too.

"Listen, I just want to know if you've heard where she could be."

"Kayla's a slut," the boy says. "Could be anywhere with anyone."

Sluts don't go missing; they just become looser sluts. I'm getting bored now. "Fine. Just guess."

The girl, with a cropped blond hairstyle that could be edgy if she'd cut the bangs a little shorter, finally speaks up. "If she didn't just take off with some trucker, then maybe she's with Little Dog. He's been gone a couple weeks himself."

"You been hanging out with Little Dog?" the taller Hispanic boy asks archly.

"Fuck off, Del."

I roll my eyes. "Does Little Dog have a real name, or were his parents giant dicks?"

More hilarious laughter. "Brodie," the younger boy finally offers.

"And where does Brodie live?"

I'm surprised when all three of them point in the same direction at the same time. Following their gesture, my eye falls on the back of a brick building. "The Laundromat?"

"Nah," the girl says, "the hill."

I follow the point of her finger again and look beyond the building this time. Past a few hazy clouds, a rise of trees climbs up a shallow hill outside town. Either Brodie is a troll in the old-fashioned sense of the word or there's a run-down shack up there somewhere. I guess I'm about to find out.

CHAPTER 8

I leave the kids at the picnic table plotting how to score more weed with their twenty-dollar windfall, and I drive in the general direction of "the hill." I lose sight of it anytime I get too close to a building, but lucky for me there aren't many structures in this town. I have a clear view in no time and realize I'm not looking for a shack at all. Just the opposite.

A fancy wooden fence runs along the road, like the kind you'd normally find around the horse farms of Kentucky. This one protects no quarter horses or Arabians. It's just a ridiculous acreage of browning grass, and its sole purpose is to use up precious water. If I ever noticed this in my childhood, I don't remember it. I probably didn't realize how much money it would take to fence in a property this size. Who the hell would build something like this outside a prison town? The warden? Even that seems a bit of a stretch. Unless he's crooked.

And it is a grand estate, though the peeling whitewash of the fence indicates the place has seen better times. I turn under a wooden archway and drive up a lane that's guarded by rows of pecan trees on either side like be-nutted sentries. Very pretty. My tires crunch over old shells.

At the top of the hill, a good forty feet above sea level, I discover a man-made pond complete with a nonfunctioning fountain and, beyond that, a low ranch house that stretches out forever. A covered porch adorns the entire front side of the house. I expect to see rocking chairs standing sentry, but the whole long porch is empty aside from an overturned bucket someone left near the front door.

Very odd.

After pulling into the circular driveway, I park in front of green double doors outfitted with honest-to-God door knockers. To entertain myself, I use one to clack away at the wood, then push the doorbell for good measure. I'm not the least bit surprised when it chimes out the opening notes of some classical arrangement I don't know. Mr. Little Dog Brodie comes from surprisingly fancy stock.

When there's no answer, I press my ear to the wood and I think I detect the rumbling bass of an action movie inside. This time I knock with my fist and hit the doorbell several times. A few seconds later one of the doors flies open to reveal some twenty-something kid with long, stringy hair, a nearly concave bare chest, and loose jeans falling off his hips.

"Monsieur Little Dog?" I inquire politely.

"Nah. I'm Nate."

"May I please speak to Little Dog?"

"He's not here."

"Do you know when he'll be back?"

"Naw, man. He took off two, three weeks ago after some big guy came by. Cleared right out of here."

A voice shouts out from somewhere deep inside the dim house. "Nate! Your turn, man!"

Nate looks over his bony white shoulder, then back to me, then over his shoulder again.

"May I come in?" I ask, and he sighs with relief and pulls the door wider.

"Yeah, man. Come in." He closes the door after I step in; then he rushes toward the voice and the rumble of bass down the short hall. "You're not a cop, are you?" he tosses back.

"Naw, man," I answer. "Definitely not a cop, dude." As I follow Nate, I recognize the cacophony of bass and explosions as a video game, and I emerge from the hallway into a living room graced with four young white men. A *sunken* living room.

The guys are draped over a U-shaped couch that looks like it was built to fit perfectly into the recessed space. Their eyes are all focused on a giant flat-screen TV above a moss rock fireplace.

The huge table in front of them is littered with at least several days' worth of pizza boxes and enough beer bottles to nearly camouflage two big glass bongs.

"Hello, boys!" I call out above the din.

One of the guys nearly jumps from his seat at the sight of me, and I notice he has a third bong clutched between his thighs. This one is shaped like a big brown penis.

"She's not a cop," Nate clarifies as he grabs a controller.

"Hey, everyone!" I call out. "Anyone seen Little Dog lately?"

They shake their heads, and their eyes drift back to the screen as Nate starts playing. "He took off," someone finally offers.

"After some guy kicked his ass," another adds.

"Oh, really? Someone beat him up?"

"Yeah."

"Was this after Kayla disappeared?"

"Yeah," Nate says, "like a week later."

I descend into the pit and nudge one man's leg until he shifts it and leaves me room to sit down. I sink into soft gray leather and realize I'm facing a huge pastel painting of the very house I'm in. "Whose place is this?"

A couple of the guys snort in answer. "It's Brodie's place, man," Nate answers. "His grandparents died and left it to him two years ago. So dope."

Jeez, what a way to honor Nana and Pawpaw's sacrifice. "So this whole giant place is his?"

"So dope!" Nate shouts.

"And you guys live here?"

All of them shrug. "Not really," one says.

"On and off," says another.

"We're watching the place for Brodie," says Nate.

Nice gig. "Can I buy a beer off you?" I ask as I toss another of my twenty-dollar bills on the table and grab an unopened can of Milwaukee's Best to pretend I'm in high school again. Of course, now I notice the stench of old weed and body odor. I've become more discerning in my old age, and the kid next to me reeks of sweat or onions, I'm not sure which.

I drink half the beer and settle in for a little while. They've been fucked up for days and don't seem to question my presence. I've appeared, so here I am.

After a few minutes, I find myself staring at a bookshelf full of tiny pale statues. They're Lladró figurines. I recognize them only because I remember watching a whole segment about them on a shopping channel one day at my grandma's house.

If that sounds like a touching moment, it wasn't. My grandmother was a stone-cold bitch who treated me resentfully when she was forced to babysit. When I was at her house, she instructed me to sit quietly and "stop being a little cunt." That's a fun word to learn when you're six. You can really shut down a whole first-grade classroom with that one.

At that age I wasn't even a monster. Not yet. My entire life was still instability and uncertainty. My parents could never be depended on, and when they disappeared for days at a time, my brother offered cruel taunts instead of comfort.

No one took care of me, so my brain helped me do it myself by eventually shutting down anything that made me weak. I grew strong. I grew invincible. I would never have let these idiot little punks pimp me out or use me. On the contrary, I would've used them for whatever they had to offer.

"What's up with Kayla?" I finally ask, and receive another chorus of shrugs. None of them even looks nervous, though I watch their faces for guilt. "Did she take off?"

"Yeah, I think so," Onion Boy says. "She was calling Brodie a lot before he left."

"So she's alive?"

Nate snorts loudly. "You think Kayla's dead? Why?"

"No one has seen her in weeks."

More shrugs, and then someone farts and the boys erupt into guffaws. This isn't exactly playing out like an interrogation scene from an Agatha Christie novel. "Did Kayla ever crash here?" I try.

"Sure," Nate says.

"Great." Without asking for permission, I get up and wander out of the room looking for any evidence of this niece of mine. There are four bedrooms, all decorated in the finest expensive eighties oak furniture, big, lumbering pieces sculpted with generic leaves and vines. All except the master bedroom, which is graced with cherrywood against mauve-painted walls. It appears that Little Dog hasn't changed a thing in two years. In fact, a portrait of his grandmother watches him sleep at night.

Jesus.

Speaking of, a big cross hangs above the headboard in a matching cherry finish. It's full-on grandma chic.

There are no bodies or bloody knives or even notes about how to get rid of a dead girl's corpse. But when I wander into a brass-fixtured bathroom, I do find evidence that a young girl has been here. There are hair scrunchies and lip gloss at the makeup table. I carefully touch a finger to a compact of glittery purple eye shadow, then a flavored lip balm.

She's just a girl. That's all. There are no pieces of me here. Nothing I identify with. I've become some kind of do-gooder.

I leave the mauve-colored room and stride down the hallway, bored with this game and done with this town. "What's your number?" I ask

Nate, whose turn seems to be over. Someone else is firing a gun now, and Nate is packing one of the bongs.

He offers his phone number without question, and I tap it into my contacts, then immediately send a text. Send me Brodie's info. While I wait, I peruse the figurine shelf, touching the pastel sculptures before picking out my favorite and sliding it into my purse. I've wanted one since I was six years old. The height of luxury and elegance. And now I have a pale, long-limbed woman reaching to drape pearls around her ice-cold neck. Just lovely. What great luck I have.

My phone lights up with the contact info, and I wave goodbye and leave, descending back into the real world down the hill and past the prison, to another grandmother's house we go.

The smokestack taunts me, guiding me home.

CHAPTER 9

I'm not putting off seeing my parents; I'm just hungry.

I drive past the power plant, taking my hands off the wheel to give it the double finger as I cruise back into my hometown and then drive right on through it, back toward the county seat. I'm craving Sonic tater tots anyway, so the heartwarming family reunion can wait.

I frown when the giant cloud of power plant steam reappears in my rearview mirror, ever looming.

My dad worked at the A&I power plant for a total of ten months, but don't get excited. That wasn't a streak. It was ten months spread out over four different years. Despite that spotty history, he called himself an "A&I man" for my entire childhood. His last job might have been at a feed distribution center that he'd quit five weeks before, but he was still an "A&I man" through and through. It was the best spin he could manage on his work history.

He staffed all the jobs around town at one point or another, but his body rejected each of them, one by one, overcome by the idea of getting up at 6:00 a.m. five days a week.

He finally threw his back out hauling a deer carcass out of season, and then his glory years of disability checks began. Funny, even after that he could still rant for days about black people on the dole. Those racism muscles of his never got tired. Truly a miracle of persistence.

Setting my father aside for now, I spend the rest of the drive to the county seat planning my perfect Sonic homecoming. Chili dog, yes. Tater tots, yes. Cherry limeade, of course. But what kind of ice cream for dessert? Hot fudge sundae? Maybe, but they might have something new I want to try. Best to save that order for after the meal to see what feels right.

I pull into the drive-in stall, roll my window down, and order the perfect meal. When it arrives, it's heaven delivered on a red tray, and I tear open the chili dog wrapper with glee. And just as I suspected, there *is* a new dessert. I chew my tots and contemplate the photo of mini-churros stuck into a bowl of soft-serve ice cream. I think I'll try that instead of going for an old standard.

When I hit the button for the second time, the voice asks for my order, and a grand idea hits me square in the forehead. I grin with the shock of it and ask for three large orders of fries in addition to my dessert. An entire overstuffed bag of french fries is delivered a few minutes later along with my churros.

"Still hungry?" the server asks as she hands my goodies over. She's not even wearing roller skates to entertain me, so I just roll up my window in response and enjoy my churro bowl in peace as the fries get cold. I'll be sure to turn the vents on them when I start the car.

Nobody in my town was wealthy or even middle-class, but their parents worked and brought home groceries and cooked meals, even if those meals were just casseroles made with ground beef and canned veggies. In fact, those church-basement casseroles were my favorite kind of meal. Warm and good and filling.

My parents rarely had fresh food in the house. They just didn't bother because they could always get in the car and pick up a meal for themselves. They also never threw food away, no matter how old it was. The oldest leftovers were reserved for me and Ricky when my parents were heading out for one of their weekend casino trips. "Still good" was a common refrain, even for old, hard fries at the bottom of a greasy bag. "There's fries in the fridge!" my dad would shout. "They're still good!"

Still good when fries got nasty and grainy after an hour. Still good when there was a box of macaroni my mom could have cooked up if she wanted to. Still good just because she couldn't bother running to the store for a can of soup to feed her four-year-old before they started drinking.

These days I don't eat fries unless they're piping hot and crispy from the fryer. The big bag of fries on the passenger seat is already cold. By the time I get to my parents' house they'll be soft, the first stage of fry death. Then they'll start drying out and hardening. I'm familiar with all the stages. Mom and Dad will keep this bag in the fridge for days, making meals out of it as long as they can. My petty spirit will linger with them over the fridge, laughing.

"Still good," I whisper as I pull out and head back to the two-lane highway out of town.

My phone rings, and it's my law office, so I ignore it. I'm on emergency family leave. How dare they?

As I drift out of town, I pass the richest neighborhood in the county. The street is lined with big oak trees shading the nicest houses and the biggest yards around. A couple of these homes even have genuine in-ground pools. More of them have aboveground pools, which aren't as nice but do offer a blue and shiny glimpse for the rest of us, like a cruel elevated mirage.

I used to covet these houses. My mouth would salivate at the sight of them. I imagined that I might seduce one of the owners—middle-aged men who were all upper management in oil companies—steal him away from his wife and install myself as stepmom to one of those blond girls who wore designer clothes to her high school classes.

But the girl and her mom would move away after the divorce, of course. They'd head into Oklahoma City and live off alimony and child support. Then I'd have the house and the pool and no stepchild. I'd lie on a cushioned lounge chair all summer, piña colada in hand, hoping my old husband had another business trip that week so I could be by myself.

I'd wanted their life so badly. And now it was strange to realize I drove past this neighborhood two or three times already without noticing it. Because the houses aren't grand at all, not to my adult eyes. They aren't estates. They're just fairly average two-story houses. Maybe twenty-five hundred square feet? Nothing to scoff at, but nothing to go tying yourself to some doughy old sex addict over.

I could buy one of these places right now if I wanted to, and I definitely don't want to. But I wanted this so much at sixteen I actually walked down that street several times one summer in booty shorts, looking for a likely conquest. I didn't see any, but a cable guy called me over to his van to show me his dick. I wrote down his license plate and called his employer when I got home, pretending to sob breathlessly over the trauma of it all. I hope he got fired and starved to death.

Ah, memories.

Now these mansions, these dreams, with brass chandeliers in the dining rooms and two-car attached garages . . . they just look like plain old houses I'd see on any street in the Minneapolis suburbs. In fact, these may be just the kind of house my boyfriend is trying to talk me into buying, and here I am resenting him.

Life is really funny, isn't it?

CHAPTER 10

I drift out of town past the one-stories and manufactured houses in no time, and once I reach ranchland, the power plant cloud is growing bigger on the skyline. Home fire, I see you and here I come!

There is no rich neighborhood in my little town. Hell, there's not even a wrong side of the tracks. There are simple houses, then the train tracks that bring coal to the plant and take luxury cars to people somewhere far away, and then, when you get past the rail line, it's all rangeland. That's it. Poor folks and cows and an obnoxious bit of industry. Not one aboveground pool to covet, though we had a deflated kiddie pool in our yard for many years.

I take a left just before the plant and head down a paved road that can only generously be called two-lane. After driving past a row of houses with neat yards, I take a left onto a packed-dirt lane just before the grain elevator. I pass behind a few widely spaced ranch homes and one small horse pasture; then the path spits me into a bare-dirt yard enclosed by barbed wire to protect the two precious rusted-out cars in front of our trailer. They're the same two cars that were there when I left for college more than a decade ago.

In fact, everything looks the same, except that there's a newer trailer home sitting directly next to the one I grew up in. The windows of the old house are covered from the inside by stacked cardboard boxes, as if the entire place has been filled up with a collection of junk. Red dust coats the white walls in years of layers like unshed skin.

The new trailer is tan and bright, smaller than the old one but definitely nicer, with bigger windows and an unfinished-wood wheelchair ramp that leads up to the front door. There's even a flower box at the top of the ramp, but whatever plant was in there gave up the ghost many, many weeks ago, and just a few sad sticks poke over the sides to greet me.

I grab my big bag of cold fries from the passenger seat and set out across the dirt and patches of crunchy grass toward the ramp. It's beautifully constructed, and the wood is smooth under my hand, so I know Ricky didn't build it. A church group probably. My mom always made sure she was in at least two congregations at a time to maximize the number of possible potlucks and charity donations. To her benefit, I mean. Not out of a spirit of generosity.

Snorting at the very idea, I knock on the metal door.

"Sarah!" I hear my father call from inside. "The door!" But when the door opens, it's Dad standing there, looking like shit. He's heavier than he was ten years ago and shorter too, but he doesn't look like a man who's been ravaged by a stroke. In fact, his bloodshot eyes and unshaven face make it appear as though the stains on his oversize Snap-on tools T-shirt are probably bourbon. Good old Dad.

"I'm helping look for Kayla," I say in greeting. "Was she living here when she disappeared?"

"I talked to that deputy weeks ago," my dad growls.

"Yeah, I'm not with the county."

"So what are you doing here?"

"I'm your daughter, asshole. Look, I even brought you a present."

"Jane?" He squints as he takes the bag I thrust into his hand. "Jane?"

"Yes, Jane. I heard you lost your granddaughter, so I'm here to help."

"Sarah!" he shouts right into my face. I can smell the bourbon now and I finally feel at home. "Sarah! Jane's here!"

"Who?" my mom shouts from a bedroom somewhere.

I roll my eyes. "It's your daughter! Returned to the warm bosom of her family!"

"What?" my mom shouts back.

"Oh, for fuck's sake," I grumble. "Can I come in or not?"

My dad shuffles aside so I can step past. The trailer is new, but the furniture isn't. I recognize the overstuffed blue sectional smashed into the tiny living room right away. I fell asleep on that couch so many times. I elbowed my drunk father awake on it far more times than that. I think I even caught Ricky making one of his children there when I was in high school. He barked at me to get the hell out or join in. I don't think he meant it, but then again, he's Ricky.

My mom finally shuffles down the hall, eyes narrowed in suspicion. Her stringy hair is gray now but still streaked with enough brown to look like moldy wheat bread. She's lost about an inch in height too. Or maybe I've gotten straighter since I left this place behind.

My lip arches in a sneer as I take her in. I haven't seen her in so many years. The last time we spoke on the phone, she called me a heartless bitch and several other names, so I blocked her number and moved on. That was more than a year ago now. Her small eyes widen when she registers that it's actually me.

"Where the hell have you been?" she barks.

"Living my best life, obviously. How about you?"

"Your daddy almost died from a stroke and you didn't do shit to save him. Now look at him! He's a cripple."

"Looks more like a drunk to me. That wheelchair in the corner has dust on it."

"You little—"

"Let's skip the endearments and drawn-out hugs, all right? I'm not here for a reunion. Where's Kayla?"

My father drops into a recliner and lets it rock violently beneath him. "You look good, Jane!" he yells, as if I'm not standing four feet away.

"Thanks." My dad never took care of us and never protected us. He could also be a mean drunk. I couldn't count on him for anything, not food, heat, transportation, or safety. But he never sneaked into my room at night to molest me, and his drunken slaps were halfhearted at best, and that's better than a lot of girls get from fathers.

My mom, on the other hand, was a cruel bitch: overcritical one day, ignoring me the next. She'd bring me a half-eaten cake from some church basement, pretending she'd made it herself, then call me a little pig for eating it too quickly. She'd take me to Wednesday services and ask the women to pray the devil out of me, then take off in the car and let me walk home wondering if I'd see her in a few hours or a few days.

My very first memory is being alone and scared at night when I was three or four. Lightning and thunder and wind knocking trash against the thin walls of our house. My brother was eight and already a bully. He told me our parents were never coming home and he was going to sell me for fifty dollars to a man he met that day. "I got him up from twenty," he sneered.

Nobody cared about us. We were the white trash of the neighborhood, and family matters weren't anyone else's business in this part of the country. It's not like we were being beaten half to shit, and plenty of kids my brother's age were cooking and cleaning for younger siblings.

I wasn't dying. I wasn't even starving, really. I was just terrified and bereft. No call to involve the authorities in that.

That was back when I still felt fear. When I still cried. When I still needed love and safety. I can almost remember what that felt like, but not really. It's more like watching a movie of some pitiful little stranger.

I hate remembering that I used to need these people. They disgust me now, and that weak little girl disgusts me too.

"Your brother's locked up again," my mom whines, trying a different tack, since confrontation didn't work, "and we're just barely getting by."

"I brought you some fries," I say, gesturing toward my dad's hand stuck deep in the bag. "They're still good."

"I don't want fries," my mom declares, though she slides right over to snag a few. "We need real help. A minivan to help get your dad around. A lifting recliner. He can't hardly get up out of that chair. Look at him, Jane!"

On cue, my dad gets out of the chair and stumbles toward the kitchen, mumbling something about ketchup.

"Tragic," I sigh. "Now, where the hell is that granddaughter of yours?"

She glares at my dad, his perfectly capable body silhouetted by the fridge light. "How the hell should I know?" she mumbles.

I drop into my old seat on the sectional and put my feet up on another corner. "Traditionally—and I know you have no experience with this—the adults in the home keep tabs on any child who lives there."

"Child?" she spits. "That girl thought she was a grown-ass woman. She treated us so badly, Jane. Her own grandparents."

"Mm-hm."

"You don't understand because you abandoned us. You don't know what she was like. Men pounding on our door at all hours of the night looking for her. She's a nasty little slut."

Having heard it all before about my own teenage self, I just roll my eyes and wait for her to move on.

"I gave her a place to stay because she couldn't get along with her mama, and that was more than I owed her."

"So she paid you rent?" I drawl, knowing full well my mom doesn't have a grandmotherly bone in her body.

She blows a raspberry through loose lips and I grimace with distaste. "Not *enough* rent," she mutters. "We had to feed her."

"Right. I'm sure there were home-cooked meals nightly. Has she come by or called even once since last month? Has she texted? Dropped by to steal something from your purse? Anything?"

"No."

Shaking my head, I close my eyes and take a deep breath. Much to my disgust, this place actually smells like home. Old cooking oil and the rose perfume my mother favors in between shampoos. The smell of my childhood, underlain by a chemical pleasantness of new walls and carpet that I never experienced in my youth.

I don't feel any of the things I should be feeling. Nostalgia or sorrow or love. All I ever felt in my last few years in my parents' home was anger and restlessness as I worked toward a scholarship just so I could rub it in their worthless faces. But even those feelings are hard to remember now. My parents have no power over me. When this discussion is over, I'll walk out of here and leave them to their misery. I guess all I feel right now is victory.

"Just tell me what happened," I say with weary impatience. "Did she leave with that Little Dog loser?"

"She didn't leave with anyone, not that it's any business of yours. She took off on her own. I'm too old to go chasing after stupid girls doing things they shouldn't be doing."

I glance at my mom. "What things?"

"What things do you think? Men. Weed. Drinking. Hell, her full-time job was hitchhiking, as far as I could tell."

"Did she catch a ride out of here?"

My questions seem to push her over the edge, and my mom snaps. "What the hell are you doing here, Jane? You don't give one goddamn about your family! Your daddy almost died and—"

"This is getting us nowhere," I interrupt, rising to my feet as I slap my hands against my thighs for emphasis. "Let me check out her room. Maybe there's something there."

"This isn't your house!" she screeches. "Why are you even here?"

"Because I love my family, Mama. Come on."

She stares blankly at me as if she's trying to puzzle out the words and the meaning behind them. Am I serious? Of course I'm not, lady; can't you tell by the thick twang I just laid on?

I push past her and march down the short hallway toward the bedrooms.

"Hey! I'll call the cops, missy. This is trespassing. You can't just . . ." Her protest fizzles out, and I hear the *swish-swish* of her polyester shorts coming up behind me.

The room is tiny and messy, just a bed and a dresser and a dark blue sheet tacked up over the small window to keep out the sun. I remember those glorious teenage days of sleeping until 2:00 p.m.

"Have you bothered to look for her?" I ask.

"*Look* for her? Even the cops think she ran away. Such an ungrateful piece of trash can stay gone."

I smirk. "Show me the worried-grandma act you put on for the cops. I bet it was a great show. You love playing the victim. Did you cry? Wail? Rage at them to do something for your little baby?"

She blows air through her teeth in a hiss, a warning that she's about to lose her temper. The wet sound would have scared little Baby Jane, a warning of screaming and slapping to come, but today it doesn't elicit anything more than an urge to shove her.

"You get outta my damn house if you can't be respectful," she growls.

I step deeper into the messy bedroom. "Speaking of: Where'd you get this house, anyway?"

"Fund-raiser." The anger in her voice immediately slides into slimy pride, just as I knew it would. "After Daddy had that stroke, he couldn't get around the old trailer in his chair. Doors were too narrow. Central Baptist was nice enough to host an event to help with a down payment and delivery fees."

"Ain't you proud."

"Yes, I am, and I have a right to be. It's a beautiful home."

"Sure is, Mama." I start sifting through a pile of crap on top of an old dresser that used to be Ricky's. His name is still carved into the front of the middle drawer. A family heirloom.

"What are you even looking for?" she snaps.

"Any hint about where she might have gone."

"She took off for the truck stop looking for a ride. That's where she went: the hell out of here."

This is new information. I'd ask which truck stop, but there's only one that needs no name around here. The first big twenty-four-hour junction in the county seat, complete with showers and laundry facilities. The year they added a KFC, the kids in my school made so many chicken runs out there after class. "So she really did run away? On purpose?"

"Sure."

I pause and turn to glare at her. "Did she tell you she was leaving or not?"

When she shrugs, I notice how much her shoulders droop now. She's only sixty-five, but she's already caving in on herself, skinny all over except her gut, and that center of gravity is dragging her in. "She didn't say anything, but she was always out there looking for a ride, looking for money, whatever she did. That girl was mean as a snake, just like you, so either she's fine or she got what she deserved. Who even knows?"

"Mean like me, huh?"

"Yeah. Sneaky. Beady eyes always watching me." She's losing her needy act completely now. "I was going to kick her out anyway. She had men coming around here like dogs after a bitch in heat. Nothing you can do for a girl like that."

"I mean, you could try to keep grown men away from her. But that probably didn't occur to you."

She smacks her lips together, then barks out a hard laugh. "Men'll take whatever anyone's giving and you damn well know it. That's just life. If you haven't learned that by sixteen, good luck to you. Hell, you gave away enough yourself when you were her age; you should know."

"Shit, Mama, I was giving it away by age seven, wasn't I? Walking around here in tight shorts for any man you might rent a room to. How are they supposed to control themselves when there's a hot ass around, right?"

"Oh please. You always were a little drama queen. You climbed up on his lap given half a chance every damn time. Didn't look too scared to me."

She told me their new friend would watch me when she and Daddy weren't home. I was so happy at first. Hopeful. I pushed the last dregs of my best feelings into that warm hollow of hope and cradled them tight. I wouldn't have to be alone in the house at night! Instead of Ricky ignoring my snotty crying, there would be an adult here to keep monsters at bay.

He was a dream come true at first. He cooked me actual food. SpaghettiOs and grilled cheese and burgers. Even homemade cookies. I can still remember the taste of warm oatmeal cookies. I was thrilled with this new arrangement. I was safe.

He told me I could call him Uncle Pete. I did. I asked him if he would take care of me. He promised he would. He said he loved me like I was his own little girl.

Then my parents left me alone with him for five days.

That was the last time I remember feeling anything much at all. They let him live here for six more months before he moved on.

Instead of punching my mother in the face, I start digging through Kayla's belongings again.

"There's no money in here, if that's what you're looking for."

"Jesus Christ, Mama. What kind of grown woman would steal cash from a teenage girl?" I flash a wide grin over my shoulder so she knows I'm insulting her nasty, greedy, grubby little fingers. "Wait a minute!" I gasp. I even press a dismayed hand to my chest. "How do you know there's no cash in here? You didn't already paw through everything looking for it, did you?"

"I was making sure there weren't no drugs in here!" she barks as I snort in disbelief. "What if the social workers came by to check on the environments?"

I open the top drawer of the dresser to find a combination of fun underwear full of pink cartoon drawings and racier white lace. Not so unusual for a sixteen-year-old. Disappointingly typical. When I shove the panties aside, I spy a little stack of business cards pushed into a corner. Not quite so typical.

The one on top is from a school resource officer she probably got in trouble with a few times. Beneath it are several more cards. One from the youth minister at Central Baptist Church, one from the head of a kids' soccer league, and one from the owner of a local equipment rental company.

Hm. "Does Kayla have a job?" I ask.

Another raspberry from my mom. The woman is truly a master of Shakespearean buffoonery.

"Okay. Does she play soccer?"

"Yeah, right. She'd get her skinny ass kicked up and down that field."

Interesting. I slide the cards into my pocket and poke around a little more. The dresser yields no more surprises, and the rest of the room is crowded with more boxes of my parents' belongings. I have no idea what they've managed to accumulate so efficiently over the years. A bunch of crap anyone else would throw away, I suppose.

"I don't know why you're so worried about some niece you don't even know," my mom snipes again as I rifle through the clothing in the tiny closet. "You can't even be bothered to worry about your own parents. We couldn't find you anywhere! What kind of a bitch changes her number after her own daddy has a stroke?"

"The kind of bitch whose loving mother calls her a bitch all the time would be my best guess."

"I call a spade a spade and a bitch a bitch. You are a goddamn devil child and you always were."

Her insults used to enrage me, but I've heard them so many times, they inspire nothing but amusement. My mother and father made me who I am, so let them experience me in all my glory.

When I consider my childhood—and I rarely do—it's strange to me that I turned out this way when others don't. There weren't years of horrific physical abuse. No incest. Nobody locking me in a crawl space or chaining me to a bed. It was just the drip, drip of emotional abuse and endless neglect accented with a dash of sexual assault, same as so many other kids in this world face.

I assume my genetics helped. My parents are both screwed up and narcissistic, and Ricky isn't far from sociopathy himself. What a nasty little genetic brew my folks created.

Ricky caused more trouble than I did growing up, but my parents mostly left him alone. I'm not sure if that was straight-up misogyny or if my mother hated me in particular for some reason. It's not even worth puzzling over. She's worthless and mean, and I'm too strong to bother with her anymore.

"Do you think that Little Dog guy could have taken her? He's gone too, or so people are saying."

"Who knows, but he didn't come around here looking for her like everyone else."

I set down the pillow I was checking under and turn to narrow my eyes at my mother. "Who's 'everyone else'?"

There's a quick flinch of the lined skin around my mom's eyes. A deep swallow as her gaze darts away from me. "Friends. Acquaintances. Whatever."

I could threaten her, try to force her into some kind of truth, but my mom is slippery if she's anything. She's conned so many do-gooders out of so many donations over the years, and pinning her down on her lies is like trying to nail snot to a wall, as the old saying goes.

She might even have less shame than I do. But she does love to talk shit about people.

"You said there were grown men coming around here. Boyfriends?"

"Boyfriends!" Her smile is a hard, mean line, just lips stretched straight over teeth. "More like customers, considering the cash they flashed around."

"Did you tell the cops that?"

"Yeah, right," she scoffs. "Like I want everyone in town knowing what my granddaughter is. One guy wanted it so bad, he paid *me* money! That girl must've sucked the chrome right off his hitch. Looked like a cop too."

"What do you mean?"

She shrugs, still smiling tight and mean. "Serious. Bald. Wearing a sport coat. And I saw he had a gun on him."

"And then you . . . *sold* him information about your teenage granddaughter." I'm not the least bit surprised.

She blows another raspberry. "All I did was point him toward Little Dog's place. Figured Mr. Man could ask his questions there and stop bothering me. You think I need all the neighbors gossiping about who's knocking on my door day and night? This is a respectable home, despite her best efforts."

"When was this?"

"Week after Kayla took off." She tugs a cigarette from her pocket to light it. "We need to talk about Daddy now that you're home. He's your own flesh and blood."

"I ain't home," I correct her, and walk straight toward the hall until she's forced to back out of the doorway and let me through.

"You owe us," she spits at my back.

"Lady, I don't owe you shit."

"We're your family!"

"Fat lot of good that ever did me."

When I pass my father, he's set the fries aside and taken up his bourbon again. The TV is blaring now, our little family reunion insufficient to hold his interest. I breeze right past him toward the door.

My mom follows me outside. "You get back here."

"A few minutes ago you told me to get the hell out of your house. I'm gettin'."

"We need help. We're out here suffering—"

"I can't imagine that Social Security doesn't treat you just fine, considering Central Baptist paid for a good chunk of this place. You ain't gonna starve, Mama, and Daddy looks like he's getting more than enough to eat. And drink."

"So do you, you fat ass."

"Oh, good Lord," I mutter, nearly skipping down the ramp. The yard might be a dried-out mess, but damned if it isn't a welcome sight now. Even the gray sky looks prettier now, but then again, I'm facing away from the steam cloud.

A glance toward the old trailer reveals the little window that used to be my room. The glass is cracked. I cracked it.

I stop and stare at the long line that reaches diagonally through the glass from one corner to another. I should have destroyed this place back then. I wanted to. But where would that have landed me? Living in an even more broken-down trailer on this same worthless land.

I leave my mom behind, still screaming my name as I drive away.

CHAPTER 11

I drop in on Central Baptist Church on my way out of town. It's a Tuesday afternoon, so I expect things to be quiet, and they are, but there's always a church secretary around keeping things running. I enter through wooden doors badly in need of a coat of paint.

The last time I was in a church, it was a shiny glass-and-metal warehouse for righteous souls, but Central Baptist is a small-town place. The chapel is dark, the pews are ancient, and I'm sure the basement meeting rooms still smell like mildew. They always did.

I'm not struck dead when I step into the small receiving area, so I continue toward a couple of open office doors I see past the bathrooms. Despite the gloomy day, it's hot in here. If memory serves, it was always hot in here. Too much furnace in the winter, and nothing but a couple of window air conditioners in the summer. At least the basement was cooler during post-service potlucks, and that was all I cared about.

"Hello?" a woman calls from a room farther down. "Can I help you?"

"Hi there!" I lay on my Okie accent as I slide into the doorway. "I'm looking for Pastor Truman? He around?"

"No, ma'am." The round-faced woman has a friendly tone, but her mouth is pulled into a perpetual frown that highlights the deep lines between her bushy eyebrows. "No. He left us several months ago."

"Dead?" I ask.

"Oh no! Not at all. He moved up to Missouri, I think. Quite a surprise, but we are working on hiring a new youth minister. Is there something I can help you with?"

"I think Pastor Truman knew my niece Kayla?"

"Kayla?"

The eyebrows draw even closer together. She looks about fifty, but a good threading would take five years off her face, and she has kind eyes.

"She's missing. You may have heard about that. Sarah's granddaughter?"

"Sarah. Oh. Of course." The lines smooth out a little when her face flattens at the sound of my mother's name.

"Anyway, I found Pastor Truman's card in my niece's room, and I thought she may have confided something to him, him being a youth minister and all."

Her face creases in genuine worry. "I'm so sorry about your niece, but I honestly don't remember seeing her around here. Pastor Truman was here for several years, though, so maybe that card was from a while ago?"

"Could've been. When did he leave?"

"Oh, six months ago, I guess. Just out of the blue! His wife was pregnant with their third, and I guess she missed her family up in Hannibal, so off they went. He only gave us a week's notice, but happy wife, happy life, right?"

"No scandal, then?"

"Of course not!"

"All right. Thanks for your help. And my mama's really enjoying that new trailer."

"Oh, sure, well . . . Tell Sarah we say hi. We ain't seen her in quite a while now."

"Since she got the trailer?"

"Well . . ."

"Don't worry, she'll be back around next time she needs something. You have a blessed day, now."

She can't quite reconcile my sugary tone with my words, and the deep lines are back between her brows, but she tries a cheerful "You too, ma'am!"

Ma'am. Yeesh. That's getting old. My kingdom for a smart young bartender who knows to call me miss. Maybe I'll find one later tonight, but the *ma'am*s are hot and heavy around here. I probably won't escape them until I fly back north.

Oh well. Onward and upward.

My phone rings as I'm getting back into my car. It's the office again. I have a brief thought that maybe I'm getting promoted, so I decide to answer it after all. "This is Jane," I say, adding a subtle quaver of vulnerability to my voice. This isn't a good time but I'm still answering the call.

"Jane," he says, and I swing the phone away from my face to glare at it. Are you *kidding* me?

"Rob?" I snap back. "What do you want?"

"Hey, sorry," he's saying when I slide the phone back to my ear. "I know this isn't a good time, but I need to talk to you about North Unlimited. Shouldn't take a minute."

"I'm busy. Whatever it is, you'll need to do it yourself this time, *Robert*."

"I just need to grab a couple of details from the numbers you threw out to the client. There's something wrong with the Google Doc."

"You want *my* details?" I ask. "Surely you have your own notes. You worked so hard on that presentation, after all."

"Jane, this isn't about me. It's about the client."

"*Your* client."

"Yeah, um . . ." Rob clears his throat. "I have some good news. They really liked interacting with you."

"Is that right?"

"Yes. Absolutely. So Jeremy and I talked it over, and we both want you to take the lead in negotiations when you get back."

Well, well, well. This is quite the news drop. And I have all the power now. No more kid gloves for Rob. "So you came up with the idea that I should take over negotiations for your client. Is that what you're saying, Robert?"

"I, uh . . ."

"You need my help," I suggest.

"Yes."

"You're asking for my help."

"Yes."

"So ask. And I suggest you ask nicely."

"Jesus," I hear him mutter before he takes a deep breath. "North Unlimited has requested that I work with you on this, and I'd really love to have you on board."

"How nice. What did Jeremy say?"

"He, uh . . . he said you should take the lead on negotiations when you get back."

"This is so strange, Robert, but I still didn't hear you ask me a question, so I'm not sure how I'm supposed to give an answer."

"Would you please work with me on this deal and take over negotiations when you're back in the office?"

"I'm not sure," I say. "You have a tendency to take credit even when you haven't done the work. This setup seems rather fraught with risk for me, don't you think?"

"I . . ." I hear him swallow. "If I've taken credit in the past for your work, I apologize."

"*If?* That doesn't indicate to me that you've learned anything from your latest missteps, and I don't think I can trust you enough to work on this project for me. I'll get in touch with Jeremy and let him know." I hang up and buckle my seat belt. Before it even clicks in, my phone is ringing again.

I wait a few seconds before answering. "Yes?"

"Jane, I'm sorry. You're right. I've taken advantage of your knowledge and leaned on you over the past year. I've really appreciated all your hard work, and I promise it won't happen again."

"I'm dealing with a family tragedy here, Robert."

"I know. I know. I just . . . I really screwed up that presentation to North Unlimited, and they're pretty insistent that I work with you on this. I'm begging you."

Begging me? Well, I do like that. I raise my eyebrows and settle back into the seat of my car. "Begging me for what?"

"I know you're concentrating on your niece, and that's what you should be doing. So I'll do the work. I'll get everything together, write up the proposals, all of that. If you could just send me your notes. Then, when you return, you're lead negotiator. But please don't freeze me out on this."

Wow. I purposefully made myself look good and Rob look terrible, but I got distracted by the excitement of hunting for Kayla, and I didn't push through to claim my place. I assumed one of the partners would step in and take charge.

Plus this whole deal is boring as hell, trying to sell smuggled chicken meat from China to a bunch of schoolkids. There's nothing particularly sparkly about that. Just imagine the bone-dry meetings I'll get to look forward to.

Still, I want it. And if I can get Rob to do the legwork for me, it will be an ideal situation. I'll sweep back into town, check his work, of course, and take my place in the spotlight.

"Are you sure about those promises?"

"Absolutely. I'm absolutely sure. You can count on me to have everything ready for you when you get back."

"All right, then. I'll forward my notes when I'm back in my hotel room. You get to work. Send me updates. I'll step in as soon as I'm done here."

"Thank you. Thank you so much. This is going to be great."

Well, he's right about that, at least. This *is* going to be great.

CHAPTER 12

It's the middle of a workday, so I can't imagine where I could track down the head of a local soccer league. That position can't possibly be a full-time job around here. League fees wouldn't support a salary.

I look up the man's name online and discover he's an assistant manager at a big chain grocery store near my hotel, so I leave my old town behind again. Can't imagine we'll miss each other much, though I'm sure the place sparkles a little less once I pull away. Hard to tell past the steam cloud.

I race a train along the highway and remember how I fantasized about hitching a ride on one when I was young. All those *things* on all those trains going to people who never set foot on these shitty oil lands. I wanted to follow the tracks and steal their lives. In the end I did.

If Kayla is anything like me, she blew the hell out of this place and will never look back. But I still can't tell. Is she strong and sick like me or just broken like half the other girls here? There was no point in pressing my mother on the issue. A bitch is a bitch is a bitch, in her parlance. There aren't exactly layers to explore.

If I don't dig up more in the next twenty-four hours, I'll have to head back to Minneapolis without hero status. I can't stay too much longer, now that I'm the new rising star in the office.

Needing a distraction from the flat drive, I call Luke on the speakerphone.

"Hey, babe," he says cheerfully, as if he misses me too much to remember we're taking a break.

I grin at his welcome and purr out a sexy hello.

"Any news on your niece?"

"Not really, but I saw my parents."

"Holy shit! Are you kidding me?"

"Nope. They're both still alive and kicking and begging for money."

"Are you okay?"

"Sure. They didn't jump me or anything."

He huffs in laughter. "I meant emotionally."

"You know me. I roll with the punches."

"Yeah, but . . . what was it like?"

Hm. I pause to think what a normal person would say, but the truth is I don't have to pretend with Luke. He knows I'm not normal. He doesn't *quite* know what's wrong with me, but he understands that I don't have the same emotions as others.

"It was good to see them," I finally say.

"Really? That's great. So things have gotten better?"

"No, it was good to see that they're the same and I'm better. I'll come back to Minneapolis and they'll be stuck right here being miserable."

He laughs again as if I'm kidding. "Okay, but you're sure you're really all right? I always feel a little sick after seeing my mom, and you've said yours was pretty mean."

"She's still mean as a bear with a bladder infection, but she looks like shit, so all in all it was a good time."

"But nothing on your niece?"

"I'm not sure. Apparently she was living with my parents when she disappeared. My mom is convinced she took off with a truck driver, and it doesn't seem to occur to her that taking off with a strange adult doesn't mean a sixteen-year-old is alive and well. Funny, huh?"

"And there's still no sign of her?"

"No. I'm running down a few leads. She had some loser boyfriend named Little Dog—Jesus, that name. He took off himself a week later, so either he's with her or he skipped town because he knows something incriminating."

"Maybe he's looking for her." Luke is a sweet guy with a bit of a blind spot, which is how he ended up with me.

"So you think a guy named Little Dog is looking out for the safety of a teenage girl to the exclusion of the rest of his life?"

"Okay. Maybe not."

I feel a sudden surge of lust mixed up with something I don't recognize. Longing? "So what are you up to?" I ask, trying for some sort of flirtatious affection. "You're not cheating on me, are you?" I'm sure he's not, but it's good to let him know I'm checking.

"Jane, come on!" He laughs like cheating on me is the most preposterous idea he's ever heard, and I smile at the sound of it.

"You basically broke up with me before I left, so pardon the question."

"I didn't break up with you. I asked you to move in with me. There's a big difference."

Maybe my anger made me play this all wrong. I should have been working his feelings to my advantage from the start, and instead I was being pissed off about it. I need to keep him tied to me as long as I want him. I need to pull him close even if it disturbs me in ways I don't understand.

"I love you," I volunteer. It's a rare declaration, usually gasped out during sex, because that's my only real form of intimacy.

"Aw, babe," he sighs. "I love you too. I'm sorry we fought, and I'm worried about you. That's a lot to take on down there. Even if you think you're doing okay, you're probably absorbing a lot of damaging crap, and that's hard on anyone."

I should be sure to act vulnerable now. He'll want to protect me. I don't need it, but I *want* him to protect me. There's no one else who'd even bother.

"My mom talks about Kayla like she always talked about me," I offer. I haven't told him much about my family. The truth is leverage, and I never give anyone that. But today the truth is a tool. "She calls her a whore and a slut. Says she doesn't care what happens to her."

"I'm sorry," Luke says, and he means it. I'm glad he feels sorry for the little girl I used to be, because all I can do is hate her for her stupid softness. If Kayla is soft, I'll hate her too, but there's still a chance she's something more. I'm getting hints of it but no proof.

"Were they . . . ?" He stops, then tries again. "Were they happy to see you? Or was there drama?" Luke knows all about drama, thanks to his mother. Only a damaged person would be attracted to someone like me, so I don't mind.

She wasn't mean or neglectful like my parents. Luke's mom is mentally ill, though she refuses to admit it or get help. She was a whirlwind of intensity when he was growing up. Manic and obsessive and focusing all her energy on Luke and his brother. That's why he likes my cool remove now. I'm a gentle breeze on burned skin.

"There wasn't much drama," I finally answer. "My mom just wanted money, of course. But my dad seemed sort of happy I dropped by. He told me I looked good."

"That's nice."

I grin at the absurdity of that one passing comment making things okay. "I'm sure I'll get my notice about the homecoming parade they've arranged any moment now."

"Have you seen anyone else you know?"

"Just my jailbird brother."

"Right," he says on a chuckle, and I'm laughing too, thrilled that he sees the humor in it and I don't have to hide my morbid giggles. It's all so ridiculous.

"What's your next step?" he asks. "Have you talked to the cops?"

"No. I can't imagine I'll bother. I know exactly what they think of troubled teenage girls. They can say she ran away, put her picture up on a website, and wash their hands of it. I'm checking out a couple of other leads tonight. If nothing pans out, this may be the end of it."

"Be careful."

"I will."

"Call me again tonight?" I can tell by the purr in his voice that he wants more phone sex, and I'm sure I'll be in the mood to give it to him, but better to leave him hanging for now.

"We'll see."

We sign off just as I pull up to the grocery store, which is doing its best to compete with Walmart by offering a drive-up pharmacy and "free cones for all kiddos!" I head right inside and serve myself a free cone before I wander the store to look for the assistant manager. If I discover he's recently disappeared too, I'll start to suspect my niece of murder.

That would be kind of fun, actually. A tiny little killer in my family. I'm just settling into the fantasy of that when I come to an open doorway and peer in to see a sandy-haired man behind a computer. "I'm looking for Frank," I say.

He brightens up and stands quickly. "Hello! I'm Frank! What can I do for you?"

Crunching into my cone, I study him for a moment. Frank looks about thirty-eight, maybe forty. He's got a little gut, but he has the healthy good looks of a guy who played a lot of sports in high school. He's white and tan and still has a full head of hair, which he spends a little time on in the morning. But there are broken blood vessels in his nose. I'm thinking he drinks at least a six-pack every night. Anything to get through this life, am I right?

"You're in charge of the soccer league around here?" I ask as Frank skirts his desk to come shake my hand.

"That's right! You found me!"

"I'm so sorry to bother you at work. Is this okay?"

"Absolutely! Come on in!" He shakes with a good grip and his hand doesn't linger. I smile up at him, but he just waves me toward a chair, not the least bit desperate for female attention. "The bosses don't mind," he assures me. "It's good for the community. Good for the store."

"Of course."

"Looking to get your daughter into soccer?"

This league had better include five-year-olds or I'll be pissed. I definitely couldn't have a teenage daughter. Then again . . . of course I could. Several of the girls I went to school with do, assuming everyone is still alive and kicking. Ha. I made a soccer joke.

"Actually . . ." I watch as he takes his seat and folds his hands patiently on top of his beat-up metal desk. What in the world did my hell-raising niece want with this guy? I cross my legs and lean forward a little. "I'm here about Kayla."

"Kayla?" His tan face goes grayish white so suddenly, I almost think the bad fluorescent lighting experienced a surge, and I glance up to see if something popped. "Who?" he croaks.

"Kayla. I believe you know her . . ." He can't possibly fake his way through ignorance when all the blood has left his head. He must be getting dizzy by now.

"Kayla?"

"Yes!" I repeat her name one more time, because each utterance lands like a bullet in his body. "Kayla. Average white girl. Really skinny. Just turned sixteen, looks much younger. Has she been by recently?"

"That was four months ago!" he says too loudly.

"Oh. Okay. *What* was four months ago?"

"She . . . She . . . I mean, she came here. Yes, I remember her. Kayla." He laughs for no reason at all, the sound a high barking that floats up to the metal rafters of his office. "Yeah, she was hoping to join the league, but she . . . I guess she didn't have much support from her family. She didn't have the fees, so she hoped maybe she could . . ."

Sweat is gathering on his upper lip as he stammers through his explanation. This man definitely had sex with this teenage girl, or something close enough to sex that he can see his life flashing before his eyes.

He coughs hard and the blood finally rushes back to his face, turning it bright red. "She was hoping there was paid work she could do for the league, but it's run by volunteers, you understand. Nobody gets paid or anything. Even I don't get paid."

"So what happened?"

"Nothing! Nothing happened! I mean, we talked about her working here at the store, maybe, to try to raise funds, but it didn't pan out. She wasn't . . . you know." A wave of hard swallows works along his throat as if he's choking down a stuck chicken bone. "You have to be sixteen to work at the store, and she wasn't . . ."

"She was only fifteen, huh?" I raise my eyebrows and meet his gaze to watch the panic swirl inside him. "So did you make some kind of deal with her so she could get those league fees waived?"

"No. No. Definitely not. She didn't join a team."

"And you never coached her?"

"Never. It didn't work out. Haven't seen her since."

"Really? Because she's missing."

Oh my, there goes his color again, though now there are red spots left behind, as if his face is a huge lava lamp, big splotches of color floating in his cheeks before getting smaller and fading. "Missing?" he croaks.

"Yes. She disappeared a few weeks ago, and we suspect foul play." The *we* will make me seem more official and more dangerous.

His mouth forms an O like the opening of a dry cave.

"Do you know why anyone would want to hurt this girl, Frank?"

"Uh . . ." I see his tongue working like a dying worm inside that cave. Gross.

"Listen." I lean forward and mold my face into understanding. "We both know she's not some average teenage girl, right? She's got issues. *Real* issues. She was . . . a *challenge*."

That's the refrain. That's the reason we give when a grown man has sex with an underage girl. She was troubled. She was fast for her age. She was the aggressor. She wanted it. She wasn't even a virgin. She thought she was grown. She's done this before.

We all know the reasons, because pussy is made to slide into; and if a young girl is there, tripping a man up, he can't help but fall straight into it. What are they supposed to do? Say no? They're just men, after all. Just men walking around like untrained puppies, semen dribbling on the floor with excitement just like a dog's urine. We expect nothing better of them. So here I am, having a conversation with this grown man about fast young girls.

I learned to work that system. I learned to be the one fucking instead of getting fucked. If men were going to do it, I was going to get something out of it.

But Kayla may have just been another victim. You let your guard down once and it's all over. Now you're not clean enough to save.

I wink at Frank. "Are you gonna tell me what happened, sir, or do we have to turn this into an official interview?"

His wormy little mouth finally snaps shut. His jaw tightens. I can almost see the thoughts turning like gears in his eyes. He's realizing now that he might be safe. If Kayla is missing, there's no one to ever tell the truth.

Damn it.

"Nothing happened." He takes a deep breath and nods. "We talked about her joining the league, but she didn't have money for the fees. It sounded like her family life was pretty bad. Sorry to hear something has happened to her. Maybe they had something to do with it. She said her mom was on drugs."

"We'll be looking at her phone records, you know."

"I . . ." A little croak before he composes himself. "Of course, we spoke several times about her fee options. Of course we did. But it didn't work out."

"You've said that."

"I need to get back to work. I'll call the sheriff's office if I hear anything."

"Oh, I'm not a cop, Frank."

"What?"

I let my mask fall for a moment so he can see the icy predation in my eyes. I don't care about him. I don't even care about Kayla. I care about the hunt. The stalking. The triumph. I smile. "Do I look like a cop, Frank?"

Lips parted so he can fit bigger breaths into his straining lungs, he shakes his head, then he nods, then he shakes his head again. "I don't know," he finally whispers.

"I'm just a friend. I'm just a *helper*." I put on a little singsong voice. "When you see a helper, ask for help!" When I reach to touch his hand, he jerks back, his chair screeching in protest. "I see you have a wedding ring. Do you have girls of your own, Frank?"

He blinks rapidly, over and over, as if he's trying to clear dust and horror from his blue eyes. "No," he bleats like a lost little lamb.

My heart beats harder, awakening every nerve in my body. I haven't felt this good in months. I lick my lips and lean closer, like a sultry movie vixen. I wish I could see myself right now. I wish I could record this and watch it later for fun. It's been a while.

"You just like coaching them, huh, Frank? You just like watching them run?"

"No. Yes. No! I'm just a coach! She was . . . This wasn't my fault." Tears fill his eyes now, despite his fluttering eyelids.

"What wasn't your fault?" I croon.

"I just wanted to help her out. She was desperate. That was all. I gave her what she asked for! I don't want any trouble!" He's crying now.

Big, ugly cries, wet cheeks, and sucking breaths. His sobs are muffled but violent, like they've been trying to escape a long time. "I don't want any trouble!" he pleads.

"What did you do, Frank?"

"It was a moment of weakness!"

"Did you hurt her?"

He chokes on one last sob and suddenly his red, wide eyes meet mine. "No. Never. I haven't seen her since. I paid the guy and that was the end of it."

I cock my head in surprise. "You paid who?"

"I dunno. That scrawny boy. He had 'Dog' tattooed on his hand."

"Little Dog?"

"I don't know. I don't know. Please leave. Please. Please. Please just leave!"

He's turned into a pitiful puddle of weakness, and I don't want to get his fluid on me, so I roll my eyes and sit straight. "Fine. But I will be in touch again."

"Please don't. I made a mistake. I'll never do it again."

"Eh. Hard to believe. But do yourself a favor and try to keep your perversion confined to the age of majority. You're getting old, Frank. Eighteen or nineteen has got to be filthy enough for you. Come on. Use your big head."

I leave him behind whispering "I'm sorry." I predict he'll stay away from needy teen girls for well over a year after this.

Look, we can't all save the world, but I do my part.

So . . . he paid Little Dog after sleeping with Kayla.

This whole thing is confusing and muddled. Was Little Dog just pimping out my niece? There's some undercurrent I'm not grasping, and I don't like that. Maybe I'll track old Frank down at his house tomorrow for follow-up questions. That will either knock loose more information or send him into the fetal position. Either reaction will make my day a little brighter.

From the grocery store, I drive straight to the equipment rental company to investigate that last business card, but the place is locked up tight. There are no trucks or strange machinery secured behind the high chain-link fence, and the office is closed, with no helpful sign on the door to indicate when they'll be back.

Not an unusual sight in this town. Everybody wants to make a buck, and not very many people actually have a good head for business, especially the risk-taking types looking for a quick fortune. Even those who do well like to take risks in other ways that don't make them reliable business folk.

I get it. I like taking risks too.

I stare at the logo for Morris Equipment for a few minutes, wondering about yet another missing member of this business card coven. Curious, I google the guy's name. Roy Morris. There's another business listing for him in Oklahoma City under Morris Industries, but the listing shows that business as closed too. The only addresses that show up are PO boxes.

When I call the number on the card, it goes to voice mail, so I hang up and head to the last stop on my tour. The Big Ol' Truckstop.

It was a magical place when I was a kid. So many lights and colors and a million opportunities for happiness. Huge trucks, giant sodas, strangers from everywhere, and individually wrapped candies that fit easily into sneaky little hands. A dreamland.

My mom always slapped my fingers and told me to stop touching every damn thing, but any tantrum I threw was a good distraction for her own shoplifting. In fact, I later wondered if she started drama so my dad could grab a couple of forty-ounce beers and slide on out the door.

The place has gotten even bigger since I left. The KFC is gone and has been replaced by three different fast-food chains all crammed into one spot. There's a big natural gas pump for fuel-efficient vehicles. And the giant parking area for semitrucks has been expanded to twice its original size.

Since it's getting to be dinnertime, I park and take a quick stroll around the surrounding area, just getting the lay of the land. In the few minutes I'm walking around, at least four more trucks pull in for a break, most of them hauling oil, though there's a big frozen-food truck too.

I spy a woman smoking a cigarette near the entrance to the shower facilities. She's wearing skinny jeans and flip-flops and a yellow sweatshirt. Not exactly how people picture sex workers, I guess, but I'm all for comfort, and these men don't need a pair of high heels to turn them on. Any warmish body will do.

"Hey," I say to her.

She looks at me and flicks her cigarette, her pale cheeks tightening as she clenches her jaw.

"I'm looking for my niece. She went missing a few weeks ago. Do you think you might have seen her?" I hold out my phone to show the picture I downloaded from the website.

The woman shrugs and edges closer to squint at the phone. "That looks kind of like Kiki."

"Kiki?"

"Yeah. She works the trucks here every once in a while. Not often, though."

I scroll to another picture. "This is her?"

"Yeah, that's her." She takes a drag from her cigarette and scuffs her sandals against the cement. "She's missing?"

"She's been gone a few weeks. Unless you've seen her since then? This was the last place she was headed. About a month ago."

"No, I ain't seen Kiki. Have you talked to her pimp?"

"Little Dog?"

"Yeah"—she smirks—"Little Dog." Then we laugh together at him and his rural white-boy bravado.

"Did she seem okay the last time you saw her around here?"

"I don't know. She was so little, we used to tell her to go on home. I mean, she's young and everything, so we worried. But mostly we didn't want her drawing the cops here neither. No one needs that kind of attention, you know?"

"Sure, I get it. What about Little Dog? Did he seem normal to you?"

"Yeah. I saw him more recently. He was hanging out in the lot, then some big SUV pulled up, and he took off like a bat outta hell."

"Who was in the SUV?"

"No one I've ever seen. Big guy with a shaved head."

Interesting. My mom mentioned a bald man too. A bald man with a gun. I glance over the lot. "Anyone else around tonight?"

"Nah, I'm the early bird." She grins. "Getting that worm."

We snort-laugh together as she grinds her cigarette butt beneath her flip-flop and shakes out her hair.

"Smart lady, waiting by the showers," I say. "That's a good tactic."

"Girl, you wouldn't believe the swamp ass these guys acquire in those leather seats. No thank you, ma'am. I'll take a clean dick any day."

I don't mind her *ma'am* at all. In fact, I hand over a ten-dollar bill. "Thanks for your help with my niece. I appreciate it."

"No problem. I'll ask around if you want to come back in a couple of days. I'll have my son tomorrow night, so I won't be here. But check in on Thursday."

"Got it."

"I hope Kiki is all right."

Kiki. Just a regular, everyday underage sex worker, maybe. But something about good old Frank's reaction is still bothering me. Time to reach out to a local pimp, it seems.

CHAPTER 13

Knowing Little Dog has been spooked by something, I decide to go with the harmless "I'm just a girl" approach to reassure him that he's in charge here.

> Hello, Brodie! I'm Kayla's aunt from Minnesota and I'm trying to get in touch. Do you know where she is or how I can contact her??? I'm pretty worried & I just want to be sure she's ok. Thanks so much!

I shop in the truck stop for a few minutes while I wait for a response. I grab a bag of Funyuns and eye the men around me in the store. And they're all men, aside from the woman ringing them up. This town has always been filled with so many strangers, men coming through for work or fueling up before a long drive into the panhandle. It's never been a safe place to be a girl.

I look at them in line, their faces unsmiling and unshaven, and I imagine any one of them might have offered Kayla cross-country passage in exchange for a daily blow job along the way. Of course, any one of them might have decided rape and murder was just as fun a pastime and dropped her body in the scrub somewhere along these two-lane highways. As a monster myself, I'm not under any delusions about the kindness of strangers.

I find it curious that men are so often the monsters, because it's definitely not about some mythological kindness of women. We can be cruel and harsh and abusive. But we don't lash out in the same ways.

I assume men's anger drills down on us so specifically because women are presented at the earliest age as withholders of pleasure. *Look at them over there, walking around with what we want. Toying with us. Denying happiness. Look at them, with their tits and pussies, just living their selfish lives like they're not cruel gatekeepers. Time to teach them a lesson.*

Even the most normal sexual interaction is framed as him getting some and her giving in. If you aren't kind enough to give a man what he needs, why should he treat you kindly in return?

Women aren't raised to be angry in response. We're raised to appease. But I don't care about pleasing anyone or being called nice, so these weird expectations have always been a bright glow in my peripheral vision. That works out fine for me. They never anticipate that I'm the one expecting to be appeased.

But I am.

As I slip into my car, my mind shifts to the decision of what to do next. I'm not good at waiting, but I'm at Little Dog's mercy here.

I'm tapping a finger against my chin when my unfocused gaze sends a clue to my brain. I stop tapping and narrow my eyes on a distant line of white. It looks like . . .

When I tilt my head, I see it. A wind turbine blade. A huge, solitary blade just lounging around like a lazy queen.

It's a quarter mile up the road, cradled on the long trailer of a truck parked alongside the highway. Another truck pulls up as I watch, slowly easing into place. The smooth white blade slides through the evening sun before it disappears behind the length of the first turbine blade. I want to touch one, so I start my car.

By the time I pull in, the driver is out of the cab and halfway across the lot, heading for a door with a sign above it that reads simply LOUNGE. The lounge is attached to a cheap motel. All these guys need on the road is a bed and a few beers, I guess.

I park my car and jump out, heart beating with excitement. The blade extends far beyond the end of the trailer, and flags are everywhere, warning of an oversize load. But there are no people. No guards. Just two Ford pickup trucks that are also decked out in traffic warnings.

I walk right up to the blade and stroke the cool whiteness. There's no one and nothing to stop me. Thrilled, I drag my fingertips over the surface and follow the long, curved line. Not metal, I assume, but fiberglass or something more modern than that. Manufactured spider silk, impossibly light and strong. Okay, it's probably just fiberglass. Whatever it is, I press my palm to it and slide my hand up as far as I can, then back down.

"Cool," I murmur. "So cool."

One more pickup pulls in, followed by a truck hauling some kind of hydraulic crane, and I immediately recognize the logo on the crane: Morris Equipment.

"Hot damn," I whisper to myself as the men hop out of the vehicles and head inside together. On the hunt now, I follow.

There are several round tables in front of the bar, and most of the men at them are wearing the same gray coveralls. They must work for the wind power company, because unlike the gas workers these guys look nearly pristine. A little dust lingers on their shoes but that's it.

I head straight for the bar and order a tequila sunrise because it just feels right in this place. The bartender is a thirty-something woman with short bleached hair, dark brown acne-scarred skin, and a flat stare. I watch her for a moment, curious whether she's like me, seeing the world through cold eyes. But it's hard to tell these days. Addicts seem nearly as icy as I am, but their ice is slushy and unstable, shifting underfoot.

She mixes my drink and hands it to me without a word. We don't smile at each other. I order some fried cheese sticks off the bar menu, and then I settle onto a stool to spy.

The table to my left already has a pitcher of beer in the middle of it, and the men are lively and upbeat. That table is an American melting pot. A black man, two white guys, and another fellow who could be Bangladeshi. They're laughing loudly about something, happy to be done with their workday.

The table to my right is quieter. Two white men wearing coveralls are nursing beer bottles, and a third man sits with them, a tumbler of whiskey in front of him. He was driving the last pickup that pulled in.

His short brown hair is mussed as if he's stressed-out, and he's wearing black slacks and a blue polo shirt with a wind turbine logo. He's the boss, and the two guys with him aren't thrilled they got stuck sitting there.

At a table on the other side of the room are two truck drivers. I recognize the Hispanic guy who was hauling one of the blades because I'd never forget that shaggy mullet anywhere. We've got a whole little wind industry convention here.

I take off my sweater to reveal the tight white T-shirt beneath it and get up to move toward the jukebox. As I pass the quieter table, I gasp. "Oh my God, are y'all with the windmill company?"

One of the men snorts derisively, but the boss smiles. He looks about thirty. Young to be in charge of a bunch of bigger, stronger guys. Dark circles age his eyes, and his teeth look a bit yellow. He's probably a smoker and maybe an insomniac too.

"Yes, ma'am," he offers politely. "That's us. But they're wind turbines, actually."

"Turbines! Oh gosh, that's right. I'm so silly. Turbines. Well, I just think they're so pretty and pale against the blue sky. Do y'all put them up and everything?"

"We oversee installation when there's one going up, yes. And we do maintenance and repairs, of course."

"I saw the trucks outside. Don't y'all just love your job? This is so exciting!" I bounce a little and watch three pairs of eyes dart toward my breasts. Well, one pair lingers more than darts, but the boss himself is far too polite to gawk. "Well," I say with a coy smile, "I'll let you get back to your drinks, but I might have some questions for you later."

"Ask away," he says. "I'm Derrick."

When he holds out a hand, I take it between both of mine and gently squeeze. "That's so sweet, Derrick. Thanks for being nice to me." His cheeks flush just the tiniest bit.

I let his fingers slide out of mine, offering the slightest warm pressure as I bite my lip self-consciously and tip my smiling face away from his. As I continue toward the jukebox, there's a moment of silence behind me, then some muffled snickering. I hear Derrick whisper something short and hard, but the snickers don't stop.

The boss man isn't an ideal target, because he may think of himself as setting a good example for his men, but he is my best bet for information. The other guys would be big on boasting and low on return.

As I formulate a way to pump him for information, I realize there's another prize for the taking here. Derrick undoubtedly has some sort of universal key to the wind turbines, and a shock of hot excitement slices through me at the thought. I can get Derrick alone to question him about Morris Equipment and I can make my windmill dreams come true.

If anyone can give me a tour, it's the boss man. And good examples aside, he might also be desperate to look like a big boy in front of his blue-collar employees by walking me out of here.

It works to my advantage that Derrick is only mildly good-looking and is a little on the short side. Maybe five-six. He wasn't such a gentleman that he stood when I came over, so it's hard to tell his exact height.

Regardless, I doubt he gets much attention—or any attention at all—from random women in bars.

I put a slow sway into my ass as I walk, then lean over to look at the jukebox selection.

I don't really like music, so I'm only making a show of it. Music is a tool used to outwardly express emotion or amplify the feelings we already have, so why would I care about it?

I tip my hips to the right and then to the left, my gaze sliding aimlessly over the rows of choices. But then I see a song I recognize! "Big Red Sun Blues" by Lucinda Williams. I liked to sing that song when it was too damn hot outside. How it managed to get so unbearably humid in this dry scrub prairieland was always a mystery to me.

Complaining about the heat ate up whole months of my life when I lived in Oklahoma. The tornado warnings were a relief whenever they came, because there was usually a cold front behind them.

I'm about to ask one of the men for change when I see an American Express sticker at eye level. Even jukeboxes take credit cards these days. How funny is that? I insert my card and choose my song and a few others. The background music dies down and "Big Red Sun Blues" fires up. Grinning, I sashay my way back to my barstool as the opening bars twang. I add a little wink for Derrick when I pass.

"Why don't you sit here?" one of the men calls out. I hear a chair scrape on the floor and turn to see Derrick shaking his head, his mouth tight as the spare chair next to him slides farther out from the table. Just as Derrick is forcing his disapproving mouth into a flash of a smile for me, the other guy's booted foot disappears back under his seat.

"Y'all are so sweet! Are you sure? I don't want to interrupt or anything . . ." I glance uncertainly back to my stool, but the guy who shoved the chair out is nodding.

"Join us. Never hurts to look at a pretty face. We'll buy you a drink, won't we, boss?"

"Sure. Yeah. Of course." He's flustered, but he can't say no to buying me a drink now that it's been offered.

"Oh my gosh," I croon. "Y'all are so nice!" I gather up my drink and sweater and plate and two napkins, all in an awkward bunch, and I swing my stuff onto their table, leaning too far over to show off the V-neck of my T-shirt. "Oh my gosh," I repeat. "This is so fun." I'm wearing a rose-pink bra that they can see through the material. I hope it makes them imagine the color of my nipples. That's the whole point.

The point! Get it? Because they're nipples.

Derrick raises a hand and calls for another round of drinks with too much volume and seriousness, as if he's unaccustomed to making this kind of request.

"So I guess you're not from around here?" I ask Derrick.

"No, we're based south of Oklahoma City, though the blades are shipped up from Houston, of course. How about you?"

"I'm from over in Norman. Out here for my uncle's funeral."

"Aw, that's too bad."

"Yeah, I think a few drinks are in order. It's all been a little stressful. Family stuff, you know? I'm just ready to wind down and forget about the whole thing."

On cue, the drinks are plunked down on our table, and the three men all clink their glasses against mine. I quickly finish my first tequila sunrise and start on the next.

"I really do get so excited when I see those wind turbines!" I say. "Do you boys hear that a lot? I just love them so much."

They all chuckle. "We don't exactly have groupies," Derrick says, but he sits up a little straighter as if his ego is plumping out.

I scoot closer to him. "It's just so cool, though. And it's so good for all of us. Those oil guys must hate you, flaunting the future right in front of them!"

More laughter. I slap Derrick's arm and scold him for laughing at me. One man gets up to excuse himself, and the other quickly shifts his chair around so he can twist and talk to the other table. His boss is distracted now and he can make a slow escape.

"Are you all done working for the day?" I ask.

"Yes, ma'am."

"Oh, please call me Jane. You bought me a drink, after all. I should be friendly. And I'm finally starting to relax!" I roll my shoulders and sigh, and this time his eyes go to my breasts and linger for a drawn-out moment. It's cold in here without my sweater, and I've got goose bumps in all the right places.

The chase is starting to turn me on, and the alcohol helps too. I let my knee rub against his and squeeze my thighs together to enjoy the lovely friction.

When the third guy returns from the bathroom, he helpfully drops into a chair at the other table. Derrick and I have privacy now. I rest my hand on his thin wrist, my fingertips sliding in slow millimeters. "Tell me everything about what you do. I'm just fascinated, Derrick."

His shoulders widen as I watch, losing any hint of the burdens he carries, and Derrick starts to talk about himself. As cool as I think wind turbines are, I can't concentrate on what he's saying. All I can think about is how good I feel.

I'm in my element, a drink in hand among unsuspecting strangers. I'm working the room, working his ego, and I'm filled with pleasure and tequila. When Derrick laughs at something he said, I laugh along, crinkling my eyes with faux warmth. "You are so funny, Derrick, oh my God."

"But it was true! He really thought he was going to get my job!"

"Hilarious. That's such a great story." I pull my hair up and shake my head. "Gosh, it's getting warm in here. Are you warm?"

"Not particularly. It could be that tequila you're drinking."

"Oh my word, I bet my cheeks are pink as cherries."

He grins, eyes sliding over my cheeks and then down to my exposed neck. "You're a little flushed."

"Oh boy, I have an idea." I drop my hair and lean in quickly. "A naughty idea," I whisper loudly, as if I have some sense of discretion but it's been lubricated loose by the alcohol.

"Whoa, really?" He licks his lips. "What kind of idea?"

My hand slides over his wrist and up the inside of his forearm. "I want to see it."

"Pardon?" His arm tenses beneath my stroking fingers as he blinks rapidly.

"A windmill. A wind turbine. Please? Will you show me? I want to see one so bad."

He pulls back a little, eyes darting toward his men. "Oh, I can't do that."

"Really? Shoot. I thought you were in charge."

"I *am* in charge."

"Then that solves it. Who's going to stop you?"

His eyes are nearly frantic now, jumping from the other table to my hand, then back to my mouth. "It's not allowed."

Now I lick my lips, wetting them so they'll glisten in the dim lighting and make him think of so many things he shouldn't think of. "What's not allowed?" I purr.

"Unauthorized personnel."

"Oh, but it's just me. And it will be our secret. I can't tell anyone I went somewhere alone with you, can I? What would they think? Picking up a strange man at a bar?" He smiles when I smile. "I couldn't say a word if I wanted to. Take me to see one? I promise not to tell. Please, Derrick?"

His gaze is moving slower now. Touching on the other table before focusing on my face, my mouth, my desperate eyes. "It's not allowed. I really shouldn't."

"Yeah, but . . . doesn't that make it feel fun, though?"

"Fuck yes," he mutters; then his eyes widen. "I'm so sorry. Excuse my language." I can tell Derrick has been following the rules his whole life. He wants to do what he's supposed to, and he always has. But what has all that gotten him? He has an education, he landed a good job, and he works hard. And now? Now he's in charge of a bunch of men who think he's a pussy. But here I am, making him feel like a man again.

"I've had such a bad day," I sigh. "My uncle . . . It was a lot. It really reminded me of my dad when he . . ." I wave my hand like I'm shooing off the saddest of ghosts. "Ugh. I have to stop thinking about that. I just want to have a little fun, you know?"

"Yeah. I do know."

I drain the rest of my drink and slump into a pout. "But I get it. I don't want you to do something you don't want to do. I'd feel so bad if I got you into trouble after you've been so sweet."

"I . . ." He looks at the other table one more time. Those men. Those assholes. Having a blast over there, relieved they managed to ditch him, when he's just here to work the same as they are.

I remove my hand from his arm, depriving him of my soft, warm skin. "And you're right, of course, Derrick. It's wrong, and I shouldn't have asked." I let my gaze wander toward the fun table to let him take in my disappointment along with my hard nipples. I smile briefly as if one of his employees has caught my eye.

Golly, what if one of them takes me up on this little field trip and reaps the rewards because Derrick was too much of a coward to seize the day? Just imagine the mockery that would ensue. More laughter. More disrespect. And more of this dreary life.

Derrick drains the last of his whiskey and sets his glass down hard. "I'm going to excuse myself to the men's room and then I'll settle the bill. Meet me outside in five."

I turn a blinding smile on him. "Really?"

"Yeah."

"Oh, Derrick. This is going to be so much fun."

"Yeah," he says, reflecting my smile again, but this time his eyes are a little hard. I've backed him into a dark corner of his ego, and his adrenaline is pumping now. Let the games begin.

CHAPTER 14

"I'd better turn in," I say in a too loud voice. "That's my limit of tequila."

Both Derrick and I stand, and I say goodbye to him before waving to the other men. I hear a couple of groans as I turn to leave, followed by a whispered "Jesus Christ, Derrick." They can't believe he's letting a desperate drunk lady walk away unmolested.

I wait next to my car and check my messages. Still nothing from Brodie. I'll drop by his house again tomorrow and knock together a few of his friends' heads. Or I'll bring a case of beer. Whichever.

I do find a text from Luke, however. He's meeting a friend for a drink and then heading to his brother's house for dinner. That's the life he wants. Secure and cozy and warm. I hate that. Hate the idea of relaxing into life and waiting for death, like a big dumb cow who doesn't know about the slaughterhouse waiting just over the hill.

But what *do* I want? This? Right now I'm exhilarated. Excited. I can't wait for Derrick to walk out and whisk me away on an adventure. Anything could happen, and I'm ready for it all.

I'm not physically attracted to Derrick, but I want danger. I want power. Should I risk what I have with Luke for this moment? I don't have a conscience, but I definitely have a good sense of self-preservation.

I don't know what I'm doing in this relationship with Luke, and uncertainty is not a feeling I'm accustomed to or appreciate. Damn it.

Derrick finally emerges from the lounge. He looks around nervously, and when he spots me, he jerks back a little, surprised I actually waited. After waving me toward him, he makes a ninety-degree turn and heads toward one of the white pickup trucks decked out in "Oversize Load" signs. I stride fast and strong. The sun is still out, but it's dipping toward the horizon, and I want to see everything before it gets dark.

"Yay!" I say as I hop into the passenger side of his truck.

"You can't tell anyone."

"I won't. I swear. You don't think they saw you?"

"If they did, I don't think they'll imagine I'm taking you to see a turbine."

"No?" I ask cluelessly.

"No."

He starts the big truck with a rumble, and I turn up the country music that's already playing. I don't know this song, and it sounds like filtered shit, but the noise makes me feel like I'm at a party. "Are you excited?" I ask.

Now that we're alone and pulling away in the truck, his shoulders are relaxing from their brief foray into aggressiveness. "I am. Mind if I smoke?"

I wave an accepting hand, and he lights up a Camel. After his first couple of puffs, I reach out and snag it from him. Then I twist and rest my back against the truck door so I can face him as I take a long drag and watch him drive. He can't help but glance down toward my spread legs when I rest a knee against the back of my seat.

"I recognize that logo," I say as he pulls past the crane. "Morris Equipment."

"Oh?"

"Yeah, it's a local company, right? I think my cousin worked there. Didn't it close?"

"I think so," he confirms.

"What happened?"

"I'm not sure. Just heard they shut down about a month ago."

"But you're still using his equipment. Do you know him or something?"

He frowns a little, confused by my interest. "No, I don't know him. He sold his gear off, I guess. We got this from another company."

Damn. That's the end of that. "That's too bad," I murmur.

"I wouldn't feel too sorry for him," Derrick says. "His brother is the lieutenant governor."

I sit up a little straighter, bumping my head into the side window. "Who? Roy Morris?"

"Yeah. His brother is rich and politically powerful, so he'll be just fine even without a lick of common sense. Those guys always land on their feet."

Well, well, well, this is very intriguing. A powerful man who had contact with my missing niece? I tap the information into my phone and hit SEARCH. This girl is more interesting now. What has she gotten herself into? Is this Morris guy the reason she disappeared?

The lieutenant governor is indeed also named Morris. Bill Morris. He's an average-looking white man in his fifties. Receding hairline, jaw going soft, a fake smile that's too awkward in this age of friendly selfie smiles. He also owns an oil company worth nearly fifty million.

"So you live in Norman, huh?" Derrick interrupts, obviously feeling neglected.

"What?" I ask.

"We work over there occasionally. Maybe I could call you next time we're in town? We could grab dinner. Get to know each other?"

"Sure," I mutter.

"I think we're scheduled to head east next month, and I make the motel arrangements, so . . . There's no reason we can't overnight in Norman. I'd love to see you."

I sigh and decide I'll have plenty of time to do research later. Right now I should concentrate on my current goal: I'm about to meet a wind robot!

I click off my phone and smile. "You'd really have time to take me out if you're working in Norman?"

"I'd make time to take you out," he says with a grin.

Soothed by his attention, I sink back into my role. "Aw, that's so sweet, Derrick."

"Life on the road gets lonely sometimes. If you're not seeing anyone . . . And you've got a place?"

"Sure. What kind of food do you like? Maybe I could make something home-cooked for you. You must get tired of restaurant food."

"I sure do. That sounds like a great time. Good food. Good company."

I'm already bored with this imaginary assignation, so I change the subject to the only date with Derrick that's actually going to happen. "How long until we get to the turbine?"

He tips his head toward the road. "There's a good, secluded approach about five miles from here. Not visible from the highway. You know, you look different out here."

I pass him back the cigarette and scrape my teeth over my lower lip. "Oh yeah?" I guess Naive Tequila Sunrise Jane wouldn't sit with her legs spread and shoulders slouched. "It's just the tequila loosening me up."

"Mm. I feel pretty good myself right now."

"I can trust you, right? Letting you take me off the highway to a secluded spot? You're not going to kill me?"

He blinks and sits up a little straighter. "No way. You can trust me. I'm a good guy."

I lean forward and reward him with a little pat on the leg, then I steal another drag of his cigarette. "All right." Just over the horizon, the turbine blades start peeking at us as they spin, so I face front again and point. "Is that the one? Right there?"

"Almost. It's just past that one. You can't quite see it yet."

"God, this is cool." The earlier clouds have cleared away, and the evening sun turns all the ugly brown scrub to gold. Each rotation of the blade catches a little yellow-orange light, and the nicotine is hitting my blood, and I feel perfect.

"You're a funny girl," he says.

"Am I?" Yes, I am. A strange girl. A puzzle. An abomination, according to dear old Ma. I'm the male fantasy and the male fear all rolled into one package.

He doesn't know I'm dangerous, of course. Because I'm a woman. But I could have lured him out with no one knowing. I could have approached him in secret with a fake name, and he would have taken me here because I asked.

He understands that I've been conditioned not to be a cocktease, not to lead him on, not to flaunt something he can't have, because then he'll have a right to take it. He believes that if I let him buy my drinks and get me alone, I'm obligated to put out. He knows he's the winner here. He's the man.

What he doesn't know is that his testicles don't imbue him with immortality, and I could easily get out a gun while he's fumbling with the button of his pants. I could kill him and leave his body in the dirt where no one would spot it from the highway. Like he's a woman. Like he's one of a million dead women.

Why did he have a drink with her if he didn't want it? Why did he let her into his truck? Why did he go off with her if he wanted to say no? What did he expect to happen?

You really have to be smarter if you don't want to get murdered by strange women.

I smirk into the sunlight and wonder why there aren't more female serial killers. It would be such a simple job.

I'm not talking about myself, of course. I like my cozy lifestyle far too much to risk trading it for prison. There are ways to make a point without committing murder. But Derrick sure would go down quick and easy.

CHAPTER 15

Derrick exits the highway onto a paved road, but a few minutes later it transitions to red dirt and isolation. There are a couple of turbines ahead of us now, and I lean forward to get a full view of them through the windshield, their giant metal bodies filling my vision.

My nerves thrum with excitement or maybe with the low vibrations of the spinning blades. Either way, it feels great. Just because I'm here to search for a missing girl doesn't mean I shouldn't have fun along the way.

Derrick drives past the nearest turbine and turns onto a track that's barely there. It dips down into a small hollow, and two tire ruts of the trail climb back out to the base of the next turbine. He stops while we're still in the depression and parks the truck.

I clap my hands. "Just look at it!"

He's grinning like a little boy now. "You were serious about this, huh?"

"Absolutely! We can go inside when it's turning?"

"We sure can. That's no problem."

Before he even has a chance to shut off the engine, I'm out the door and looking up at the tower. The beat of the blades is like a giant mechanical heart filling me up with happiness. "Let's go!" I call as I head up the low rise.

I hear the jingle of keys behind me and then Derrick catches up and brushes past me to clang up the stairs first. I follow, making as much racket as I can on the metal grates just to entertain myself. There are twelve of them, carrying us high above the foundation.

While he tries to find the right key, I turn and survey the area. He's right: I can just barely make out the highway from this elevated point. His truck definitely isn't visible from any road. No one will catch us.

"Are you ready?" he asks as the lock slides open.

"I'm so ready."

"Don't touch anything. There's a lot of voltage coming through here." And then he pulls the metal door wide.

I hold my arms out, hands and face raised to the sky in triumph as he walks through the opening. I love getting what I want. Then I collect myself and follow, stepping right into the cool white beast.

The first thing I see are what look like banks of lockers. "Grid inverters," he says as we walk by them; then he starts explaining that they convert the electricity generated by the spinning blades into some other kind of electricity that can be sent to a central location, but all I can hear is the thrumming power.

"It's so loud!" I say.

"Ear protection." He reaches toward a shelf, but I'm shaking my head.

"No, I like it!"

"Suit yourself."

He walks me farther in, past the lockers, and I see a control panel with lots of numbers on it. I'm disappointed to find no spiral staircase winding up. There's just a high ceiling. I point to a giant metal box. "What's that thing?"

"Elevator."

"There's an elevator?" I hurry toward it, but he shakes his head at me. "It's only safe to use when the turbine is powered down."

"Can you power it down, then? Take me to the top?"

"There's no way. An alert will be sent to the main station with my code if I stop it. Everything will be on the record."

"Awww. Please?" But I can see by the set of his jaw that it's not happening. I don't want to beg for something I won't get, so I move on and wrap my hand around a metal ladder that climbs up the wall. Now I feel the real pulse of the robot deep in my bones.

I wish I could look up and see the whole chilling height of it, but the ladder disappears into an opening in a platform only fifteen feet up. "Can we go there at least?" I shout.

"We need climbing gear."

"For that? It looks harmless. I bet you could catch me if you stay right behind me."

He cuts his eyes toward the door, then up the ladder. His jaw isn't set so firmly anymore.

"Come on," I urge. "We're all alone here. And I promise to hold on tight, Derrick."

We both know he's thinking of his penis right now, but he hesitates for one more valiant moment. "There's not much to see up there."

"Oh, I bet we'll still have fun."

He shifts like I'm making him feel funny things, but then he nods. "All right. But go slow and careful."

"I definitely will."

I climb just as slowly as I can make myself, glancing down to smile at Derrick past my ass. He smiles back and starts climbing too. Then I'm crawling out onto a gray metal floor before I pull myself to a standing position and tip my head back.

"Yes," I hiss in delight. I can see up another thirty or forty feet now, and I'm thrilled.

Derrick pops up and stands with a lot more skill than I did, but I ignore that as I turn to take in the rest of the space. It's not much. A few boxes of replacement parts, maybe, plus a bunch of cables snaking up the walls. There's a big hole for the elevator in the high platform above us, but the area beyond it is dark.

I turn to smile my gratitude at Derrick. Now that we're on a level surface, I see that my estimation is right. He's about five-six or maybe a hair shorter, and he's pretty fine-boned. Not ugly but not cute. Frankly, he's just not noticeable at all.

"So . . . ," he says, his cheeks reddening as he rubs his hands together. "Do I get a thank-you for the tour?"

"A thank-you?" I ask as if I'm confused. "Of course! Thank you so much. I'm having a great time."

"Me too." We smile at each other until his mouth wobbles into a twist. "I thought maybe . . ." He pauses, too self-conscious to say more, waiting for me to fill in the blank. But I'm not the type of girl to get worried and try to fix an uncomfortable silence, so I wait. And wait. Until he actually gestures to his groin with eyebrows raised.

I nearly burst out laughing, because it looks like he's politely offering me a seat on his penis. Poor Derrick. He's really not used to such a tawdry interaction, but he's certainly willing to try.

And that's when I see it. Not his penis, though it's there. What I see is the right way to play this. I've been going for low-hanging fruit this whole time, and yes, I do mean genitals. But I can have my fun *and* play it safe for the sake of keeping Luke, and that will be a more challenging form of excitement.

Maybe I don't have to settle down completely. Maybe I can have everything I want and not die of boredom.

Gasping over the noise of the turbine, I widen my eyes. "Did you think . . . ? I mean . . . I don't know what to say, Derrick. I'm a good Baptist girl following Christ's path. I'm saved! I can't do . . . *that* . . . until I'm married. It wouldn't be right."

"Huh?" he croaks.

"Derrick, don't you believe in our Lord and Savior, Jesus Christ?"

"Of course I do! Of course!"

"Whew. Then you totally understand."

He touches the front of his pants, cupping his erection, puzzlement sliding into grief on his face. "What?"

When I see the shape of his bent fingers and the mass behind it, my eyebrows fly high. Well. Now that he's outlining the whole thing, this is quite the surprise. And, to be fair, he isn't being aggressive. I'll give him that. He hasn't even called me a bitch yet. He just looks a little heartbroken. Poor guy, standing there politely with all that enormous expectation.

"Well," I offer with shy reluctance, "I guess I could watch?"

"What?" That seems to be the only word he can force out at this point as he's trying to process his grief.

I'll have to spell it out. "I could watch you masturbate, Derrick. I mean, if you want me to."

His lips part, jaw going slack before he shakes his head, his brow creasing into a deep V between unremarkable brown eyes. Another "What?" passes his lips.

"Would you want me to?"

"I . . . I've never done that."

"You've never jerked off? Color me surprised. My mama always told me men had *needs*."

"No, not that. I mean . . ." His face is beet red now but I can see his breath quickening. His eyelids growing heavy. He squeezes himself through his slacks. "Of course I've done that. Oh, Jesus Christ."

"Exactly. I just can't touch it, you know? I'd have to tell Pastor McAllistor, and how could I live with that? He'd think I was the worst kind of fallen woman. But if you do it by yourself . . . You don't think that would be a *huge* sin, do you? It wouldn't even be *my* sin, really."

He's positively panting now, his eyes sliding down my body, and I realize I've pressed a hand between my own legs. "You'll watch me? Really?"

"Sure."

141

That one tiny syllable is all it takes to set his hands scrambling for his belt, the metal clinking as he works frantically at the buckle. Once the belt gapes free, he drags the zipper open and shoves his Hanes briefs down and the great white whale emerges. Okay, it's ruddy pink and not actually a whale, but it is a shockingly ferocious beast.

"Oh wow," I cry.

"Yeah," he groans. "Yeah, look at it."

Gone is the slight, mild-mannered manager. As he takes himself in hand, his mouth draws back into a slash of lips and his body hunches, curving around his proud prize. Lust has shaped him into a rutting werewolf, and I love it.

"It's so big!" I exclaim.

"Yeah. Look at it. *Look.*"

This poor man walks through life every day being disrespected, dismissed, barely seen at all by society, and the whole time he has this glorious *thing* in his pants that he can't show anyone. How utterly frustrating that must be.

I laugh in pure delight. "You really are huge," I say, figuring he deserves a little praise.

"Fuck yeah." He's positively snarling now, his eyes cast down at his own show. "Look at it." His gaze flicks up every once in a while to be sure I'm watching, and I definitely am. The turbine buzz surrounds my head as I watch ol' unnoticeable Derrick put on the best performance of his life.

And I'm glad it's a performance. I'm glad I'm not participating. Not because I'd feel guilty, but because this is a new level of the game, and I'm winning it.

I'm also glad because, impressive as he is, Derrick wouldn't be a good lay at all. He's all clumsy big-dickedness, which is a problem a lot of well-endowed men have. There's that one great tool in their toolbox, and they think their hammer trumps all other instruments no matter what the job is.

142

"This is so hot," he growls, rubbing himself rough and fast, going right for the goal. No easing in, no subtlety, no teasing. He's probably afraid I'll change my mind if he gives me a moment to think. Another problem a lot of men have during sex.

But a show is a show, and I'm worked up with sex and power and the hum of electricity. I ease my back to the metal wall, let the vibrations purr through me as I press the heel of my hands to my jeans.

I got my giant robot, and I love getting what I want so damn much.

I start to slide my hand down the front of my jeans to get myself off, but when he sees me, Derrick bites out a strangled "Oh God," and then it's all over, Derrick painting a ridiculous splotchy mess all over the gray metal floor. "Oh God, oh God," he chokes, his skinny body in spasms, face a comical rictus, and my fingers haven't even reached their destination.

"Oh, Derrick," I sigh in disappointment, drawing my hand free. He definitely wouldn't have been worth the chafing if he was that out of control with his own right hand. Yet another great decision on my part. I'm killing it today.

Derrick is starting to come to his senses, returning to reality from that place people go when they're aroused beyond all reason. The behavior makes perfect sense in evolutionary terms. Sex is a weird, messy act with a likely outcome of saddling the participants with a needy creature that will be dependent on them for at least a dozen years and could, in fact, result in the death of the female. Of course we have to lose our damn minds to enjoy it. That's just good design.

But now Derrick's sanity is returning, and he's still standing there with his pants and tighty-whities collapsed around his knees, softening penis in hand and the sad evidence of his expulsion at his feet. I even spot a dribble on his shoe.

"Uh," he grunts as he starts to reach for his pants and then pauses to stare at his soiled hand. He looks so hopeless for a moment. So lost. I swallow a giggle.

143

Finally he reaches gingerly for his underwear and pulls them up, then wipes his hand on the white cotton so that he can pull his pants up without sullying them. This is why Derrick is in management. He's a problem-solver.

"Can we go up higher?" I ask as he buckles up.

"Excuse me?" he mutters.

"Can we climb a little higher now?"

"No, it wouldn't be safe." He only glances at me before looking sheepishly away. "Let me go down the ladder first so I can spot you." He starts toward the opening, then stops short to gape at his little Pollock painting of semen. He's frozen again. Lost.

"That'll dry right up," I say. "No worries."

A blush conquers his entire face, but he eases around the mess he's made and heads for the ladder.

Now I wish I'd recorded the whole thing. If he'd noticed, would he have let me? Probably the idea would have turned him on even more, but he'd have immediately regretted it, and I'd hate to wrestle him for my phone. He hasn't even washed his hands yet.

Once I hear him jump the last few feet to the floor below, I head down the ladder myself, whispering, "Goodbye, my favorite turbine," into the tall space above me. I pat the ladder railing. "I'll miss you."

We're back in the cacophonous buzzing of the base, so Derrick averts his eyes and silently gestures me toward the door, but I hold up one finger. I need a moment to turn in a circle and take it all in. I finally offer him a blinding smile.

"Thank you!" I shout before leading the way out.

I step out into the beginnings of dusk, then I rush down the stairs and the hill so I can turn and see the spinning blades above me against an orange sky, my robot soldier beautiful and still ferocious. Before Derrick can reach me, I take out my phone and snap a couple of pictures so I can keep this power with me forever. In the first one, I capture the top half of Derrick as he walks down the hill, but he's holding up a hand to cover his face.

"Let's go," he says gruffly, all business and no charm now that he's satiated. Which is utter bullshit.

People always call women manipulative, and I count my skills as a point of pride, but constant manipulation for sex is considered normal for men. Their behavior isn't *called* manipulative, of course. Or sneaky. It's not even twisted or deceptive or plain old lying. It's just the way it's supposed to be. They want sex and they'll do anything to get it.

Sweet talk and falsehoods and affection and such pure fascinating *interest* in you. You're beautiful and insightful and promising! This could be something. This could become *anything. I'll make a special visit to see you. We'll go out. I'll try your home cooking. This is so fun!*

Until they come. Then nothing.

Then: *Why is she so clingy? I just wanted sex. Why is she talking to me and making this awkward? Why can't she just shut up and go away now?* Such cruel manipulation, and it's so constant, it's considered regular old life. Suck it up, bitch, you knew what he wanted.

I set my jaw and follow him to the truck. He doesn't open my door. In fact, he gets in first and starts the engine, impatient to be gone.

I lied and used him, but at least I have the goddamn courtesy to keep up the fake politeness afterward. Jesus. Fucking monster.

After I climb into his truck and close the door, he starts backing out before I even have my seat belt on. "Where to now?" I ask in a friendly chirp.

"I need to get back," he grumbles; then he actually turns up the music to shut me down.

Oh, fuck no, Derrick. This is just outrageous.

Setting my jaw, I let him listen to his music as he reverses down the trail. I let him hold his silence for the last little while of his normal life. I even send him a small, shy smile once we're on the side road and cruising toward the highway.

But Derrick stares straight ahead, his jaw an unforgiving line.

I just gave this guy the best work night of his gray, pitiful, endless life, and now he's freezing me out?

I turn down the music as he accelerates onto the highway. He graciously spares me a narrow glance.

"Derrick," I say hesitantly. I reach out to briefly touch his leg.

"Yeah?"

"I was wondering," I start, then I exaggerate holding my breath before blurting out the rest. "Do you think we should get married?"

"*What?*" The truck actually jerks a little to the side, and they don't believe in shoulders in this part of the country. Whoa, buddy. "What?" he bleats again.

"You know! After what we did! Back there! It was pretty naughty . . . *really* naughty . . . and I was thinking maybe we should get married to make it right."

"What *we* did?" he practically shouts. "I didn't even touch you!"

"I know, but . . . I mean, it was definitely a sin. You touched yourself, and I watched, and I even . . . you know . . . rubbed myself *down there*." I widen my eyes. "And, Derrick . . . I liked it."

His forehead is practically collapsing in on itself, trying to eat his eyebrows alive. His mouth is a marvelous writhing oval surrounding a wet, dark hollow.

I try to reach for his hand, and he jerks it away.

"You crazy bitch. I'm married! Jesus Christ! What are you talking about?"

My gasp sucks the air from the truck like a reverse scream. Derrick, you dirty, cheating dog. How could you? "No!" I cry. "You're not married! You can't be! You don't even have a ring!"

"I can't wear a ring because of safety issues!" He's ramped up to shouting now, and sweat beads above a throbbing vein in his temple. "I have a wife and a baby, you psycho!"

"Oh! *Oh!*" My compromised soul wails the words in anguish. "Then why did you *do* that with me? Oh my *God!*" I drop my face into my hands and start to cry. "Derrick! *Derrick!*"

"I didn't . . . I . . . This was a mistake. I made a mistake. That's all."

"I've sinned. Oh, my sweet Lord, I've sinned and I'm going to hell. And so are you. You especially! Your poor, sweet wife. How will she ever get over this?"

"She won't know! I won't tell her! Nobody will!"

"You asked me to dinner. You said we'd hang out. I thought we were dating, Derrick! And you have a wife and a tiny perfect baby?" I keen with grief and betrayal, then increase the volume when he tries to speak. I keep it up for a while, but ever so slowly my sobs begin to subside.

"I'm sorry," he says desperately. "I'm sorry. I've never done anything like this. And I did like you. I swear. If I weren't married . . . I just got carried away, that's all."

I sniff as if I'm crying real tears, but I'm just no good at summoning them. I never have been. I pretend to wipe my face on my sleeve to compose myself. "You knew I'd assume you weren't married. You *knew* that, Derrick."

"No, I didn't think of it, I swear to God."

Another sin to add to the rest? Tsk-tsk. "The Lord is always watching. Why would you debase yourself like that and betray your sacred vows? If I'd let you, we would have had *sex!*"

"I just . . . I'm sorry. I swear I am. My wife's always so tired. The baby's only three months old. We haven't . . . It's been a long time. And you were just . . ."

Right there?

"Nice," he finishes weakly.

"I *am* nice!" I slump down, pouting. "Are you still going to call me?"

"What?"

"Will you call me so we can talk sometimes?"

"I . . . Sure. Yeah. Just write down your number. I'll call you."

I slide a clipboard off the dash and jot down some numbers. "You promise?"

"Yes."

"That's good. Thank you. We'll figure this out. We will."

He makes a muted noise like he's swallowing his tongue. I just smile toward the twinkling lights of the town as we finally reach the outskirts.

Derrick pulls into the big gravel lot and parks far away from the other trucks. He shuts off the engine and we sit in the ticking silence for a few seconds. This could be the moment he decides to strangle me to eliminate this problem I've created before it can fly away from his hold. He can try, anyway. I'll go right for the eyes, and I have a good quarter inch of thumbnail. Then there's the knife in my purse.

"I'd better get back," he says instead of lunging toward me.

"Okay. Call me tonight?"

"Yeah. Yeah, I sure will."

"Bye, Derrick!" I open my door and start to slide down to the ground. "Oh, hey," I say at the last minute, my feet perched on the chrome step. "What's the name of that new rental company?"

"Excuse me?"

"The one you rented the crane from."

"Uh. I think it's Dayson's?"

"Cool." If nothing else pans out, I can always get in touch with them.

I walk jauntily to my rental car. I didn't really have a dinner, but I'm too sleepy for a night out, so I think I'll pick up something delicious and take it back to my room. Dinner in my underwear with a good book. What a treat.

I've got my eyes peeled for decent options as I pull out, but my gaze is drawn to a figure walking through the dark toward the lounge. I roll down my window as I pass. "Bye, Derrick! Don't worry, I won't post those pictures online!" He slides right out of my vision when he stops dead in his tracks, remembering my phone raised to snap a few photos.

Derrick won't pick up any strange women again, and this is going to be good for his life in the long term, especially if his career continues to take him on the road. Honestly, it was a lesson he needed to learn. I glance into the rearview mirror and wave again.

But what did I learn tonight? Well, I found out more about Roy Morris, for sure, and that would've made this whole excursion worth it, even without any other benefits. But I also learned something deep and important about myself, I'd say. I can never be good or honest, but maybe I can actually be faithful? As long as that definition is . . . slightly looser than normal. So the bigger question is: Does this mean I want to keep trying?

I pass a gas station with a Popeyes franchise inside and decide to go for it. It's hard to find red beans and rice in Minneapolis. Fifteen minutes later I'm back in my room and digging into dinner. Fifteen minutes after that, I'm idly flipping through the TV channels. I should have grabbed more cookies on the way in. The last one from yesterday is hard now.

I feel strange and restless, on some sort of precipice, and I'm wondering if I should get dressed again and go out. Maybe I could go back to the truck stop, ask more questions about Kayla, and throw in a few about Roy Morris.

Kayla could be in real danger from this guy. That soccer coach was pushed into some kind of corner. It wasn't just a friendly transaction for sex. That's also not the kind of deal that would send a youth pastor running for another state.

If Little Dog and Kayla were shaking men down, that would've been a dangerous move with a man like Roy Morris. His brother's fortune and political career would be put at risk, and girls have been killed for far less than that in this world. Hell, even I could be in danger from a guy like Morris, but I like that. Bring it on, asshole.

I'm considering getting up and putting on my shoes, but a call comes through from Luke. "Hey," I say.

"Hey yourself, beautiful. Did you solve any mysteries today?"

I grin because he knows I like being called beautiful. "Not really, but I'm getting closer. I think Kayla is a sex worker and that may be the crux of it. I'm trying to track down her pimp."

"Holy crap. Really? That's so sad. The girl is just a baby."

"Yeah," I agree, though I doubt she's been allowed to be a kid for years. She had to learn to survive. To protect herself. To hurt people to stop them from hurting her. We're from the same damn family, after all.

"Be careful," Luke says softly. "It sounds like she was mixed up with some dangerous people. I wouldn't want you to get hurt."

"Because you love me?" I ask.

"Yes. I do love you."

"What if I told you I flirted with another man tonight?" This strange mood is making me lash out. I want to stir the pot and force a reaction out of him.

"I'd think maybe you're telling me that to make me jealous because you want some attention."

Well, damn. "You shut up!" I cry, giggling now.

"Is it true?"

"Shut up," I repeat, but then I add, "Maybe. Did it work?"

"A little. What else did you do?"

"I didn't touch him, if that's what you're asking."

"No? Did you want to?"

"Eh. Only a little."

"Did he want to touch you?"

"Very much so."

"Yeah, I bet." I can hear him smiling through the phone, and it makes me smile too. "Remember when I ran into you last year?" he asks. "Here in the city? You were the hottest thing I'd ever seen. So sure of yourself. You scared the hell out of me, and I couldn't get enough of you."

Now I'm positively preening, stretching out in the bed, pointing my toes, arching my back. "Is that right?"

"It's one hundred percent right. So yes, I'm jealous. But no, I'm not surprised. You're like a panther, Jane. Wild and gorgeous. And I definitely don't want you touching other men, but I can't imagine you being some contented housewife either. That's not what I'm asking of you. Do you know that?"

"Not really." I'm slightly irritated that he's not more jealous, but I'm also thrilled that he knows so much about me . . . and he still wants more. "You'd let me cheat?"

"Would you let me cheat?"

A vision of Luke pumping into some weak replacement flashes through my mind and fills me with murderous rage. He's mine. He's really mine, and all my imaginings of letting him go are nonsense. "No."

"Then no, I wouldn't let you cheat. Keep it in your pants, Jane." I snicker that he's so close to the truth. "But you're a sexual being. Like, a *really* sexual being." He distracts himself with that for a moment and mutters a curse that makes me laugh. "You like it rough sometimes," he mutters.

"I really do."

"So when you get home, you tell me what you did, and I'll make sure you get in big trouble. Will that work?"

I'm grinning so hard now that my cheeks hurt and my whole body aches with immediate arousal. "Is that a promise?"

"Yes. And be careful. It may be more anger than you actually want."

"That's impossible, you idiot."

"You make me feel crazy sometimes. But we'll think of a safe word."

"I won't need it," I promise. "God, this is so hot."

His choked laugh sounds edged with pain. "I don't want to lose you, Jane. I want to *keep* you. That's what I'm trying to do. There's no one else like you out there."

"That's true," I say.

"So are we all made up? Everything's better?"

"Maybe, but please shut up, Luke. I don't want to talk about feelings right now."

"No?"

"No. I want to have sex."

Always the magic words. And abracadabra, they work.

CHAPTER 16

I wake up at 5:00 a.m. because I fell right to sleep after my intimate talk with Luke. I guess I was worn out from all the excitement.

There are voices and footsteps outside, and I glance out the window to see the atrium teeming with men leaving their rooms. Wow. These people don't mess around with waiting for sunrise. Now I realize why the breakfast buffet starts before dawn.

But I don't want thick biscuits and gluey gravy, so I take a quick shower before getting dressed and pulling on my boots. When I check my phone, I find that Little Dog still hasn't written back, and, frankly, I'm starting to get irritated. That shithead had better be dead somewhere.

Figuring I have all the time in the world, I head out to grab a good breakfast at Sonic, and then I cruise out of town in a line of petroleum workers eager to get to their fracking sites. My little sedan in a parade of big trucks. It makes me feel like a princess.

The sky ahead of me is purplish pink. The sun rises behind the smokestack cloud like I'm entering some sort of futuristic dawn hellscape. I glare at the tower and keep driving toward the small prison town beyond.

Instead of bothering to sneak up on the boys, I pull right up to Little Dog's mansion on the hill. Assuming a group of twenty-something stoners doesn't have the common sense to use a lock, I walk straight to the front door. Voilà. It opens on quiet hinges, letting me in to do anything I want.

For a moment I take in the house in darkness, the dank, lingering stench of weed and sickly-sweet hops. The ticking of a grandfather clock in the dining room. The heavy air that tells me they haven't cracked a window in weeks.

Once my eyes adjust, I move deeper into the house. One guy is passed out on the couch amid a hailstorm of crumpled beer cans, but he's not the person I'm looking for, so I keep walking. At the first bedroom I crack open the door, but it's another guy in there and he's actually managed to score some female companionship. Not Kayla, though. This girl has dark-brown skin and black twists of hair.

I shut that door and continue on through the open doors of the master bedroom, pulling them closed behind me. It's too dark for me to see well, so I shove aside the curtains that cover a sliding glass door to let some of the rising sun in. When I turn, I find Nate sprawled across the king-size bed in sweatpants and a sleeveless T-shirt. Little Dog still isn't home, it seems, but Nate doesn't seem worried. He's content as an innocent babe and snoring slightly with each breath.

I sit down on the bed with him and grab his phone from its resting place on the mattress near his arm. Hoping he has a fingerprint lock on his passcode so I can use his hand for entrance, I wake up his screen. Lo and behold, this guy has no lock whatsoever. He really is an innocent babe. You don't often find such trust in a pothead.

Upon opening his texts, I find a thread from "LD," and, sure enough, Nate texted him the first time I dropped by.

Where you at? Some lady just came by. You still alive?

He sent that text as soon as I left, but it looks like Little Dog didn't respond for hours. But he did respond.

Still alive & kickin. What lady?

"Well, well, well," I whisper. If it ain't Lazarus Pimp himself, back from the dark beyond.

Dunno, Nate responded. She was looking for Kayla.

Was she alone?

That seems like an odd question. Not *Was she a cop?* or *What did she say?* but *Was she alone?* Hmmm.

His friends already said that someone came by and beat the crap out of Little Dog about a week after Kayla went missing. It seems like he's on the run from that bald guy as opposed to fleeing from something he might have done to my niece.

Nate reassured him that I had come alone, then asked if everything was cool.

Jus layin low man. Hope we can head back soon.

We! "A clue, a clue," I sing softly before scrolling back through previous texts. Little Dog has indeed been pretty quiet this month. The last text before this round was two weeks earlier, when he asked Nate to bring him clothing and some cash he had stashed in the crawl space.

I'll meet you haffway. Enid cool?

Interesting. The town of Enid is halfway to Tulsa if you go by the back roads instead of taking the tollway. And something tells me Little Dog doesn't have an EZ Pass.

Yeah man no worries. Wtf is going on?

Did that guy come back?

No.

Ok, tell you in Enid.

Hm. Nate knows more than he let on. I nudge his shoulder. "Hey. What did Brodie tell you when you met him in Enid?"

He grumbles into his pillow, and I'm highly irritated that I had to come back to this stink-ass house, so I raise a hand high and bring it down hard on his ass with a satisfying crack. "Wake up."

Nate squeals and flips around, seeming to hover in midair as he twists with a wordless cry.

"What did Brodie tell you in Enid?" I repeat. "I know you saw him there, so don't bother lying to me."

"What the fuck, man? Who are you?"

"I'm a fancy lady, not a man, dude. And I'm not here for fun and games this time. You'll tell me what you know right now or I'll make your life a living hell, starting with calling the sheriff to report all the drugs strewn around this house. I'll tell them you've been dealing, and I don't think they have video games in jail, *Nate*."

He's awake enough to be scared now and scooting back to press himself to the headboard while his hand slides back and forth under the sheets. I hold up his phone. "Are you looking for this?" When he doesn't answer, I raise my other hand to reveal the knife I brought along. "Or are you looking for something more like this?"

"Eep," he bleats out, and I snort-laugh at the sound.

"Just tell me what Brodie told you in Enid and I'll leave. No big deal."

"In Enid?" he gasps. "Uh. He asked if that guy that beat him up came back and I said no."

"What else? And don't lie or you could wake up anytime and find me watching you in your sleep again. I'm sneaky that way."

"Jesus," he whines. "I don't know. He said Kayla had fucked up. That's all. He said, 'Kayla fucked up and we need to lay low.'"

"So he's with her?"

"I think so."

"And he was her pimp?"

Nate swallows with comic loudness. "Something like that. I mean, it was weird."

"Weird how?"

Nate presses a hand to the front of his sweats. "Can I pee, man? I'm gonna piss myself."

"I don't care. You've probably got a gun stashed in the toilet tank or something. Piss yourself if you're going to."

He shakes his head and swallows again. "Brodie used to say he was her pimp. But he didn't act like that around her. But, like, I don't even know if she even *gave* him any, you know? She slept in a separate room and smoked all his weed."

"But he claimed he was pimping her out."

"Yeah."

"They're in Tulsa?"

"Yeah, but I don't know where. I swear. He didn't say anything more than that." He's actually squeezing himself hard now as if he's trying to stop water coming out of a hose.

I aim my knife at his groin. "What else do you know?"

"Nothing! I swear! Brodie came by my place three weeks ago, and his face was a mess. Lip split, black eye. He told me he had to get the fuck outta town, and he said I could stay here if I wanted but that dude might be back. That's all I know!"

"Did he hurt Kayla? Kidnap her? Sell her to someone?"

"I don't know. He left town for a day around the same time she disappeared. Maybe he took her somewhere, or maybe he was lying and something bad happened. I seriously have no idea!"

"Okay. What did he tell you about the guy who beat him up?"

"Nothing!"

"Maybe a guy named Morris? Roy Morris?"

"I don't know anything, I swear!"

"Ugh. Fine. I need to use your phone. If you stay in the house and don't cause trouble, I'll leave it in the mailbox at the bottom of the driveway."

"The mailbox," he repeats, nodding violently.

"You gonna be cool?"

"Yeah. I'm cool. Mailbox. That's fine."

"Don't follow me."

"I won't. Swear to God."

I take his phone, and before I've even made it to the double doors, I hear his feet hit the ground and pound away toward the bathroom. Just in case he's playing hero, I slide past the doors and watch through the crack near the hinges. If he comes barreling out with a gun, I'll just trip him and kick him in the head.

But Nate isn't playing hero. I hear the wild flow of urine hitting water and then his guttural sigh of relief, so I bounce down the hallway and out of the house, and I even close the front door politely behind me.

I do watch the house carefully as I get into my car, and I glance constantly into the rearview mirror as I drive, but the door stays still and unmoving.

Since he didn't try anything and he was kind of funny, I actually stop at the bottom of the driveway to send a text to Little Dog from his phone so I can put it in the mailbox as promised:

That lady came back! With a huge dude! They just left!

I wait a few moments for the ellipses of response, then send a WTF man in case he didn't wake up with the first text.

Finally, I see a *dot dot dot* and then Nate's phone dings.

Fuck! Whatd you tell them?????

I hit the telephone icon and raise the phone to my ear. "Hello, Mr. Little Dog," I drawl when he answers. "Don't hang up."

"Shit!" he yelps. "Who is this?"

"I'm a relative of Kayla's, and I have a law degree and more than enough money to hunt you down and send you to jail for the rest of your life for trafficking a minor child. Tell me where she is right now or I'll have this text traced and you'll lose the one hiding place that you've managed to dig out for your sorry ass." I pause for a beat and add a smile to my voice. "Nice to finally meet you, Brodie."

"I don't know where she is!" he screeches.

"Don't be a lying little bitch, Brodie. I know you're in Tulsa; I just need your address. And if you don't give me your address, I'll let that big bald guy know what I've discovered and he can help me find you. Is that what you want?"

"Fuck off!" he tries, but fear makes his defiance squeaky.

"I've got Roy Morris's number right here, Brodie. One phone call and he'll know you're in Tulsa."

"I want a thousand dollars," he blurts into the phone.

"I'm not giving you a thousand dollars, Brodie."

"Five hundred. Five hundred and I'll send you the address. You can have her. This stupid bitch has been nothing but trouble. Fuck this."

"I'll give you two hundred dollars when I get there *after* I see that she's fine."

"Deal."

"I'll be there by tonight. Don't move or the deal is off."

I write down the address he gives me and warn him that he'd better damn well answer any texts from me in the future. Then I very kindly get out of my car and slide Nate's phone into a mailbox that's shaped like a red barn.

159

It's not until I'm turning away from the miniature barn that I notice the black SUV driving slowly down the road toward me. As it approaches, I lock eyes with the big bald white guy behind the wheel.

Very interesting. It's scary mystery man himself.

Well, Nate definitely isn't getting his phone back now. I snatch it from the mailbox as the SUV passes, then get back into my car and watch the truck turn around. He's welcome to follow me if that's what gets him off. I'm a grown-ass woman with a law degree and a camera, not some scrawny two-bit hustler scared to go to the cops.

I've got only one more stop before I go pack up my hotel room and head for brighter horizons. There should be several luxury hotels to choose from in Tulsa.

The SUV follows me onto the highway, not on my tail, but not bothering to hang back. There are two possibilities here. Either Little Dog came up with some scheme that got him in trouble with Roy Morris or Kayla did. I'm really, really hoping it's the latter, because that's what Baby Jane would have done at Kayla's age. But Brodie seems to be the one calling the shots and taking the beatings, so it's hard to tell.

Considering what the soccer coach blurted out under pressure, I assume that Kayla or Brodie made some sort of extortion attempt after he paid her for underage sex. And I assume they did the same to Mr. Morris, not realizing he actually had deeper pockets and dangerous connections behind his failing business.

Big Baldy here has got to be working on that side of things. He's approaching all of this like a hired goon, not a panicked middle-aged man. He tracked down my mom, used her, and then tracked down Little Dog and put the fear of God in him.

Once my car approaches the familiar environs of my old hometown, I pull into the ancient gas station and sit there to see if Baldy wants to chat. He pulls in and parks but doesn't engage.

Just to be sure, I do an image search for Roy Morris to confirm he's not the guy behind the wheel, but no. Morris is a fifty-something guy with a full head of salt-and-pepper hair and disturbingly pink lips in his round face. He's smiling in the PR picture I'm looking at, but his smile is snarky and self-satisfied instead of friendly.

Shutting off the car, I get out, figuring this is as good a place to handle this as any. There's a pretty steady stream of people stopping in for gas and coffee on their way to work, so he can't shoot me here.

The guy in the SUV is momentarily distracted by his phone and doesn't notice me approaching. He actually jumps when I knock on his window, my phone raised to snap a picture of his face. I descend into a fit of laughter as his heavy brow falls into a frown like an iron curtain dropping. He rolls down his window, and I find out immediately that I've underestimated him when his arm shoots out, hand grabbing for my phone.

"Hey!" I jump two feet away so I'm out of his reach, then hold up a hand when he starts to open his door.

"Don't do it. I've emailed your picture and your license plate to my attorney's office, so if you're planning to murder me, you might wish to reconsider."

"You're fucking crazy, lady."

"Crazy or just not an easy mark? They're not the same thing. And now you've made an attempt to steal my phone."

"Good luck with that claim," he says, but he shuts his car door.

I'm back in control, but I hate that I underestimated him. "Why are you following me?" I snap.

"I just stopped for gas, lady."

I take another picture. "I guess I really *am* crazy, then! So are you working for the Morrises?"

That finally makes him blink. He starts to roll up his window.

"Which one? Bill or Roy?"

I watch his stubbled cheeks turn red as the glass seals him off. When he starts his truck and pulls out, I wave cheerily to see him off. Still, he doesn't look harmless. His collar is unbuttoned, mere fabric and thread unable to constrain the muscles of his thick neck. His hands look ridiculously oversized around the steering wheel, the knuckles ravaged with scars. And then there was that gun my mother spotted.

I guess she's good for something after all.

After he pulls out with a squeal of tires, there's really nothing else for me to do but grab my stuff and get the hell out of this county, so I fill up the gas tank and buckle my seat belt. But just as I'm starting my car, I see a familiar face. It's not often I'm surprised, but you could knock me over with a feather with this doozy. It's my old English teacher, Mr. Hollingsway! What an unexpected delight!

He's walking back to his car with a big coffee in his hand, and he looks just as miserable and hangdog as he did the last time I saw him. Older, though, and thinner and grayer. He was never an enthusiastic teacher, but I liked him fine because he was fairly hands-off in the classroom.

Hands-off. I snort at my little joke.

Mr. Hollingsway gave me an A my senior year because I had sex with him. He was all regretful tears and self-hatred afterward, but the truth is that we both got what we wanted. I wonder if he's still married to Mrs. Hollingsway, my favorite math teacher. She was way too good for him, so I hope they're divorced by now.

When he gets into his beat-up gray Hyundai, I follow him to the high school. It's probably safer for me to stay off the highway for a few minutes anyway. Give Baldy a chance to get confused.

High school is an admitted exaggeration when it comes to my former educational institution. The town is just too small at this point to support individual schools, because most people don't have families of a dozen kids anymore. One wing is an elementary school and the other houses grades six to twelve.

Every year that I went here, there was talk of shipping the older kids out to the big secondary schools in the county seat, but, frankly, they didn't want us. Long bus routes and low test scores aren't on any school's wish list. That's why they left the prison town's kids to us, but there were only about twenty-five of them when I went here.

I park in the teachers' lot and hop out as Mr. Hollingsway slumps toward the school. He was a plain man before. Slim. Quiet. Slightly miserable with his existence. But now he's reached middle age, maybe forty-five, and he's slowly being molded into the shape of a man who knows that this is it. This is his whole world. He'll never teach at a well-funded school. He'll never go back and get that PhD. He'll never even have a group of smart liberal friends he can kick back with on Saturdays to share a joint and have a great debate with.

Mr. Hollingsway, welcome to the rest of your life.

Twenty feet behind, I follow him through a side door of the school and find that everything inside looks the same as it ever did. Drab gray and green and dirty white. The colors of an institution. The perfect way to torture restless minds and remind you that no one wants to be here. Not you, not the teachers, not the administration.

I pass metal-framed doorways and realize I've been in almost every one of these classrooms at some point or another. Had lockers in almost every hall in both of the wings. But I feel nothing as I glide along.

I came to this place and sat in these rooms because that was the ticket to escape, and I was smart enough to use it. I could have earned that A in Hollingsway's class easily, but I resented the boredom and the busywork, so I chose a shortcut. Plenty of students would. Even normal teenagers are known for bad decisions and impulsivity and spitting on the rules of the Man. The onus, of course, is on the adult. The teacher. The golden holder of authority.

Funny thing, that. There's a reason they had to pass strict laws to punish the transgressions of teachers and clergy.

Mr. Hollingsway disappears into his classroom. Same classroom. Same view out the window of some pipes on the exterior wall perpendicular to his. He collapses into his chair and begins to arrange his papers.

163

I wonder if I was a bright spot. A moment of terrible guilt and vulnerability, yes. An utter betrayal of his societal duties. He could have lost everything in that afternoon or even in the months after. He still could.

But, oh man, he had a tight little teenager right there on his sad metal desk. Right there, where he has to put up with their hot pants and back talk and scornful eye rolls every single day. What an exhilarating disaster.

Perhaps he thinks about me still.

"Hey, Mr. H!"

"Hi," he says automatically. He shifts his coffee and sets his laptop case on the floor before looking up. "What's up?" he asks, and then he sees me. Sees my face and my smile and raised eyebrows. For a moment I watch the thoughts crawl over his face like spiders. I look familiar, but who am I?

"It's Jane!" I offer helpfully. "All grown up!"

His face freezes into a blank. Nothing moves. Not his eyes or his hands or his chest. He's turned to stone as I stroll inside the room and drop into my old seat in the second row. Not that I came to his class much after that little rendezvous. Why bother? I'd put in my service.

"Listen," I say. "I'm looking for my niece Kayla. She's missing. Is she one of your students?"

"Who?" he whispers, eyes fluttering strangely.

"Kayla Stringer. She's my niece."

"I don't . . . I don't know that name."

"Really? She wasn't in your class yet? But you've seen her around."

"I don't know."

I smile at his continued shock. He thinks I must be here for him, his own little nightmare finally scuttling out from his bad dreams. "This is weird, huh?"

He shakes his head but his eyes get shiny, tears magnifying the blood vessels creeping through the whites.

"I was worried if she was your student, you might have slept with her or something."

"No! Never. Never!"

"Well, come on. Not *never*, Mr. H."

"I . . ." He stops there, lips parted, throat working. For a moment I think he's going to vomit, but then he bursts into tears instead.

"Oh, good Lord," I mutter as he weeps in strangled, heaving gulps.

"Please don't tell!"

I shrug and wait for him to quiet down. It takes a while.

"It was a mistake," he gasps. "I'm sorry. I never . . . never again. I swear."

I really don't understand this part of human fallibility. I have no idea what it's like to have this much regret, but if it hurts so much, wouldn't you just avoid it? If something will make you so sad, don't do it. But of course he *wanted* to do it so much more than he *didn't* want to do it, and that's the eternal problem.

The truth is that Mr. Hollingsway had a fine life when I knew him. A steady job. A nice wife. A halfway-decent house, even. He also has a teacher's pension waiting for him at the end of it all. He's fine.

He hadn't had kids when I knew him, but if he did, he would've been able to feed and clothe them and send them to college. Maybe even take a modest vacation once a year.

But all he could see was what he didn't have. What was in front of his face and couldn't be touched—that was the thing he yearned for. A young girl with firm breasts and wide eyes and soft skin. I was the thing *denied* him, and he wanted it so much.

The tears came after, of course. After he said yes. After he pulled off my panties. After he pushed up my top and kneaded my breasts like rising bread. After he shoved himself gleefully inside me again and again, lasting longer than I expected. He got through all that without guilt or hesitation. He managed to waltz enthusiastically through all those very delicious steps before he bothered to break down.

Yet I'm considered the one with the fractured brain. I'm the one who's dangerous and broken. At least I'm *consistent*. How could anyone ever predict what a human being like Mr. Hollingsway might do when backed into a corner? Or even when he's just plain horny?

So-called normal humans have spent millennia trying to explain themselves into innocence with stupid tales of magic and Satan and bad things that burst out of them during the full moon. Curses and possession and spring madness. All of it to explain away their true desires and pass them off as mere temptation by the devil. Or maybe just temptation by little ol' me.

Lies. It's all inside them, just beneath the surface, hidden in their tight throats, straining to get out. I hate them all for thinking they're any better than I am.

Rolling my eyes at Mr. Hollingsway's snuffling, I get up to leave. "See you around, Mr. H." He has nothing to say to me.

When I slip out, I pass a scruffy boy heading into the classroom and imagine what Mr. Hollingsway's explanation will be for his wet face and red eyes. Maybe the kid will be too self-absorbed to even notice.

The narrow halls are starting to fill now, so I slow my pace and let the crowd surround me. I like lots of humanity. The greasy energy of emotion rubs off on me, leaving a film I can wear as my own for a moment.

Look at that redheaded girl laughing hysterically at a text. She shows her friend, and now they're both laughing, touching each other, experiencing affection. They look so happy and feel so bright.

And check out that young Hispanic boy carrying a bouquet of carnations. They're tacky as hell, stored in colored water to turn them blue, but he looks beyond thrilled, a wide smile cutting across his pimpled face. He's in love with some girl or boy. He feels a connection. He feels hope and anxiety and thrilling lust.

Farther away, a group of girls is huddled around a locker, their shoulders bent toward one central figure, all of them concerned with whatever fraught story she is explaining with twisted mouth and big gestures. The tallest girl glances down the hallway with a vengeful frown, a ride-or-die sister out to make things right for her injured friend. They're so close. So bound together.

So many feelings, and I spread my arms as I walk, trying to absorb all of them.

The kids aren't sympathetic. They brush past my slow stroll and send me irritated glares. I smile in return.

One boy says, "Move it, fat-ass bitch," identifying my size-ten-to-twelve ass as a point of deep insecurity. Cute, but I'm better at the insecurity game than he'll ever be.

"Oh my God, it's you!" I say loudly. The boy, wide shouldered and red-necked, lurches to a stop as his friends look from him to me. "Long time no see, little guy. I sure hope you didn't inherit your daddy's tiny dick! I haven't seen him in a while. How's he doing?"

His friends burst into immediate uncontrollable hoots of awe and laughter.

"Fuck you, you slut!" he counters, clearly already clawing the rocky bottom of his repertoire. And now he's lost this game. There's no glory in calling some random older woman a slut, and his friends are hysterical now, slapping his back, lurching with laughter.

Hot blood creeps all the way up his face and into his buzz cut. "You fucking bitch. Who the fuck are you?"

God, maybe I should come back to high school. It would be so much more entertaining if it were my choice to be here. But even I'm not arrogant enough to think I could pass for eighteen. Gravity does have its way with you even when you're as saucy as I am.

A woman steps out of an office a dozen feet away. "What's going on out here?" she snaps.

The boy's friends tug at his stiff, flared shoulders until he reluctantly turns to leave. I smile and approach the woman. Her brown skin and broad face point to Native American heritage, and if she's working in this school, then that counts as progress around here. When I went here, racism was a feature and not a bug. In fact, I spy a Confederate flag T-shirt passing me by as we speak. If she sees it, she's gotten very good at pretending she doesn't.

"Hi," I say sweetly as I hold out my hand. "I'm Kayla Stringer's aunt."

"Hello. I'm Vice Principal Sky. What can I do for you?"

"I don't know if you've heard that Kayla is missing?"

"I'm so sorry. I know she hasn't been in school, but our phone calls haven't been returned. I did send notification to the sheriff's office about her truancy, but . . . Well. Please come into my office."

"Thank you." I follow her through a small reception area to a tiny rectangle of a room. "So the police never came by to speak to you?"

"No. I certainly would've remembered being told if one of our girls was missing."

"They consider her a runaway, but with such a young teen, I'm not sure why they'd find that a less-than-alarming explanation. Anything could've happened to her by now. I've come down to help look." I slide one of my business cards across her neat desk. "Is there anything you can tell me about Kayla?"

"Not really. This was only her second year here. She was a little . . . Well. I can't violate privacy laws, of course . . ."

"Of course."

She leans into her desk and meets my eyes. "I don't believe things have been very stable for her."

"My parents took her in a few months ago, and they are no one's first choice. I can tell you that from my own experience."

She presses her lips together sympathetically.

"I would imagine she's quite troubled," I say. "But of course those are the girls who are so often made victims."

"That is the unfortunate truth. Predators identify the troubled girls right off the bat. And she certainly acted out. She got in a fight her first week of school here. She came off as very aggressive, but she was likely just looking to protect herself."

"Certainly. Anything in particular stand out?"

"Not really. She was pretty quiet. A few in-school suspensions. Quite a bit of truancy and lateness."

Before I make my way out of the school, I thank her and ask her to get in touch if she hears anything. I don't really need more information about Kayla. I'll meet her myself in a few hours. But at least I explained my presence in the hallway and nobody called the cops. I consider that a good day at school.

I wish I could find that jock's car and slash the tires, but I'd better go while the getting's good. I always enjoy pushing things further than I should, but I don't have the free time today.

After heading back to my hotel, I spend half an hour looking into Roy Morris and the lieutenant governor, assessing my danger, but the only interesting thing I find is that Roy Morris has filed for bankruptcy twice in his life. Other than that, there was a DUI at age twenty-five and one more at thirty-one. A fairly average businessman's life if one accepts that most of them have mediocre financial skills at best. They consider bankruptcies the cost of doing business, even though anyone else who doesn't pay their bills is a freeloader.

I check my work email to see if there are any responses to the information I helpfully sent Rob on the North Unlimited case. Distracted, I open my first email just to skim the details before I hit the road, but when I see what it is, I growl low in my throat.

"That motherfucker." Someone from North Unlimited has forwarded something to me with a response, only I never saw the original email. The original email is an apology from Rob and he's apologizing for *me*. "Oh no," I breathe. "Oh no, sir, you lying little shit."

He screwed something up and didn't get them a number they'd requested, and then he blamed it on me. *Sorry, my colleague Jane is out of town with some personal issues and didn't get to this. Here's the document you requested.*

This is his whole shtick. He hasn't learned his lesson at all. He rides on the backs of others and then takes credit for being tall.

That's it. No more. I gave him his chance and agreed to help him out and he failed spectacularly at redeeming himself. Good old Rob has fucked with the wrong woman for the very last time.

I log into his email account with a smile.

CHAPTER 17

After that surprise from Rob, I get out of town later than I expected, and then I stop for a leisurely lunch along the way at an adorable cowboy-themed café I spy from the road, so I don't hit the outskirts of Tulsa until six. Not that I'm worried about making Little Dog wait. I'm in a better position if he's anxious for me to show up.

The address I finally pull up to is quite a surprise. It's a suburban two-story brick house with an old-fashioned portico that is far too fancy for the size of the place. It's the kind of ostentatious eighties house that oil industry people loved in the era of the TV show *Dallas*.

Now that I think about it, this house fits in perfectly with Little Dog's estate out in rural Oklahoma. Perhaps it's another gift from his dead grandparents. Hot damn, this kid is living the mauve maven lifestyle! What a gangster he is.

There's no other car to be seen when I park in the covered driveway, but there could be one in the windowless garage. Or he re-kidnapped Kayla, and the pair are even now racing toward Mexico so he can sell her into the sex slave trade before I get my hands on her. Ugh.

I'm ready to get back to Minneapolis and see my cat before I settle in to enjoy the new pecking order at the office. Still, I'm so close to parlaying this into a moral triumph. If I can find my missing niece and return her to safety, this whole trip will pay off in spades at work even if the girl herself is a disappointment.

I knock on the oversize black-painted door and wait. Crickets chirrup desperately for mates around me, and that's the only sound I hear. I'm not the least bit surprised that no one answers the door.

Damn it. Now I'm gonna have to make Little Dog pay.

Sighing, I knock again, just in case, then ring the doorbell. Amazingly, I hear a *ding-dong* version of "The Saints Go Marching In" echo around somewhere inside. This family is a true wonder of throwback kitsch. Maybe I actually am on the set of a 1980s evening melodrama.

I'm bored with this stupid chase, so I get out my phone and start to text Little Dog's number, but then I hear the soft *pat-pat* of feet approaching. I tip my head to the side and catch movement through the frosted sidelight. Well, hello. There's someone home after all.

"Who is it?" a tiny voice squeaks gently through the door, sounding for all the world like a timid cartoon mouse.

"It's Jane," I say. "Open up."

There's a long moment of quiet, and then a lock slides. The brass doorknob turns and the door opens one inch. One muddy-green eye stares out.

Finally! It's the lost little lamb from the picture! I did it!

"Who?" she asks through the gap. Does she think opening the door only an inch protects her in some way? Does she think I can't kick the wood straight into her head and knock her out? This girl has no common sense at all. She's already a letdown. I sigh and shake my head. "Are you Kayla?"

"Yeah."

"I'm your aunt Jane. Your daddy's sister."

"I ain't never met you," she says in a slow Oklahoma drawl, chewing on the word *you* like it's taffy.

"Be that as it may, your family got in touch with me and here I am. You ready to get out of here or what?"

"I can't. Little Dog said to wait here."

I raise an eyebrow. "He's gone?"

"He left this morning. I don't know where."

"Great. Can I come in, or are you going to stay rude and keep me out on this street all day?"

I see one bony shoulder shrug, and then she swings the door wide and waves me in with a lazy hand. She looks even younger in person. Delicate, her wrists thin, her elbows big lumps of bone in her arms. She's got no meat on her thighs at all under the sweatpants hanging off her narrow hips, and her pointy chin gives her a pixieish quality.

She's not pretty, though. She just looks like a frail dullard. No light to her at all.

My hard little heart sinks. This girl isn't anything like me. She's a limp washrag passively waiting for someone to tell her what to do. That's it. Gross. My psychotic boredom has struck again. I chased after something that has nothing to do with me, just to distract myself from the slog of everyday life.

To be fair to my ego, though, my restlessness often pays off with spectacular fun. I don't want to be too hard on myself. And I did find her, so I'm still a hero.

I turn in a slow circle under a brass chandelier. Every light is ablaze in it, and the interior of the house is a bit more updated than Little Dog's rural estate. I may as well appease my curiosity now that I'm here, because this house might be more interesting than this girl. "What is this place?"

Another bony shrug. "Little Dog said his aunt and uncle are down in Arizona, so we should stay here."

"Just a quick vacation for young lovers?"

"Whatever."

"Everyone's looking for you, you know. Did you run away?"

"I guess. He said we should get out of town for a while; that was all."

"Why?"

"Cops or something. I'm not sure."

Good Lord, this girl is dull as sandstone. I can hear her brain scuffing over the rough spots in her intellect. All this time wasted on a kid destined for the scrap heap of life.

My mother was right about Kayla, and just imagine how triumphant she'd be if she knew I was thinking that. Of course, I'd eat shit before I'd ever admit it to her.

"So Little Dog dropped you off here; then he joined you a week later. And now you're just sitting here, waiting for what?"

Yet another shrug.

"Where did he say he was going this morning?"

"I don't know. Maybe Enid."

Enid? Was he meeting Nate again for something? More cash or clothes? A gun? "You got a Coke?"

Kayla moves slowly to the fridge, the ironic claim of JUICY across her backside barely moving with the motion. I follow her into the main living area and glance around for any clues. There are no piles of powdery drugs or cash. No weapons in sight, not that I'll take that for granted. All I see are fast-food wrappers in the trash and a dirty ashtray on the kitchen counter. The TV is flashing the bright colors of a commercial, but the sound is down.

She hands me a cold can of Coke.

"So this is it for you?" I finally ask. "You just want to stay here with your loser pimp? Wait to see what he tells you to do?"

That's when I see a flash. Just the briefest twitch of the muscles in Kayla's face. "No." Then a few tense seconds later, she grinds out, "He doesn't tell me what to do. He's not my pimp."

"Really? Because you *are* working, right? Picking up tricks at the truck stop? Sleeping with dirty old men? And he's ordering you around like you're property. *Go here, go there.* He's your pimp, baby girl. Or did you believe it when he said he was your boyfriend?"

"I don't fuck Brodie," she spits out, and the dullness vanishes like dissipating mist in that sudden gust of anger. So does my boredom.

I perk up and study her closely. Her sleepy eyes are bright and sharp now, her bony shoulders tight. "Well, that's an unusual arrangement," I say with a smirk aimed dead into her pointy, angry face. "How does he know if you're a good enough piece of ass to turn out if you don't give him a taste of the goods?"

"*He* works for *me*," she says, and the words are compact as rocks, no more working the vowels through her lazy mouth. She glares at me through narrowed eyes, and she's thrust her head forward as if she's about to barrel straight into a brawl, tiny size be damned.

"Well," I drawl. "Aren't you an uppity little slut?"

She snarls, her thin lip easing up over teeth to show off canines just like a vicious dog. "Grammy always said you were nothing but a worthless cunt."

A hard bark of laughter escapes my throat. "A cunt? My, my, what happened to the helpless little girl who opened that door? Where'd she go? Off to church for the evening?"

"Screw you."

I step back to take her in, the fisted hands and tense shoulders. She looks more wiry than frail now, tendons standing out in her neck, eyes like dirty green ice against her white skin. She's not helpless at all. It was an act.

The nape of my neck prickles and my pulse rate picks up to a pleasant trot.

"Well, Kayla, maybe we have something to talk about after all. What exactly does Brodie do for you, if you're actually his boss?"

"None of your fucking business."

"Oh, it's got something to do with fucking business. Come on."

She seems to get a little bored with her own outrage and rolls her eyes before she pads barefoot back into the pinewood-and-granite kitchen.

"This place is nice," I say as she slides a pack of cigarettes from a drawer. She lights one with a bright pink lighter and takes a deep drag before blowing it out in my direction. I watch her like she's a movie about to reveal a secret.

"Good place to hide out," I press. "So who exactly are you running from?"

"What are you, a cop?"

"No, I'm not a cop. But I am smart and well-connected, so if you need help, now is the time to ask."

"I don't need your help. I'm doing just fine." To emphasize that, she saunters over to a wide recliner in the living room and drops into it, hooking one skinny leg over the padded arm. The window behind it looks out onto a treed side yard, and it's a good setting for her argument. Everything certainly looks peaceful and affluent out there.

"Okay. So why is Roy Morris after you?"

Her neck straightens from its slouchy curve and she turns her hard little eyes to me. "How the hell do you know that name?"

"I told you I was smart. And your life isn't anything like *The Da Vinci Code*, sweetie."

"The what?"

"Yeah. Exactly." I take a seat on the sofa and face her. The couch smells like clean laundry. It really is a pretty nice place. "Look, Kayla, I'm not some social worker here to save you. Life is a bitch and the world is a terrible place, and the fact that we're related doesn't make your life more tragic than any other forgotten girl getting abused and destroyed on every street in this sick goddamn world. Got it?"

She rolls her eyes and takes another drag.

"You're a sex worker, and that means no one gives a damn about you whether you're eighteen or sixteen or fourteen. No one will help you. The cops will arrest you and send you to juvie as a criminal even if you're not actually old enough to consent. Or, hell, they'll arrest you and send you to jail as an adult. I'm the only person who's even looking for you. You know that? Nobody cares. So I'd suggest you wipe that smirk off your face and tell me what you did."

She ignores me, flicking her ash onto the hardwood floor.

I feel like I'm stalking her now, and I like it. "Did you blackmail them?"

Oh, she can't hide these cards, because her pride won't let her. A slow, wide smile spreads across that narrow face until she's almost cute. Her eyes scrunch up into pleased little crescents. "No idea what you're talking about."

"Sure, sure." I smile at her. "Just tell me how you did it." I know her ego can't resist the prompt. I know because mine wouldn't. "Come on. You worked those men. We both know it. Just tell me how."

She enjoys her proud satisfaction for another silent moment, and then she gives in to the siren call of her ego with another flick of her cigarette. "They all knew how old I was, so don't try saying I tricked them. Some of them thought I was even younger. One sick bastard kept insisting I was eleven until I played along and agreed. Wanted to pretend it was my birthday party. 'I can't believe I'm finally turning eleven! Did you get me a present?'"

"Gross."

"Yeah. Gross. It was their fault, not mine."

"I agree with that. I just want to know how you pulled it off."

She sets both her feet on the floor now, and her eyes sparkle like emerald chips in dirty rock, though she's still trying to keep her face blank. I'm fascinated watching her and wondering if this is what it's like to watch *me*. "It wasn't exactly difficult," she says. "They all thought I was *nothing*. Nobody worth noticing at all. Just a victim."

"Because you let them think that."

She shows all her teeth in a grin, and I see that the bottom ones are crooked and spotted with cavities. No dental care or orthodontia for poor folks. I'd had to spend several thousand getting my teeth fixed in my twenties. And it was worth it. Good teeth are another point of access many people in the world are never granted. I made sure I punched that ticket.

"I gave them what they wanted," she says. "A poor, helpless underage girl they could use and throw away. What a thrill. And why bother looking under the surface when the surface is exactly what you dreamed of?"

No, she's not so dumb after all. My body tingles with the thrill of it.

"The best part is it's all so exciting to them that it's over in a few seconds. Easy money. But"—she pauses to wink at me—"video lives forever, of course."

Aha. Not the least favorite of my own tricks. "So you recorded them?"

"Sure." Another shrug as she relaxes back in the chair. "I don't understand why everyone doesn't record everything. Like, you hear about people being bullied or harassed, and, like, come on, record that shit! What the hell? That's your first step right there."

Wow. This is like hearing my own thoughts played back to me. A surge of pride rises inside me.

I've done plenty of my own recording, though oftentimes it's just for my personal enjoyment. But, boy, those tapes do come in handy when you need them. Especially sex tapes.

Guilt doesn't live on the same plane with erections, and neither does caution or common sense. You'd be amazed what people don't notice in the heat of the moment.

"So," I push, "the soccer coach?"

Another wide smile. "Yeah."

"Youth minister?"

"Sure."

"Were there others?"

"Not many. Half a dozen."

"So you recorded them, and then what happened?"

"I'd email them a clip from the video and tell them that someone would be in touch. Then Brodie would collect the cash, usually a thousand bucks, and we all lived happily ever after."

"And then you'd split the money?"

"Yeah, right! I'd throw Brodie a hundred. I was doing the hard work, after all. He was just there as insurance. If I showed up to collect the money on my own, they'd think they could kill me and toss my body in a ditch to fix the problem, right? There was nothing they could do to Brodie to make *me* go away. I'm not an idiot."

"No, I guess you're not." There's no guilt on her face. No self-consciousness. My nerves are alive with excitement like tiny waves of shivers. "So with all those plans in place, what happened with Morris?"

She blows a raspberry and I wonder if she learned that little tic from living with my mom.

"Jesus. I didn't know he was related to the damn governor or whatever. I just thought he was another businessman with deep pockets and a perverted mind. That sick fuck had a little schoolgirl costume for me to wear and everything. He owned his own company, and the video was clear as hell, so I told Brodie to ask for five thousand instead of one."

"Oh, you got greedy, huh?"

"I figured he'd pay a premium."

"And did he?"

"No. When Brodie showed up to collect, that big bald guy got out of the car and pulled a gun on him. Ordered him to go get me and my phone and bring me back to the meeting place or Brodie would get a bullet in the head. He texted me as soon as he left and I took the hell off. Packed a bag and Brodie picked me up down the street and brought me here. I've been here ever since."

"Smart."

"Yeah, I thought so."

"But Brodie just went home?"

"Yeah. He told me I could chill here and he left; figured they didn't know shit about him, not even his name. But they tracked him down. He gave them my grandparents' address, but they already had that, I guess, because that bald guy beat the crap out of him. Told him it was his last warning."

"Were you worried for your grandparents?" I ask out of curiosity, because if she's like me, she doesn't worry about anyone.

"Oh sure," she spits. "As worried as they've always been for me. Dad in prison. Mom on drugs. But those assholes couldn't even be bothered to invite me over for Christmas unless Daddy just happened to be out of jail in the month of December. Fuck them."

She ain't wrong. I don't bother telling her my mom sold her out and gave the bald guy Brodie's whereabouts. That was how they found his place. That fact won't reveal anything she doesn't already know about the world. "So do you have a plan? You don't think Morris is just going to forget about you two, do you?"

Her face tightens up into a bitter little scowl. No, she hasn't figured it out. She's stuck. "Maybe I'll stay here and work for a while. Start googling my clients before I take them on so I don't run into any more surprise bullshit."

A lifetime of that smokestack cloud really socked her in. If she's truly like me, she can be so much more than a two-bit hustler, but she hasn't yet seen beyond the stifling bubble of her environment. Maybe she got some dumb genes from her mama, or maybe she was exposed to too many drugs in utero and she can't fight her way past the poisoned air she's been breathing deep her whole life.

The question is: Why do I care? Is this just a fun flash of time travel back to my youth? Maybe. Probably. But I suddenly feel invested, and I'm not sure I've ever felt that before, and I love the way my skin burns with interest.

Left to her own devices, she'll be her father all over again, in and out of jail and useless. But she doesn't have to be. She's better than her father. Just like I was.

"What are your grades like?" I ask.

"Grades?" she sneers. "Who the hell cares?"

"I'm asking if you're dumb."

"Fuck off, you snotty bitch. I know you've always thought you were better than everybody else. Everyone says that."

"Yeah, I'm sure you've heard it a million times."

"You've got that right. My dad really hates your guts."

"The feeling is mutual. And look who hasn't spent half her life in prison. Spoiler: it's this snotty bitch out here showing off her freedom. Leaving his trifling ass behind in that visiting room a few days ago really warmed my bitchy little heart."

That coaxes a small smile from her.

"Our family can't think past their next hit or handout. That's all they've ever been good for. 'What's going to happen tonight, and how can I get a piece of it?' Is that the life you want for the next eighty years?"

"I'll get the biggest piece of it, whatever it is."

"Three-quarters of a shit pie is still just a giant piece of shit, Kayla. Do you get that? Or are you as dumb as the rest of them and that's why you're so angry and sneaky?"

"Screw you, I'm not dumb."

"Then why are you still scrapping for your chance at that delicious shit pie?"

She's mad, her jaw jutting out with stubbornness, but she stays silent, listening now, waiting to see what I want from her.

What *do* I want from her?

I cross my legs and sip my Coke, returning her gaze for a long moment before I pose the next question. I stay calm, though. If she knows this is important to me, she'll lie. "Have you always felt different?"

"Like how?"

"Different from the people around you. Your mama. Your siblings. Your friends. If you have any friends."

"I got friends," she snaps, so I'm pretty sure she doesn't.

"Do you feel . . . ?" I try to think of the best way to express it. I'm not exactly great at tapping into my innermost depths. "Do you feel *removed* from the world?"

She stares.

"Removed. Like the people around you are on a TV show that you don't particularly like that much."

"Sure. Why would I care about them at all? They've never cared about me."

That's just logic, as far as I can tell, but most people don't seem to feel that way, even if they've been raised by monsters. Most people seem to want their mommy's love despite cruelty and neglect. Or because of that. Most people raised in shitty environments are determined to find love, by proxy if nothing else. A daddy leaves, so the daughter falls in love with any screwed-up man who'll tell her she's a good girl. A mom drinks and whores, so the son shacks up with the drunkest floozy he can find.

Most typically, of course, a family is dysfunctional and it creates in them a sticky need to stay close, stay in touch, keep trying to make it better. We've all seen it a million times.

I've never understood it, though, because I don't have any guilt or regret that makes me want to make things better. Maybe Kayla doesn't either.

"You might be young enough to fix," I say, testing her a little. Is she ashamed? Does she want to get *better*, whatever that means?

There are therapies for children edging toward this condition. Ways to learn how to behave empathetically even if you can't actually feel that. If a baby sociopath is caught early enough, they can be trained to . . .

conform. Maybe even to thrive. I'm not sure about sixteen, though. That seems a bit long in the neuropathic tooth.

"Fix what?" she scoffs. "There's nothing wrong with me, lady."

"You're probably a sociopath," I say simply.

For the barest moment she looks startled. Her eyes widen for a split second before she narrows them again. "I don't know what you're talking about. That's some serial killer shit right there."

"No. It's not. It's actually fairly common. One in a hundred people or so. Most of us don't kill people; we just have great skills at getting through life."

"'We'?"

"Yes. We."

"You're some kind of psycho bitch?"

"Yes, I am," I say with only the barest hint of pride.

She snorts and gets out another cigarette. She feels disadvantaged here and she doesn't like it. I haven't said what she expected me to say, and now she's scrambling for a new plan.

"What do you want from me, huh?" she demands; then she leans forward suddenly, blowing a stream of smoke to the side so her mouth is free to offer me a coy smile. "You like girls?" she asks, running her gaze down my body. "Is that what all this is about? I've been with girls before."

"Jesus Christ, you really are a one-trick pony, aren't you?"

"What's that mean?"

"Sex. It's all you know. All you're good for."

"I mean, I'm great at it, if that's what you're asking. I'll do anything you want. Anything at all. But it'll cost you. I need a little money to start over here, you know?"

I stare at her, flat-mouthed.

"If you're scared, you can have my phone so you know I'm not recording it. Right here. Right now. One thousand dollars."

Slapping my knees, I push up to my feet. "All right, I'm leaving."

"Five hundred," she says. "Family discount."

"Good Lord. You can come with me if you want. We can have dinner. Talk."

"I'm not going anywhere. I don't even know you."

"Are you waiting for your man Little Dog to return to your loving arms?" I ask.

"No, I'm just not getting in your car so you can drive me over to CPS."

"Girl, I'd take you straight to the cops. Child Protective Services!" I laugh. "As I said, I'm no do-gooder." I'm not, but I do need to turn her safely over to the authorities to get a nice, heroic ending to this story. I can't let her know what I want, though, or she'll run off again just to spite me.

"Whatever," she mutters. "I'm fine here. Go back to wherever you came from."

"Listen, Kayla, I get it. You're tough. You want to take care of things yourself. Fine. But I'm going to rent myself a nice hotel room and stay in town for the night. You'll be much safer if you come with me. You really managed to piss off the wrong guys."

"I'm fine."

"Okay, but we could have a nice chat about ourselves. Wouldn't that be fun? Talk about what's going on in that weird head of yours?"

"There's nothing wrong with me," she snaps. "I'm just stronger than everyone else."

True. Very true. "Yes," I say, "you are. And you're going to waste that strength. You've got a gig for now. You can use the thing that would normally make you vulnerable to men and turn it on them as a weapon. But that will only work for two more years, if you stay alive that long. After that, all you'll be is an eighteen-year-old dropout with a long rap sheet and a body that's worth the same dollar amount as every other whore over the legal age. You want to be queen of the state prison system? Or do you want something better than that?"

"Fuck off."

"Got it. But here's my number anyway." I tear a scrap of paper off a coupon in the kitchen and jot down my cell phone number. "Little Dog might have decided to sell you out to Morris. They might already have this address. But I'm tired of you right now, so just call if there's trouble. Or don't. Your decision." I head for the door. "Sleep tight."

"Wait."

I turn back, my hand on the cold doorknob, a little disappointed that she's come to her senses so quickly. I was starting to look forward to a long soak in a nice bathtub and a few drinks at the hotel bar.

"Could I have twenty bucks? We're out of food, and Little Dog took the car, so I need to order pizza."

There's plenty of food in the fridge, but I appreciate her attempt to scam me, so I flick a twenty at her and leave with a wave. It's time to upgrade my accommodations and take a long night of luxury to consider the stupid idea squirming at the back of my mind.

Stupid . . . but it could be fun.

CHAPTER 18

A dull buzzing wakes me from a sound sleep. My body is cradled in a luxury mattress and warmed by a perfectly fluffy comforter. I feel amazing. Powerful and right.

When I crack my eyes open, I see that it's morning, but the colorless light coming through the sheer white curtains indicates a fairly early hour. I ignore the buzzing and go back to sleep.

When it wakes me again, the light is yellow enough that I decide the hour is more civilized and turn over to grab my phone. Eight a.m. I got to bed before midnight, so I stretch hard and scroll through my alerts. Nothing from Kayla and nothing from Luke.

I'm not surprised about Luke. We had a long conversation while I was in the bathtub last night. I told him I'd found Kayla and he was so damn happy. Choked up, even, and that only inflamed my ridiculous idea.

"She's a lot like me," I told him. "I think I can help her." I didn't tell him how. I didn't even hint at it. The idea is dangerous and I enjoy the secret rush of it.

"You absolutely should," he gushed. "You should help her any way you can. Jesus, I can't believe you found her. Actually, yes I can. I don't know what I'm saying. You're amazing, Jane. Just let me know if I can help."

He *might* be able to help. He just might. But I haven't quite decided yet.

I pee and I'm taking my birth control pill when I hear the buzz again. It's not my phone. My phone is quiet on the bed.

Frowning, I dig through my purse and find a light emanating from inside it. I wrap my hands around the mysterious stowaway and pull out Nate's cell phone. "Oh, hello, little guy! I forgot about you!"

I drop into a cozy chair by the window and open Nate's text messages.

LITTLE DOG IS DEAD MAN

Oh shit. That's quite an eye-opener. What the heck happened while I was asleep? Is Kayla dead too?

I scroll back to find an initial text from last night from an unfamiliar number, but it must have been Nate, because it just asks, Where's my damn phone????

After that, there was silence for several hours, before more texts started early this morning from three people. "B," "Rodney," and "K-man," all conveying the same message: Little Dog is dead. LITTLE DOG IS DEAD!

Rodney is the only one offering the additional info that someone "took him out." Looks like it wasn't a natural death. Intriguing.

I need to find out if Kayla was affected by this, but I forgot to get her number. Still, if I had it, I wouldn't want my information on her phone at this point. Even if she's fine, I can't have another clue linking me to a dead guy. Bad enough that I called Little Dog a couple of days ago. I'm so glad I didn't text him last night.

Nate is definitely going to tell the cops that a strange middle-aged woman broke into his house and stole his phone while on the hunt for Brodie, so I power down Nate's phone, then pop out the SIM card and the battery. I'll ditch it on the road later.

They'll be able to trace the texts the phone received to this area where I've spent the night, so I'm thankful I have legitimate business. I've been looking for my missing niece. *Of course* I tried to call Brodie. *Of course* I went to his house. And Nate can say whatever he wants about my breaking in, but I'll say I knocked and knocked and then I got worried. Who are the cops going to believe? A drugged-out kid crashing at a dead boy's house? Or professional, successful me?

When there's a rap on my door, I get up silently and take careful steps to look through the peephole just in case it's the police or maybe the murderer. But it's just my breakfast.

Breakfast! I forgot I left an order on the door hanger last night.

I fling open the door and grin at the petite man carrying the big tray. "Thank you!" I'm suddenly starving.

He's nice enough to look everywhere except at me as I sign the bill, and I realize I'm only wearing panties and a tank top. It's hard to remember these kinds of things when you have no shame. I give him a big tip for being a gentleman; then I switch on the TV and settle in at the table to eat.

The French toast is perfect and they brought me two tiny bowls of soft butter, which is the height of breakfast service as far as I'm concerned. A little stingy with the bacon, but the side of fresh fruit distracts me from my annoyance.

I'm done with breakfast and halfway through the pot of coffee when I remember that I should be hurrying. Something went very wrong overnight, and there's a good chance I shouldn't have left Kayla alone no matter how snotty and defiant she was.

Then again, if Kayla was in danger, she's already dead; and if she's dead, she won't care if I hurry or not, so I pour one more cup of coffee and turn on the financial news to see if anything interesting is going on.

Nothing. It's all boring.

I made an impulsive decision last night and called in a reservation at the most luxurious hotel I know in Oklahoma. I've never stayed there myself, but even in my teenage years I'd heard of it. An Oklahoma City high-rise hotel popular during the roaring twenties that is still frequented by oil executives today.

I imagine that Kayla has never seen anything like it, and she definitely needs something shiny to set her eyes on. Something to tempt her toward good behavior for a greater goal. It's not easy for people like us to be patient. *If* she is like me. I still want to study her a bit more before I commit.

When I was her age, keeping up my grades so I could get the hell out of my town and go to a good school was the most challenging part of my life. I had to sit tight. Had to study for tests and do my homework or at least find ways around it like Mr. Hollingsway. I had to tolerate my parents and my brother and every nasty asshole in my town. And I had to stay out of trouble.

Well . . . I had to not get *caught* in trouble; let's be clear. *Staying* out of trouble would have driven me off the deep end.

I stole cars for a joyride every once in a while. And I shoplifted constantly. But I never got caught. I was white and I was female, so it was easy to fly under the radar while quietly entertaining my dark side.

Kayla hasn't been that smart. She doesn't give a damn about anything, which is totally understandable. I get it. But it won't keep working for her forever. She was right about being stronger than other people, but she needs to be smarter than them too. They expect her to end up in prison just like her daddy, and that's exactly where she's headed at this rate, the dumb-ass.

Well . . . if she's headed anywhere at all and not lying there dead in the home of a stranger. What a shock that would be for Brodie's aunt and uncle after a couple of months in Arizona.

If she was killed, I won't be able to return a hero, but I will be a sympathetic and tragic figure, at least. I tried to help, but I was too late!

I finally get cleaned up and dressed and pack the few things I took out of my suitcase, and I head on out to the leafy avenues of the nicer areas of Tulsa.

The neat and tidy house looks the same when I pull under the portico, which is good news. No cop cars, no police tape, and no Brodie-like vehicle, which I can only assume would be a muscle car with patches of primer showing. Or maybe he's been driving his grandma's 1988 maroon Mercury Grand Marquis all over the great state of Oklahoma.

Snorting at the image, I get out of the car. All I can do is knock on the door and see if she answers. If she doesn't, then I'll need to make some serious decisions. Walk away and wash my hands of this whole thing? Sneak around back and see if I can spy any clues through the windows? Break in to discover the truth? Maybe not a great idea if there's a dead body in there, but it does appeal to my reckless side.

In the end I get quite a surprise. Kayla answers the door within seconds of my knock. Her hair still looks stringy and unwashed, but she's changed into leggings and a long blue T-shirt.

"Hey," she says flatly, smacking on gum that's putting off clouds of grape scent, likely her solution to brushing and flossing.

"Did anyone come by here?" I ask.

"Nah."

"That's good news for you, because Little Dog is dead."

Her eyebrows twitch up, but that's her only reaction. "He's dead?"

"Yeah. Murdered, apparently."

"Wow."

"Yes, wow. So I think it might be a good idea to get you out of here. You can come with me or you can strike out on your own and hope for the best, if that's what you want." I feign indifference. "Like I said, I'm not here to save you or be your social worker."

"Where would we be going, exactly?"

"I thought we'd get a nice hotel room and chat. A fun girls' night."

One side of her mouth lifts in a smirk. "So you changed your mind, huh?"

"No. This may seem surprising to you, considering what you've seen in your life, but I'm not at all interested in an incestuous relationship with a child. I don't need to steal your false innocence in order to feel power. I've got more than enough of my own. Got it?"

My speech only warrants an eye roll. Damn. I thought it was pretty good.

"I'd like to find out if there's anything more to you than this menagerie of sexual tricks you trot out at every given opportunity. Do you think there could be something more in there?" I point toward her chest.

She blows a huge purple bubble before sucking it back into her mouth and cutting her eyes to the side. "If Brodie's dead, I definitely can't stay here. Give me a minute to clear my shit out."

"Fine."

I use my jacket sleeve to open the fridge and grab another icy can of Coke. When I spot my previous can still in the trash, I fish it out to toss later along with Nate's cell phone. No point in leaving my fingerprints in plain sight, just in case.

Fifteen minutes later Kayla is back with a backpack and a garbage bag full of clothes. She seems ready, flip-flops on her feet and everything, but she's studying her phone as she meanders slowly across the living room. "Kevin says he was stabbed just outside of town yesterday."

"Which town? Here or there?"

"Here. In Jenks. Other side of the river."

"Hm. You said you thought he was going to Enid."

"Yeah, I don't know. I heard him talking to someone, planning to meet them."

"You didn't ask who?"

"I did, but he was already out the door and told me not to worry about it."

"Selling you out?" I guess.

"If he was, the deal didn't go through."

"Let's get going, just in case." It makes sense. He thought I was coming with two hundred dollars in exchange for Kayla. That deal would've taken Kayla off his hands, but it wouldn't protect him from Morris. That big bald guy would still be waiting for him when he got home. So, instead of handing her off to me, he decided to upgrade and turn her over to Morris's guy for more money. He was smarter than I gave him credit for.

No. Of course he wasn't smart. He *tried* to be smart, but now he's dead and he failed to actually pull off his scheme. No money, no safety, no life at all.

We're in the car and pulling out of the driveway within a minute, though I check my mirror until we actually make it out of the tree-shaded neighborhood. "The first time I came to Tulsa, I couldn't believe how green it was," I say. "It's still nothing like where I live now, though. In Minneapolis there are trees everywhere. Lakes everywhere. Waterfalls and rivers. It's gorgeous."

"Isn't Minneapolis like . . . Siberia?"

"No, it's not like Siberia."

She kicks off her sandals and props her feet on the dashboard. The tacky glitter pink polish on her toes has chipped off to the middle third of each nail. "Where are we going?"

"The Skirvin in Oklahoma City. You ever heard of it?"

"No." She blows another bubble.

"Want to put on some music or something?"

"No."

Unlike most teenagers, she doesn't seem to have earbuds constantly shoved into her ears. I imagine that, like me, she doesn't identify with the emotions in songs. And she doesn't seem to need a way to shut out the world. Other people don't affect her. Other people *really* don't affect her. She hasn't shown a hint of emotion about her dead friend.

"What's this?" she asks, picking up the Lladró figurine I stashed in the cup holder of the center console.

"It's art," I answer. "Put it back."

"I think Brodie has these things at his house."

"Had them."

She sets it back down as I glance at her face for any reaction. There is none. "Do you think Morris had Brodie killed?" I press.

"Probably. They threatened him with a gun and beat the shit out of him already. Who else would it be?"

"And just so things are clear between us . . . you don't seem torn up about his murder."

"Why would I care when he was meeting that asshole to betray me? That doesn't even make sense."

It doesn't make sense to me either, but it's not how most people would respond. Certainly a normal teenage girl would be more upset. More scared. And more sorry. This whole business was her idea, after all. Her moneymaking scheme. She dragged Brodie into it as muscle and now he's dead because of it.

She stares placidly out the windshield, her eyes watching the river as we drive toward it before curving around for the bridge. I pull a small bag of chocolate mini-doughnuts from behind my seat and offer her some. She eats six before I grab the bag back and finish the last two myself.

Teenagers.

Neither of us feels the need to fill the silence with small talk, so we're quiet nearly the whole way to Oklahoma City. Luke calls once, but I let it go to voice mail. I don't want Little Miss Sneaky Pants listening in on my personal calls.

Flying down the turnpike, I miss the view of wind turbines. There's nothing to see on this drive but billboards and fast-food signs. Oh, and cows. Lots of cows.

At long last we're in the city, and I exit deep into the interior of downtown. We pull onto the wide drive of the Skirvin, and I stop my car for the valet. Kayla loses some of her placidness and looks around with big eyes. I notice her watching as I toss my keys to the boy in the Skirvin polo shirt. I hand a few dollars to the man who grabs our luggage—and Kayla's garbage bag—and I breeze inside, Kayla hot on my heels.

"Whoa," she says when we get inside the lobby. I don't know anything about architecture, but everything here is fancy. Everything is gilt against rich colors and polished wood. The elevator doors look sculpted from brass and jade. Eight-foot chandeliers hang from the three-story ceiling. It's cool and echoey in here, with little pods of murmuring businessmen gracing the furniture like leisurely painted ladies. Kayla's sandals slap obnoxiously against the glossy marble floor as she trails behind me.

The air smells of cool lemons and fresh flowers, and I breathe it in and smile. No cloud of pollution here.

"Good afternoon!" the girl behind the chest-high wooden desk sings as we approach. I give her my name, and she's all gushing politeness as she checks us in and scans my card; then she steps out from behind the desk and personally leads us to the elaborate elevator doors. "Your suite is already prepared. Right this way, ladies."

"Oh, just the one lady," I correct her with a wide smile as we step onto the elevator.

Her grin falters as her brows dip in confusion.

"We'll see about this one here." I tip my head toward Kayla, who glares back.

The tiny elevator car finally spits us out on the highest floor, and the clerk leads us down a carpeted hallway spaced with beautiful wooden doors, each of them framed with painted vines and flowers. We walk all the way to the very end, where a plaque reads *Presidential Suite*.

Sure, I'm showing off a little, but consider it my version of *Scared Straight!* Stunned smart? Pampered into politeness?

The woman swipes the key and swings open the door with pride. "Here we are! Our finest suite!"

I breeze past her and stride down a short wood-floored hallway into a huge living room with expansive views of the downtown buildings that surround us. "Lovely," I say.

"Holy shitballs," Kayla chimes in.

We get the grand tour, of course. I've paid for the privilege. This place is expensive, and I want Kayla to know that, but it's not extravagant by, say, New York standards. In fact, I couldn't get a junior suite for this amount in Tokyo. But this one-night rental is presenting Kayla with an entire universe. *You too can have this; all you have to do is learn to concentrate your psychological specialty.*

People are afraid of us. Afraid of the idea of sociopaths, lumping us in with serial killers and mass murderers. But I've never killed anyone. I probably never will.

Still, if they knew the truth, they'd be even more afraid. There are so many of us. We're everywhere. Sure, we're petty criminals and fraudsters, but we are also CEOs and surgeons and military brass. More than that, we are the most successful CEOs and surgeons and military brass. The very people the world admires. Why do we have success? Because we're not scared of anything, and we're willing to accept the kind of risk/reward exchange that pays off in millions. We're *eager* for it.

Of course, we're also the worst CEOs and surgeons and military brass, and you definitely shouldn't marry one of us, but you have to take the good with the bad.

And if we can't care about people, is that our fault? How is it different from any other psychological condition? I'm not wired to feel regret. I'm not capable of sympathy. I couldn't pity you if I wanted to, but—lucky me—I just don't want to.

My brain grew this way naturally, my genetics helped along by years of abuse and neglect, layered over with my brief, awful experience of feeling any emotion in this shitty, shitty world. Teachers ignored my dirty clothes and sunken eyes. Grown men saw my desperation as fun opportunity. Family laughed at my trauma-induced bedwetting. Politicians ignored my most basic animal needs.

I had to take care of myself. And I fucking did.

With her father in prison when he wasn't spraying his seed on every ovulating woman in the state, Kayla may have had it even worse. I can't imagine the number of men who rotated through her home. The number who considered her a nice little family bonus. I won't ask. We've all heard the story a million times and only the details change, and I can't feel sympathy anyway.

So I watch the wonder take her face and I let it fill me with satisfaction. *Yes, girl. I can have this anytime I want. Yes, this is who I am and what I can give you. Look at that sunken tub. Look at that five-foot-tall headboard. Look at the tray of fresh fruit someone rushed up here to make me feel special.*

Are you good enough to have this too?

There's a knock on the door, and the hotel woman jogs off in her heels to answer it. "Your bags are here!" she calls.

I leave Kayla spinning in a slow circle in the master bedroom and give the bellboy and the clerk ten dollars each so they'll leave. When I get back to the bedroom, Kayla is about to flop down onto the bed. "Stay off it. There's a pullout couch in the living room. The bed is mine. Like I said, I'm not a do-gooder."

Kayla huffs. "Whatever. I don't care. There's a TV out there too."

"Yes, there's also a TV in the bathroom. Why don't you wash your hair, have a long soak in the tub, and then we'll go shopping. Sound good?"

"Hell yeah."

"Have you ever had a manicure?"

Her brows dip into an angry V like she thinks I'm making fun of her.

"We'll do mani-pedis too. Girls' day. I'll call the front desk and ask for recommendations."

"What's this about?" she demands, but I walk away to get some work done. I've got a lot of emails piling up from the office. Seems something big is going on there.

I hear the bathtub start up as I open my laptop, and I hum happily to myself. At least she's willing to wash, even if she's not particularly self-motivated.

I open an email from one of the partners and exclaim "Oh no!" into the empty room. I even put a dramatic hand to my chest and try it again with more feeling. *"Oh no!"*

It seems Rob's client has run into some huge problems! A scandal, even! And, horror of horrors, it was caused by Rob himself!

He made a classic mistake, really. He was trying to forward some documents to two of the school districts interested in the deal with North Unlimited, but he attached the wrong files. And one of them— oh, Rob—one of them contained evidence that the frozen raw chicken product originates in China and not in Brazil as the client promised!

The deal has completely fallen apart. There's talk of a lawsuit from the state prison system. And the school districts are horrified. This company was putting children—vulnerable little children—in danger of consuming adulterated, smuggled food!

All because of Rob. My God. This is a fatal mistake. A career ender, even.

The client has been assured that swift action will be taken. Rob will definitely get fired, but I doubt anyone is the least bit worried about him. He'll land on his feet and find work again soon. He's great at nothing if not selling himself.

The important thing is that Rob will never again stand in my office, talking and talking and passing along work that he should've been doing himself. And he will never, ever lie about me to another client.

I type out a quick email to the partner, letting him know that things are still dire here, but my missing niece has been located, and I should be able to help do damage control this evening once I find a place to stay and get this little girl settled.

Please don't hesitate to call me. I'm familiar with this case and I'll do whatever I can to help. I can step outside her hospital room to take your call if needed. Please know I'm here to assist during this crisis, and I'm very sorry I'm not there to do my part right now.

Once that's sent, I take my time reading through the rest of the emails. I cc'd myself on that email I sent from Rob's address, so I'm able to take in all the alarm and recrimination from the two sides. And of course the most delicious dish I've ever been served is Rob and his many exclamation points, swearing that there was some sort of sabotage afoot. He never sent that email or that file!!! It wasn't him!

As if any of the parties cares how this came about. The deal is over now. And so is Rob.

I tried to help him. I honestly did. Well, not *that* honestly. I helped him because I thought it might help me, but Rob had to go and screw that up. He made his bed, and now that he's unemployed, he'll have plenty of time to lie in it. Sweet dreams, Rob.

I did this for myself, of course, but it's really a service to every person who'll ever encounter Rob in the future. Without this setback, he would have spent his whole life leaning on others and taking all the credit for himself. That tactic was working very nicely for him. He became successful because of bad habits, and those habits needed to be corrected.

Now, when he finds work at another, lesser law firm, he'll be the low man on the totem pole. Forced to be on his best behavior to make up for his tarnished past. Forced to try hard and get better.

You're welcome, Rob.

I hear a shout from the bathroom and tip my head to concentrate. "What?" I yell back.

"What's the Wi-Fi password?" she screams.

I yell it out for her, then open the email that has just dinged in from the office. *Thank you so much, Jane. This is wonderful news about your niece, and we all hope she will be okay. Please take time with your family today and I'll call this evening if we need anything urgent from you. We're eager to have you back as soon as you're able, of course. Rob's cases will be redistributed, and I know you are familiar with most of them.*

I type back a quick and earnest reply before closing my laptop with a grin. What a day.

I've already showered, but I want to change into something more stylish for our shopping trip, so I carry my luggage to the bedroom. When I pass the bathroom door, I hear the dulcet moaning and tinny grunting of porn being viewed through a small-screen device. I guess the girl has needs, and it's none of my business, but I make a note to use the shower tonight instead of the tub.

I dig out some black skinny jeans and a pink sweater to wear with my black boots; then I settle in with the room service menu to plan a delicious lunch. Flatbread, a spicy-chicken-and-avocado sandwich, french fries, and several desserts. I also add a glass of wine for me and a Coke for her, and then I stretch out to doze until the food comes.

A drop of water wakes me. I open my eyes slowly to find Kayla standing over me, wrapped in a robe, her hair hanging in wet ropes like the goddamn ghost child from *The Ring*. "What?" I snap.

"There's someone at the door."

"Yeah, it's room service. I ordered lunch. Answer it."

"It could be the cops," she says calmly.

"Why would the cops be here?"

She shrugs, and I elbow her out of the way so I can answer it. It's room service, just as I thought.

I don't trust Kayla not to steal it, so I sip the wine as the server is laying out the meal on our dining room table. I offer Kayla half the sandwich and half the flatbread, and she happily accepts both and pulls the platter of french fries to her side of the table.

Fine. I've got my wine.

"This place is cool," she says between bites.

"You like it?"

"Yeah. It's nice."

"It *is* nice. Tell me why you were worried about the cops. You didn't seem concerned when I knocked on your door this morning. Is this about Brodie?"

She shrugs and stuffs more food into her mouth.

"Kayla, I want you to be honest with me."

"Why?" she asks simply, and it's a great question. I'm sure she's never been truthful with anyone in her life—and, really, what is the point of truth?

Who have I ever been honest with? No one.

Luke has no idea I'm a sociopath, just as he has no idea of the double life I was leading when we reconnected in Minneapolis.

My best friend is dead now, but when she was alive, I mostly told her what she needed to hear so that she'd keep being my friend, because she was my only anchor in this world.

I tell people things that benefit me and keep them close, and I'm sure Kayla has learned the same trick. If she and I are going to get along, it will take months of proving to her that she can be herself with me. Maybe years. And I do want us to get along.

This is a shallow, reckless idea, but that's my specialty. That was how I ended up with my cat, and look how happy we are together.

And now a family. Just for me.

Some people want to have children so they can create people who will have to love them. People they can be around constantly, with no question of divorce or betrayal. A spouse is fine, but a *child* . . . That's so much more permanent. Any tiny thing can send a friend or lover or spouse far away, but you really have to screw up to lose a child completely. They'll love you through your worst days, even if the "worst" is just your natural personality. I've seen it a million times in the warped relationships of those around me.

But I don't want love. I want that other big thing people search for in their own children. *Themselves.*

She is like me, I've decided. A wild little me. A flattering, fascinating mirror. A *legacy*. That's what I see in Kayla. That's what excites me. This wouldn't be settling down, not at all.

Just look at her, stuffing her face. Her friend died, a boy she spent countless days with, a boy she used for her own benefit, and she hasn't missed a step at the news of his death. After all, he was likely in the act of betraying her when he was murdered. Why should she care at all? I get that. I feel it in my deepest spots. I wouldn't care about him either.

Kayla has been taking on grown men since she was fourteen or fifteen at most, shaking them down for their money. Imagine what she could do at twenty. At thirty. With education and class and an expansive understanding of how the world works, she could have it all. Because of *me*.

I'll need to be careful. The girl is lightning in a bottle, and she could be very, very dangerous to me. But danger is intoxicating, isn't it? What's the fun in living a safe life?

That was what I was resisting with Luke, after all. The stultifying horror of settling down. As far as I can tell, settling into your life is just waiting patiently for death. Slowing everything down until you just don't care and you welcome the sweet embrace of eternal darkness.

Screw that. I'll fight that nothingness until the day it violently strangles me into submission.

Kayla isn't nothingness. She's excitement. Possibility. Risk. If I take her under my wing, who knows what could happen? What a little treat she could be. Maybe there could even be affection between us and real understanding.

People think we have no feelings at all, but that's not true. We get lonely. We crave companionship. We chase after it, hoping for a real connection *just this once*. Kayla and I might click together like dangerous puzzle pieces.

I push the desserts at Kayla and tell her to pick one. She snatches up the fried ice cream sundae without saying thank you. She hasn't said it once. She's waiting for the moment when I reveal the catch, because this girl knows damn well that nobody in this world is nice without a reason. There will be a catch, so why offer gratitude and then look like a gullible idiot later?

She's right. Even love comes with strings attached. We fall in love with people because of how they make us feel. We don't just fall in love with any random kind person we encounter. It's more than admiration. It's sizzling need. Your need, not theirs. Your crush, your wants, your desire for *them*.

Everyone is a monster, as far as I can tell. I'm not alone in this.

Luke is a good and decent person. He works hard and does the right thing, and he loves his brother, and his brother-in-law, and his adorable niece. He loves them all so much because they bring warmth and joy to his life. His mother? He stopped loving her when she became too much of a nightmare to live with, and good for him. It's more than most normal people can manage.

But do you want to know why he loves me? I know. It's because my coolness reassures him after years of his mother's erratic, obsessive love. Because I pump up his ego when he needs it and I make him laugh. And because I give the most mind-blowing blow jobs he's ever experienced and I'm down for sex at the drop of a hat.

That's it. That's love. No need to write poetry about it; I've solved the riddle.

So no, I don't need Kayla's love. But I really, really want the spark of her companionship.

I smile widely at her as she hums over her first giant bite of ice cream. "When you're done with lunch, we'll go shopping and get you all fixed up. Some new clothes. A haircut. Beautiful toes."

Kayla nods and smiles back, a dollop of whipped cream adorably perched on the end of her little nose. But her eyes stay cold and careful, waiting.

Good girl.

CHAPTER 19

We have a fantastic day on the town. There's no need to relive the boring details and write them in our diaries. Everyone knows what a fun shopping day is like.

Kayla's hair has been tamed. It's nearly the same length, but it's cut at a sharp angle now, the front sliding about two inches longer past her shoulders than the back. The dirty blond is brighter too, with a few light streaks near the front that Kayla asked for. Her eyes look less muddy and more green.

Her fingers and toes are aqua blue with tiny green crystals on the pinkie nail of each hand. They look nice against her expensive new jeans and white rhinestone flip-flops. Her new ruffled black shirt cost nearly one hundred dollars, and it makes her pale skin glow.

She's flushed with excitement, and the rush of blood has chased away her sickly waifishness. Now she looks like a healthy little colt of a girl instead of a hungry child raised on the streets. This relationship might be just what we both need.

"Do you want to go out for dinner or order in?"

She glances around the living room with an assessing eye as we drop our bags next to the big dining table. "I liked the lunch here," she says.

"It's good food, but it's much more exciting to go out and show off your new hair and nails and clothes after a big day. You get to enjoy the fruits of someone else's labor."

"Can we go somewhere fancy?" she asks, her jaw jutting out as if she's ready to challenge any denial.

"Obviously. I already checked Yelp and found a high-end Northern Italian place nearby. Does that sound good? Or would you prefer steak?"

"I like meatballs," she says, so I shrug and grab a reservation for fifteen minutes from now. Northern Italian or not, I trust they know that folks in America would expect meatballs.

"I reserved a table. Let's go."

When we get back to the lobby, her flip-flops slap the granite with the same echoing volume of her old shoes, but at least these sparkle and shine as she walks. I watch her gaze slide over the happy hour crowd in the hotel bar. There are dozens of men in there, all in dark suits, all loosening up their already loose morals with booze. Her eyes narrow as if she's counting their money.

"Come on, girl. You're off the clock right now."

"What?" she snaps back in a sharp whine. "I wasn't doing anything."

"Do you think you can get past this sex-scheme phase, or is this it for you?"

"Whatever," she mutters. "I was just looking around."

"Okay, sure."

The wind has picked up since we were out shopping, and she's obviously cold as we walk, but she doesn't admit it because I told her to grab a sweatshirt or something and she didn't. She doesn't want to cover up her cute new clothes. I understand that completely, and I admire the way she just clenches her fists and refuses to even cross her arms against the wind. I grin at the mountains of goose bumps that erupt on her skin as I lead the way around the corner.

A few minutes later we're sliding into a booth with a street view. I order myself a fancy gin fizz and tell Kayla to try an Italian crème soda. The server brings bread, and Kayla grabs a slice as if she's afraid he'll return to take it back.

Chewing, she watches me with a cool stare.

"Warming up yet?" I ask.

She ignores that and lifts her chin. "So are you going to explain what all this is about or not?"

I tilt my head and study her for a moment. "Do you like your nice clothes?"

"Sure."

"Your new hair, new nails?"

"Obviously."

"You can tell when people have money, right? You can see that they look different and carry themselves differently?"

She shrugs.

"They pay for that look. The shiny hair, gorgeous nails, perfectly hemmed and tailored slacks. They look good because they can afford to pay for those things. They can afford suites at the Skirvin and massages to help them rest and relax. They get vacations. Time off to lie on the beach. Skin care. Personal trainers."

"Yeah, I know."

"You can have that too. You don't have to scramble every damn day of your life. But you have to be willing to work for that money."

"I already—"

I hold up a hand. "Not that way. Not if you want real money, Kayla. Sex has its place in ambition, but it's not the only tool."

"Whatever," she growls.

"I came from the same place you did, and look at me." She doesn't. "I mean it. Look at me. Look at my hair, my skin, my boots. I own a gorgeous downtown condo. I drive a nice car. I go out to dinner anytime I want. Travel overseas. Shop without a budget. And I do it all on my terms, not by negotiating with some wrinkly-sacked sugar daddy who'll throw me a coin now and then. It's *mine*, Kayla. You get that?"

She turns her eyes resentfully in my direction.

"I earned this life. I'm not rich, not by one percent standards, but I sure as hell will never again in my life need to hitch a ride with a pervie truck driver so I can get out of some shit town. Never."

"Good for you. So . . . what? You're going to write me into your will or something?"

"Boy, that would be a huge mistake, wouldn't it?" I grin until she finally grants a tiny smile before ducking her head to hide it. Not out of shyness, but because she can't conceal the hard amusement of picturing me dead and passing on my belongings to her.

"Thankfully," I say, "I'm smarter than that. No, what I'm saying is you need to work hard in school and learn to control yourself if you want a better life."

"Oh, Jesus Christ," she moans, eyes rolling so hard, I wonder if she strained them.

"This isn't a pep talk, so shut the hell up, little girl."

The server was sliding up along my side to take our order, but I watch him freeze and hesitate now.

"We'll need a minute," I say, then wave at Kayla to look at her menu. "Decide what you want." Picking mine up, I spy lobster ravioli, but I'm sure it won't be the lobster ravioli I like, so I take a few minutes to study the food. "Osso buco," I say aloud.

Kayla frowns. "What's that?"

"It's sort of like the best pot roast you've ever had in your life. But don't ever explain it that way to anyone. They'll think you're hopelessly ignorant."

"So it's fancy?"

"Sure."

She keeps frowning at the menu.

"If you want to try it, we can order meatballs as an appetizer. Then you'll have the meatballs you wanted and you'll get to experience something new."

"Yeah. Yeah, let's do that. I want to try it."

"Good choice." I shoot a look at the server and he darts over as if he's been anxiously waiting. I order the food and remind him about my gin fizz. He's back within thirty seconds with our drinks. Kayla eats more bread.

"You and I are the same," I say. Her eyes rise and watch me impassively, waiting for more. "Or close enough to the same. I called you a sociopath before. Do you know what that means?"

"I looked it up."

"What do you think? Does it fit?"

She only gives me a shrug and takes a sip of her soda, still waiting. Still assessing. She doesn't have the self-consciousness other people have. She can stand the quiet.

"I'm not a doctor, of course. I've never even been to a shrink myself. Why bother? So I suppose I could be way off. But we both know I'm not, don't we?"

"What's your point?"

"I came to find you because I heard you might be like me. I was curious. And now I'm even more curious. Would you like to come live with me in Minneapolis?"

That finally gets her attention. She lifts her mouth from her straw as her eyes squint into a glare. "*Live* with you? In fucking Siberia?"

"You live in a desolate prison camp now, so I don't know why you're turning your nose up at a change. Yeah, it's cold during the winter, but it's a hell of a lot nicer than your current surroundings."

"I have a shitty, psychotic mother already. I don't need another one, but thanks."

"I don't want to be your mother, shitty or otherwise. I have a cat, and that's enough nurturing to last me decades. I'd be your mentor. Teach you how to navigate the world using your unusual skills."

"Why?"

It's my turn to shrug. "Because it sounds fun, actually. Right now my life is very *stable*. And sometimes when things are stable I act out. I hate being bored."

"Yeah," she responds.

"You're rough right now. Unpolished. I want to show you a big picture and help you place yourself in it. You still haven't told me if you're smart."

"Smart enough."

"How did you do in school?"

The waiter brings our Caesar salads, and I dig in while Kayla shoots a glare out the window. She's still avoiding the question, but I love garlic, so I eat happily. I guess she's not a fan of veggies.

"In fourth grade they wanted to put me in a special class," she finally says. "For dumb kids."

"And? Did you go?"

"No. My test results were really high, so they couldn't send me, and they didn't know what to do with me."

"I see."

"But I hate school. I don't want to go and I shouldn't have to. It's fucking stupid."

"Of course you should have to go. Am I supposed to put up with gangs of wild, uneducated kids running in the streets at all hours of the day? Look, you've got two more years of school. You've had a rough patch until now, and your grades probably blow, but you can turn that around. A big comeback story works wonders. Two years of hard work, and then you can get a scholarship to college."

"Bullshit. That money is for black kids and Indi—"

"Stop. Just stop. You haven't believed anything these assholes have told you your whole life, but you believe *that*? All they're doing is giving you an excuse for why they haven't done shit with their lives. You're a poor kid from an abusive home. Mom on drugs. Dad in prison. Colleges eat that crap up like chocolate. You bring up your grades and write a good essay about how you finally learned how to separate yourself from destructive family dynamics and *thrive*, and you're automatically in."

Chin down, she watches me through her lashes, ice in her eyes. I finish my drink and my salad and finally snag a piece of bread. When the meatballs arrive, I order another gin fizz and sit back.

"I could really go to college?" she asks.

"Yeah. Maybe not Harvard, but a state school? Definitely. Maybe even an expensive school somewhere else if you can get some scholarships. Hawaii? Florida? California?"

Her eyebrows rise in interest.

"But you have to work for it. Plan and scheme the same way you did with these men. This is a long game, Kayla. You get to college and you can have so much more fun than in high school. You just have to toe the line. Do the work, or at least *pay* someone to do it."

"You can do that?"

"Sure. Learn how to work the system from the inside. That's where the money is. That's the power. You act like *them*. Get it?"

"I still don't see what's in it for you. Unless you really do want sex."

"I really don't want sex. Even aside from the fact that you're my niece and a *child*—Jesus, I can't believe I have to say that—I like penises, and my boyfriend has a great one. So no, I don't want to collect you like some orphan sex doll. I'm not an asshole trafficker. I get great sex for free, thank you very much."

"Okay. So . . . you've always wanted a baby or something?"

"No, I've never wanted a baby. Have you seen those things? But I think we could . . . Shit, I don't know." I tilt my head and meet her gaze. "We could be friends. Or like . . . well, like an aunt and a niece, funny enough."

I laugh at my own joke. "No one knows what I am, Kayla. I've never told anyone. And even if they did know, they couldn't really *know*. I'd just be like a weird animal in a zoo. But you and I get each other. Or we could. I wouldn't have to pretend with you and vice versa. We understand what it's like, how we each think and feel."

She spears a meatball and puts it on her plate. I do the same.

"You might not care about that at sixteen. I wouldn't have either. But I'm over thirty now, and it feels good to look in your face and know what I'm seeing. Other people are just fucking strange."

"Yeah. That's true."

My second drink arrives and I take it from the server's hand with a muttered "Thank God." I'm not used to giving sincere speeches, and frankly it took far too much energy to pull off. Either she gets it or she doesn't. I'm done being honest for tonight. My face feels tight and prickly and I don't like it. Ugh.

We finish the meatballs and both keep our mouths tightly closed until the entrées arrive. I point at my empty glass again and the server nods. No driving tonight, so I can get comfortably blitzed.

"I'll have another crème soda too," Kayla says. "Cherry this time."

She sounds older than sixteen suddenly. Calm and completely in control. I smile at her, feeling a lovely frisson of pride as I imagine molding her into greatness.

"What would all this mean?" she asks. "Living with you? I'd have a room? Food? All that?"

"Yes. And I won't charge rent." Let's be honest, I haven't planned this out. I always go with my gut and act quickly. But I'm an expert at getting what I want. "But first things first. There will be rules. I have a boyfriend. He's a good guy, not a creep. You don't ever screw with him."

"Oh?" Her eyes gleam for a bare moment.

"Listen to me. You don't lie about him. You don't record him. You don't flirt with him. You don't even look sideways at him. And you don't tell him what we are. Luke is a normal guy. He's a little naïve. And he loves me."

She snorts.

"Yeah, I know. It's dumb. But it's true. Think of him as my prized possession and that makes it easier to understand. This is a deal breaker and I'm willing to go to the mat over this. You don't try to make either of us look like something we're not or I will ruin you and everything you've ever wanted."

"Wow. Calm down, maybe."

"Look, I don't understand the way normal people work, but Luke will do his best to be a good, devoted uncle to you. Let him."

"What if he's secretly a creep and you don't know it?"

I snort. "He's not. I recognize creeps, I promise. But if he is, you come to me and tell me immediately. Other than that, he's under my protection and you'll treat him with respect even if you have to reach into your darkest unplumbed depths to fake it."

Kayla doesn't respond, but I will get that agreement out of her before we move forward. I will make her say it out loud.

"Second, right now I live in a downtown condo. I have a cat. Do not hurt that cat or I'll hurt you. And don't trash my condo. For a few weeks you'll have to sleep on the couch. But we're looking for a house right now."

"'We'?"

Yes, we. I've decided to take Luke up on his offer to move things forward. Settle down. Like a quiet little spider. "Me and Luke," I say.

"So you'll definitely have your own room and a nice big house to live in. With food. Lots of food."

"Okay."

"Three, you'll try hard in school and not create unnecessary trouble. Everyone gets in fights and loses their temper, but don't start a prostitution ring or set up the vice principal to take the fall for embezzlement or something."

"Ha!" She lights up a little when she laughs. "Good one."

"Are you starting to believe that I just might know how you think?"

"I'd say you have promise."

I pause for a moment and watch her eat. "Do you like the osso buco?"

"Yeah. It's good. What's this stuff?" She pokes at a yellowish mound under the meat.

"It's risotto. Fancy rice. You'll like it."

She takes a tiny bite and nods. "It's okay."

I dig into my own risotto before it gets cold. It's delicious, so I take a few minutes to shut up and enjoy my food.

I haven't told Luke my plan yet, but—worst-case scenario—I buy my own house in the suburbs and keep dating him. Or I could get a slightly bigger place downtown. That would work out too.

But downtown means more trouble for Kayla to get into and more directions for me to watch. It would be doable, because I wouldn't trust her at all, but it would take more work. Cameras all over the house. And I could set a private investigator on her once a month to make sure I'm in the loop on all of her neighborhood shenanigans.

I imagine the little spy game she and I will play and I feel a surge of affection for this troublesome person.

"Are you interested in my offer or not?" I finally ask.

"Maybe."

"It would get you the hell out of this damned place. I'm not asking you to live a moral life or be kind or generous. I don't care. Just keep your nose clean and apply yourself."

"I see."

"And do not fuck up my life. That's all. Understand?"

"Whatever."

Good Lord, teenagers and their one-word answers. "You're annoying the hell out of me. Do you want in or not? And a 'Thank you for saving my stupid life, Aunt Jane' wouldn't hurt anything."

"You didn't save my life."

"Shit, girl. A few months ago you moved in with *my mother* because that was your best option. I'm very clear that you haven't started living any kind of life, even if *you're* not."

"Fuck off," she mutters, but she keeps on eating. For a tiny thing, she can pack it away, and I really admire that. You've got to get while the getting is good.

Her shoulders hitch up in a shrug, though I haven't said anything. "So what's the plan? Smuggle me out of state?"

"No. I need to do this legally so we can get the documentation to enroll you in school. Joylene would testify that I'd be a good influence, I think. But I don't know what your mom would do."

"I can take care of her," Kayla says.

"Oh?"

"I know about several buildings she burned down to help people file insurance claims, and one drug dealer she ratted out to the cops. I'll just threaten to tell everyone if she doesn't sign me away."

"Nice," I say with genuine appreciation.

"Thanks."

"Obviously, everyone in our family can be bought off if necessary. But it won't be necessary. I'm not worried about them. My biggest concern is that the lieutenant governor has your name and could make trouble."

"I can take care of that," Kayla says, finally sitting back to press a hand to her belly as if she can't eat another bite.

"What do you mean?" I ask.

"I mean I have the tape and I've decided it's time to use it. In fact, I edited it this afternoon. It's ready to upload. Once Roy Morris is exposed, they'll be too busy scrambling to worry about me."

I have to admit, I'm surprised. The sound I heard from the bathroom today wasn't her watching porn. It was her preparing blackmail material.

Listen, I'm a big fan. I've pulled off similar schemes myself for fun and profit. But this is dangerous.

"That's child pornography. It's illegal to make it, view it, or share it. Even if you're in it. You can't just send it out."

"I'll use a fake email address and a throwaway ISP. It's fine."

"And what if your face gets out in the future and you're trying to land a big job?"

She shrugs. "Whatever. It's illegal to view, right? I'm not worried."

"But you didn't send it out yet?"

"Not yet. I wanted to figure out my next step first."

"Yeah? What is your next step?"

"Moving in with you," she says, just like that.

I guess we have a plan.

Still, I shake my head. "Look, I like throwing out filth for public consumption as much as the next girl does, but that's not going to work this time."

"I plan to send it to newspapers."

"Newspapers would be extremely careful about this, and at best they might write an article hinting at what they've seen. But if they can't prove you're underage, they'll consider it sordid gossip that isn't their business. If they *do* suspect you're underage, they will send the video to the police and run away like their hands are on fire, because they're not legally allowed to view that."

"So I should just distribute it online?"

I tap the table and try to think it through. I do love a puzzle, and she's on the right track, at least, no longer sitting around in an empty house, waiting for something to happen.

Kayla dips her straw up and down in her glass and watches me. "Well, you haven't said anything about how wrong it is yet."

"Wrong?"

"Yeah. You know . . ."

"Using your body? Making the tape? Putting it out there?"

"All of it."

I laugh. "Yeah, I'm not real great at figuring out right and wrong. I'm more interested in what works and what doesn't. Or what I can get away with and what I can't. What it comes down to is *he* can't get away with this, and that's *his* problem."

She smiles in answer.

"As for whether you were wrong . . . Hell, I'm a sociopath, and I can tell what's *most* wrong was him paying a child so he could rape her. I mean . . . Jesus. If you think about it, your filming it was really just self-defense, wasn't it?"

Her smile thins into a sneaky little grin. "You sure could say that."

"If we can keep your identity and face out of this, then maybe it's usable collateral. But I'm not getting within ten feet of any device with that video on it. I can't see or know. But if I were giving you advice . . ."

"Yeah?"

"This is just hypothetical."

"Okay."

I bob my chin in her direction. "Put your phone on the table and turn it off."

"Why?" she asks with so much wide-eyed innocence that I know she knows exactly why. But she takes out her phone and powers it down, so I proceed.

I cross my arms on the table and lower my voice. "You know it's illegal to blackmail people, right? What you've been doing is a crime."

"Yes, I know that," she says.

"Okay. But there is nuance here and you can work with that. If you were, for example, to send a file to the lieutenant governor's office, a file that has been edited carefully to keep your face out of it, that could be used as leverage. Not to blackmail or extort, but as a guarantee of your safety. You could include a sad explanation that the poor girl in the video shouldn't be victimized again by having the unedited tape go public. Make clear that no one wants that and the victim should be protected. His people will understand that it's a threat without you having to make a threat or ask for money."

"So I send it to his office anonymously to let them know they need to back off."

"Yes. But . . ." I hesitate for a moment, considering what I'm about to say. Inserting myself into this could put me in danger, but I want to see this man. To look him in the face and let him know that I've beat him at his game. Not the little pervert Roy Morris, but his powerful brother. The muscle and money. The rush of it flows into my blood.

I smile. "I could follow up with a visit to the good lieutenant governor to explain that you're an underprivileged little girl who lives in a trailer with her grandparents, and if any tape goes public, you would be revictimized and many criminal charges would be filed. It would be less a threat and more a courtesy to him, really."

"Hm. I won't get any money, though."

"No. But you won't get dead either. We have to go back to that county to start the court process moving. He could stop it if he wanted to, or he could hire someone to shoot you dead on the highway out of town."

"True." She's quiet as I accept the check from our server, but then she nods. "I'll think about it."

"Thanks for taking it under consideration," I say dryly as I open the bill portfolio.

When I get out my credit card, I notice her gaze slide to the receipt total to take it in. She wants to know exactly what kind of lifestyle she's buying for herself with this little deal between us. More signs of intelligence.

"Do you really know how to cover your tracks online?" I ask.

She nods. "It's no problem."

"All right, then." I snap the portfolio closed and slide it to the edge of the table. "We might have ourselves a plan."

CHAPTER 20

Kayla is settled on the pullout couch in the living room of the suite with blankets and fluffy pillows and, most important of all, the television remote. When I leave her, she's holding up her newly painted nails and admiring them in the blue light of the TV.

She's uploaded a very short clip to a password-protected server on the dark web, and she assures me that her face isn't visible but Roy Morris's is. I've left that decision up to her. Despite what she thinks, I don't want to be anyone's mom. More to the point, I'm not capable of it.

We've decided to write the IP address and password on a little card and hand it off to the lieutenant governor as entrée into his office. That will give him less time to come up with a counter-scheme to cut us off at the knees. I imagine he'll be quite interested in seeing me as soon as he spots his brother in flagrante. I chuckle softly at the thought. I can't wait to see his face.

After shutting the bedroom door behind me, I climb onto my big bed to call Luke. I can manipulate him into accepting Kayla's relocation, but there's no urgency, really. If he doesn't say yes now, he will eventually. I'm more than willing to use intense persuasion and the very shallow well of patience I possess. And honestly, Luke is too kind to say no.

You up? I text to Luke.

When he sends back an excited little smiley face, I hit the call button and listen to barely one full ring before he answers. "Hey there, sexy," I drawl.

"Hey, yourself. What's going on? I've been dying to talk to you all day. Is Kayla doing okay? Are you?"

"Yes, we're both great, to be honest. I took her shopping. Got her hair cut. That kind of thing. She was in pretty rough shape." I mean, she was fine, but let's face it, her cuticles were a mess.

"Oh, wow. Is she . . . Jeez, Jane. Is she *all right?*"

"I think she'll be all right with a lot of care and a little security, but it will take time, you know?"

"Yeah. I do. She needs peace and support. Did you figure out what happened to her? Where she's been?"

I sigh and stretch out on the huge pile of brocade pillows. They're a little scratchy, but I still feel like a beautiful princess. "This has all been so crazy, Luke. A whirlwind. Pathologically independent as I am, I almost wish you were here."

"Aw, that's the sweetest thing you've ever said to me." We both laugh at that. He knows I'll never be a sweet girlfriend, and he doesn't care. He likes that I don't demand much. I don't *need* anything from him. Not really. I just *want*.

In some ways, Luke is as damaged as I am, but the jagged edges of our broken parts fit together nicely. He wants icy calm, and I'm incapable of providing much else. Except, of course, when I'm ready to stir things up.

"She's a lot like me," I say on a sigh. "Same family, of course. Same issues. And she's very smart. Very capable."

"I bet."

"But no one is looking out for her here." I toe off my boots and let them thump onto the floor. "She got mixed up with that pimp, an older guy, and he got into trouble, and he basically took off with her. She's been sitting in an empty house, doing whatever he told her to do."

"That's where you found her?"

"Yeah. I tracked down the guy and offered to just . . . buy her back from him."

"Jesus."

"It gets worse."

"Oh no. Is she hurt? Is she pregnant?"

"No." I hope not. "No, it's not that. The guy. Her pimp . . ."

"Little Dog?"

"Yeah. He took off after I called. We think he meant to strike a better deal with a third party, sell Kayla out to someone else. These men trade girls like they're cars. Except he never made it back to Kayla. He was killed. Stabbed to death."

"Okay, Jane. You need to get the hell out of there right now. I'm serious. This is dangerous. Come home now."

"I know it's dangerous. I'm fine, I promise. We left Tulsa this morning. We're in a hotel in Oklahoma City now. No one knows we're here. We're completely safe."

"Maybe I should come down there, then."

I smile at his words, because he really does want to take care of me—and he'll want to take care of Kayla too, because that's the kind of man he is. That's good news. Really good news.

"We're all tucked in for the night," I say soothingly. "Tomorrow we're going to the authorities."

He blows out a long breath, and I can imagine the way he's rubbing his forehead right now. He did the same thing when he heard that his niece had to be rushed to the emergency room with a high fever.

Luke is a good man. I haven't known many of those in my life. To be honest, I haven't known even one before Luke, and I somehow managed to collect him along the way. Lucky me.

"Kayla needs a home," I say simply.

He draws in a breath on the other end of the connection. "Okay. But what does that mean? You're staying there?"

"Here?" I nearly screech. "No. No, that's not what I mean at all! I mean that I'm going to try to get custody and bring Kayla home with me. If I can guide her through the last two years of high school, be a mentor to her, she'll be in a great place to get into college and make something of her life. If she stays here, she doesn't have a chance. These people . . ." I growl instead of ranting about them.

"Oh," Luke says. "I see."

"These people are eating her alive. She has the same challenges with emotion that I have. I know what that's like. I can actually help her, and I can't really say that about too many kids."

"Yeah." The word is a little faint, but then he clears his throat and lets go of his shock. "Well, of course you have to."

"Oh. Of course. I can't just abandon her. That would be wrong."

"Whatever you need from me, you only have to ask. This is going to be a huge change for you."

I explode in a hard laugh. "That's probably the understatement of the year."

"Listen." I can hear him settling in to help already, his voice edging into determination. "She's practically an adult already. And you're her aunt."

"True."

"All she needs is a little bit of support for a couple of years and a nudge in the right direction. You can do that easily. No problem."

"Right. I can do it."

"Absolutely."

In that moment I really do wish I were home with him. I'd even cuddle right into his arms for a few minutes before turning his attention toward sex.

He treats me like I'm real even if I'm not, and sometimes just being near him feels like intimacy. I've always needed sex to access that feeling, and I certainly need it with Luke too, but sometimes, on very special occasions, I feel close to him without it. Right now he wants to make my life less stressful, and even a sociopath can appreciate that.

It's time for the biggest step, and I have to approach carefully. "I'll need a bigger place." I let it sit there for only a moment. "Kayla can't live on my couch for more than a few weeks. That wouldn't be fair. She needs to feel like she has a home."

"Sure," he says faintly.

"But listen, that's not your problem. We'll discuss all those complications when I get home. It's not something I need to figure out now."

"You don't. You have enough on your plate. Don't spend any time worrying about it at all, okay? You just concentrate on Kayla."

I feel another surge of anticipation at the thought of this fun new adventure.

"What will you have to go through to get her moved?" Luke asks.

"I looked into it," I say. "If she were in foster care, it would get complicated. Tons of paperwork and court hearings and agreements between the states. But on first glance it looks like her mom can give me temporary guardianship, especially if Kayla agrees. All I have to do is get everyone to buy into the idea that Kayla belongs with me."

His chuckle is warm and soothing. "I'm not sure it will be as simple as you make it seem."

It won't, but I don't mention our planned meeting with Bill Morris. "Eh, the approach is always the same with my family. They'll want to be bought off. We just need to find the right combinations of levers for threats and rewards. Kayla says she can get her mother to agree."

"Stressful," he sighs.

"Yes. But I might be home within a few days if it all works perfectly."

"God, it will be so nice to see you, Jane. My bed is lonely as hell without you."

"Well," I drawl, "I won't be able to spend the night, but I bet I can make a little field trip to your place when I get back. If you don't mind a quickie."

He laughs. "You know I don't."

"Okay. I'll check in tomorrow. And I'll see you soon."

"You'll be great at this," he says.

Yes, I believe I will.

CHAPTER 21

Kayla insists on accompanying me to the lieutenant governor's office, and I'm quite proud. I told her it would be safer for her to stay hidden, but she brushed me off. "Like I'm gonna let you secretly sell me out to this asshole while I eat french fries at a random diner."

Good girl.

In this day of digital menace, her presence won't put her in true jeopardy anyway. The threat she presents won't vanish even if she does. Not at this point. Not with me involved. Roy Morris and his brother have let this go on too long and it's gotten very messy.

Bill Morris's best bet by far is to cut his losses with his loser brother and wash his hands of the whole thing before it gets worse. But privilege comes with a hell of a set of blinders. It's my job to tear those off and let the full picture shine right into his eyeballs.

A visit to the lieutenant governor sounds important and stately, but the Oklahoma senate isn't in session, so it really just means a trip to a downtown Oklahoma City office building where Bill Morris runs his drilling company. There are no marble halls or bas-reliefs here, just gray carpeting and an elevator ride to the ninth floor.

The internet says the lieutenant governor earns more than $100,000 a year to serve as president of the state senate and fulfill "other duties assigned by the governor." The senate meets for only a few months a year, so that's nice work if you can get it.

Kayla is padding along in her sparkly flip-flops beside me, but she's not wearing short shorts or a fancy new blouse today. Instead we stopped to buy a new outfit: a frumpy knee-length skirt and a yellow T-shirt with a unicorn on it. She looks frail and young, especially with her edgy new haircut hidden by uneven French braids that cause her ears to stick out from her narrow head.

She smiles shyly when we approach the receptionist's desk.

"Hello," I say quietly, "we have an appointment with Lieutenant Governor Morris."

The white woman with the short gray haircut maintains her polite smile but shakes her head. "I'm afraid I don't have any appointments on the schedule today, Ms. . . . ?"

"He told us to drop by today, and I rearranged my schedule for this visit. I'm sure he's just forgotten. If you could give him my card, he'll remember."

"I . . . I suppose that would be okay. Please have a seat. I'll be just a moment."

I hand over my business card, which identifies me as an attorney with a law firm in Minneapolis. The card on which I've written the IP address is tucked just behind it.

Kayla and I take seats on two leather armchairs, and I grab a fancy architecture magazine to flip through.

"He's on the phone," the woman says when she returns to her desk, "but I left your card with him."

"Thank you."

I take the time to reach out to the partners of my law firm with an ingratiating email answering a few questions about Rob's cases that I've seen floating around in group emails. Kayla plays a game on her phone and swings her feet until one of her sandals flies off and she has to retrieve it. I smile indulgently, then aim a lovingly exasperated eye roll at the receptionist. She laughs quietly.

About ten minutes later she perks up with a start. "Oh! He can see you now. Would you like to wait here, young lady? I can find you a Coke somewhere."

Kayla gives a quick shake of her head and darts to my side to hold my hand.

"She'll come with me," I say, clutching her little hand tightly, and we follow the woman down a long hallway toward a closed maple-wood door.

"Mr. Morris," she says as she sweeps open the door to let us in. Kayla stays glued to my side as we enter, her pale hand holding tight.

"Hello, Bill," I say darkly, giving the woman something to gossip about later. I'm on a first-name basis with him and I'm bringing a child along for a mysterious personal appointment? *Oh, Bill Morris, what have you done?*

The man tries to keep his glower aimed at my face, but his eyes can't help a few darts toward Kayla.

"It's okay," I say softly as I lead her over to one of the chairs. "Sit down. You'll be fine."

She makes a show of letting go of me reluctantly before she takes a seat, scooting back too far in the chair so that her sandals dangle above the ground.

I take my own seat and cross my legs as the receptionist draws the door slowly closed behind her.

"What the hell is this filth?" Bill Morris growls, slapping the card down on his desk.

"I wouldn't know, Mr. Morris," I answer. "It's illegal to even view that kind of content, as I'm sure you understand."

"I had no idea what I was looking at!"

"This is Kayla," I say, gesturing toward the pale girl with her head bent in shame. "Did your brother explain exactly what he was getting

227

you into when he asked for help further terrorizing my niece after sexually abusing her?"

"Your niece." He's still angry, his eyes shaded by a cliff of furious brow, but the words come out as a resigned statement instead of a question.

"Yes. Kayla is my niece, and she was fifteen years old when she . . . *encountered* your sick brother. Since then she's been stalked by a bald man in an SUV who I believe is in your employ, and that same man assaulted her childhood friend Brodie. Did you know that Brodie was found murdered two days ago? Because I find that very interesting."

He blinks hard and sits back a little in his huge leather chair. "Excuse me?"

"He didn't tell you?"

"Who didn't tell me? I have no idea what you're talking about."

"Why don't you call up your brother and ask him about Brodie, then? He might know him as Little Dog."

"Ms.—"

"Sir, I've worked overseas helping victims of sex trafficking, and I never thought I'd come home to find that my own little niece has been victimized by the same type of monster I fought so hard against in other countries. I assure you that I have taken steps to protect this child, and those steps include storing the proof of this assault in several different safe places, both online and in multiple secure locations with instructions on how to proceed if anything happens to us. This problem will not go away no matter the threats of violence. Kayla is not alone anymore. She's not the helpless child she was a month ago."

Kayla sighs and reaches out to touch my hand. I grasp her fingers briefly before she slumps back in on herself. This girl is a master actress, and I have to fight not to let my mouth lift in amusement.

Morris crosses his arms on the table and studies me for a long moment. "And yet you're here in my office. You haven't gone to the police." I see his eyes dart down to the phone on his desk. I imagine he's recording this, hoping I'll make an extortion attempt.

"To what end?" I ask. "I have no idea how far your tentacles reach. The only guarantee of consequences to your brother would be making this public, and that would further damage a vulnerable child."

"I see. So you're not going to the authorities."

"Not yet."

"Right. So how much do you want?"

"How dare you?" I snap. "How dare you treat this as some seedy financial matter! I'm an attorney and an aunt and a decent human being. But, considering your family, maybe you've never encountered one of those before and have no idea how to interact with one."

His confidence has finally slipped a notch. I watch his shoulders drop and I pounce.

"Your brother is a pervert and a danger to the community. If I had any hope at all that we'd find justice, I'd see this through. But look at you, still treating my niece as if she's the cause of this instead of your predatory, rapist, pedophile brother!"

"I didn't—"

"You most certainly did. We don't want your tainted rape money, Mr. Morris. I want your brother to get extensive treatment and my niece wants to get the hell out of this state to somewhere safe. A boy is dead! Do you understand that? My niece might have been murdered already if I hadn't been the one to find her."

"I don't know anything about that. And I can't force my brother to—"

"Oh, you can make your brother do whatever you want. Don't feed me that bull. Your specialty in life is pulling strings. Chair of the state board of development, head of the council on economic growth, a member of the insurance council. You've got more strands to pull than a spider, and you use them to devour everything you can. Try using your power for good just this once."

When I go quiet, I can hear him swallow even from ten feet away. "I'm not a bad man, and I am certainly not my brother's keeper. I don't know anything about this death you mentioned. But I will try to direct Roy into treatment. He has trouble with alcohol and it causes him to . . ." His gaze darts toward Kayla and then back to me. "To act out."

This time I'm the one to reach for Kayla's hand. I grasp it in mine and nod. "My niece has been traumatized, and I want to help her leave this violation behind her and get a good education. I have reason to believe her mother will agree to a change of guardianship, but there will still be a hell of a lot of red tape to work through. All I ask is that you call off your attack dogs and do what you can to help us leave. It will be good for everyone to get Kayla into a new environment."

His eyes narrow. "That's all that you want?"

"Yes. I'm not here to blackmail you. I'm here to ask you to do the right thing, if you know what that is."

"And the . . . evidence?"

I shrug. "There's nothing to be done about that. There's no physical tape I can turn over. No proof that it's really gone. The best you can do, Mr. Morris, is distance yourself from your brother in every way possible. Reject him. Let him sink or swim on his own. If you do that, then his criminal evidence has no hold over you, because your future isn't tied to his. You won't have anything to worry about."

He uncrosses his arms and presses his hands flat to the desk. "So you can't give me any assurance that this won't come out."

I lean forward and let him see the natural darkness in my eyes. "Let me make something clear. You are not the victim in this situation, and I'm not here to assure you about anything. *You* don't need protection. *You* are not the one who has been damaged. What I'm giving you is the opportunity to do right by a young girl who was raped by your brother and further victimized by your support for her rapist. You will get no reassurance, and I have put automatic safeguards in place in case of any further malfeasance on your part, and I promise those protections are airtight and legal. Is that reassuring enough to you, Mr. Morris?"

"Yes. Yes, it is." He says the right thing, but he's angry again, backed into a corner and hating it. But that's fine. He can hate it as much as he wants as long as he understands that I hold the power here.

"And those strings we spoke about?" I press.

He clears his throat and I see him set his anger aside. He's a businessman, and this is business now. "I'll do what I can to make sure your application for guardianship is expedited."

"And you'll call off your dogs?"

His jaw clenches. Clenches again. "I'll speak to my brother and make sure there is no further contact of any kind. *If* he was the one responsible."

He's too smart to admit he was involved, and I can respect that, so I dip my head. "If anything happens to me or to Kayla, this will not work out well for anyone."

"I understand."

"Good. I hope your brother gets the help he needs."

It's his turn to incline his head.

I stand and tug Kayla up too. She keeps her head down as we exit, her sandals slapping against the floor. My neck prickles, my animal senses warning me that Bill Morris is watching from his desk.

He can watch all he wants, but there's no good way to solve the problem his brother has dropped at his doorstep like a decomposing rat. If they'd gotten to Kayla while she was alone, maybe. But now she's got me.

I'm grinning widely as I wave goodbye to the receptionist and step onto the elevator.

Kayla jerks her hand away. "We could've gotten so much money from him!"

"He's a politician, Kayla. If we pushed him too far, he would have turned us in to the cops for blackmail and painted himself as an innocent victim in his brother's crimes. Then he probably would have started a task force against child exploitation while we were still waiting for a trial."

"Whatever," she snaps.

"You've still got the recording. Do whatever you want when you're eighteen."

"I can do whatever I want right now."

"Not if you want to get out of this place. You start throwing that video around and you're on your own. I'm not going down in flames so you can score five thousand dollars and a permanent audience on the dark web. I have a law license to protect, and you *might* have a future if you listen and learn. *Might.*"

Rolling her eyes, she pops a piece of grape bubblegum into her mouth.

"You were amazing back there," I say, and that brightens her expression.

"Yeah?"

"Great acting."

"Thanks."

"You should try out for the school play."

"Dumb," she answers, but her anger is gone, smoothed out by praise. I know what a little girl like her wants. Praise and admiration. I know because I want the same and I always have.

She blows a purple bubble. "If his guys try to grab us on the way to the car, you're on your own. I'm quicker." She flashes me a mean, narrow look, but I smile. Then I giggle. Then I'm laughing so hard, I have to hold myself up on the elevator rail.

"Weirdo," she mutters, but I don't mind. She likes me.

CHAPTER 22

I completely forgot about dealing with the police.

With Kayla reported as a missing child, there were interviews and written reports and talk of child neglect charges for her mother. There was even a murmur of charging Kayla with truancy, but I shut that down.

They spent so little time looking into her disappearance that they never even connected her to Brodie, so there are no questions about his death. I assume they don't care about him at all either. I wonder who his house will go to now.

Kayla and I made up a much more palatable story to tell the authorities, of course. Something about her hitchhiking and then living on the street for a while. The intense questioning about her circumstances did help move her mother's decision along. The woman was eager to assign me temporary guardianship by the end of that first day and wash her hands of the entire situation. A true case of parental devotion.

Permanent guardianship will take longer, but we've greased those wheels. A judge immediately approved Kayla's voluntary move to Minnesota, expressing gratitude that an attorney was taking this troubled girl under her wing.

A temporary situation is better for the two of us regardless. She'll be slightly more malleable if there's a chance she could easily lose all her new luxuries. And with a budding little sociopath, malleable is better.

It's our third day back in the boonies, and there's been no sign of trouble. We could still be gunned down on the highway back to Oklahoma City, but my hunch is that Bill Morris decided to take my deal. The emergency hearing with the judge came through suspiciously quickly.

We've got one last stop before we head to the city to catch a flight. That's right. It's time to say goodbye to Grandma and Grandpa!

That's a joke, of course. Kayla wants to pick up the belongings she moved to their trailer. I've advised her to leave that shit behind, but I guess she has some useless crap she wants to drag to Minnesota with her. Fine. I drive her to my parents' place and we both step out into the crunching brown grass.

My mother, ever a lover of drama, rushes out of the trailer as soon as she spots Kayla. "Oh, my baby!" she cries. "I heard you were back!" Today she's wearing baggy white jeans and a pink Hallmark sweatshirt. How apropos for our touching family reunion.

She throws her arms around Kayla, who stands stock-still and waits for it to be over. "My sweet little Kayla! Where have you been?"

"Mom, there are no cameras or social workers here. Cut the crap already."

She snarls like a vicious dog over Kayla's shoulder before letting her go. "Look at these fancy-ass clothes," she says in a sharp whine.

"Yeah, they're great," Kayla answers.

"Go on and get settled in," my mom says. "I put a few things in your room, but you can just shove those boxes out of the way, no problem."

"She's coming home with me, Mom. Seriously, cut it out."

The kindly grandmother act falls from her face for good now, and she swings around to glare at me. "What are you yapping about?"

I wave her off wearily as Kayla slips past her grandmother to bang through the metal storm door.

"You can't take my granddaughter away; I only just got her back."

I glance around with huge eyes. "Seriously, who are you playacting for? There's no one else here, and I heard all the shit you talked about Kayla the first time I dropped by."

"I have custody, and you need my permission to take her out of state no matter how high and mighty you think you are, and I'm not giving it."

Permission. What she means is that she wants money; she always wants money, and she's not smart or steady enough to work me for it. All she can ever do is lash out and attack, because she resents having to beg for what she wants.

I used to send money sometimes. I used to do it because my best friend told me I should. "They're your family," she'd insist. "The only family you'll ever have." True, thank God. And Meg was the only conscience I ever had, but she's dead now, so Mom is out of luck.

They raised me, yes. But puppy mills raise animals too, offering paltry shelter and shitty food, just enough to keep them alive, and no one ever thinks the owners of those places are owed any love. I have no idea why it's supposed to be different with parents.

"You don't have custody, Mom. She was crashing here and you were charging her rent. We've already worked all this out with Kayla's mother."

"You're a liar just like you always have been."

"I'd show you the signed court document, but I honestly don't care that much. Kayla is getting her stuff and we're leaving."

Mom's face is drawing tight and desperate now. As much as she hated me, she always wanted me under her control and in her orbit. She's pulling the same thing with Kayla now. "I held her room for her! I stored all her clothes! Someone needs to pay for that."

"No one is giving you any more money, Mom. Least of all me. Maybe you can con some of your other grandchildren, but I'll warn Joylene about you, at least. God knows how many others there are at this point."

"You listen here, you little—"

"No, *you* listen. I didn't even tell Kayla that you gave Little Dog's name to that thug. She doesn't know about that. Do you want me to tell her?"

Her face twists, freezing in an ugly mask for a moment before she smooths it out into helplessness. "I didn't know he was dangerous."

"That boy is dead, by the way, so your judgment is hopelessly skewed. You'd better drop it right now, lady."

Miraculously, she does. She takes two short steps to the trailer, then glances to me as if she's worried I'll steal everything if she turns her back. I'm not even sure what she's going to try to pull with Kayla, but I remember now how she tried to sabotage my escape to college. She threw away letters from Minnesota. Told me she got a call that I'd been rejected after all.

Some sort of fear of abandonment, maybe. Who cares?

My eye catches one last time on that crack in my old bedroom window. I remember the rage behind it. The bloodlust.

"What was his name?" I ask.

"What?" my mom asks, her hands fluttering. "Who?"

"That man. Your boarder. He told me to call him Uncle Pete, but he wasn't related to anyone I know. What was his name?" Maybe I'll look him up. Maybe he's still around. He seemed old at the time, but fifty could have been ancient to a little girl. He could very well be alive and kicking.

"*Pete?*" She scowls. "I don't know. Low? Lowell? Something like that. Haven't seen him around in years."

"Maybe he was sent to jail for raping little girls, Mom."

236

"Oh Lord," she mutters. "You keep that filth to yourself. Climbing all over that man like he was your daddy."

My filth. The filth of a seven-year-old girl who just wanted to be safe and warm. Monster that I am, they're lucky I didn't burn them all alive in that goddamn trailer.

I cock my head because . . . I still could. I stare at that window, which I cracked in that rage tantrum when I was ten because I hated everyone. It wasn't my fist. I'm not that self-sacrificing. It was my brother's stupid remote control for his stupid toy truck that he'd run straight into my back on Christmas morning.

My parents had told me they didn't have money for gifts and I was a nasty little bitch anyway. All I'd gotten was a set of cheap flavored lip gloss and a fake Barbie doll from the thrift store. My teenage brother, on the other hand, got the exact remote-control monster truck he'd wanted.

He ran it into me all day long, leaving bruises on my legs and back. Then he offered to let me "play with it" while pointing at his crotch. "Five minutes for five minutes." My mother just laughed.

The minute he went outside to sneak a cigarette, I stole the remote and threw it at the wall hard enough to break it. Then I threw it again. And again. Until it finally ricocheted off the window with a satisfying snap. At the time, I wished I'd cracked his head instead of the glass. I still do. I wish I'd cracked them all open.

That old trailer is packed with trash and could easily ignite and spread flames to the brand-new trailer next to it, still stinking of flammable chemicals. Spread to the elderly woman inside and her stroke-victim husband, unable to navigate out in the smoke and heat. A clean slate. For me and Kayla and the rest of the goddamn world who've been subjected to these people for almost seventy years.

But no.

Not worth it. I have a real life now. A gorgeous condo and a beautiful cat and a new car and a niece full of promise, not to mention a successful boyfriend who wants more. The fucking American dream. Everything my mother will never have.

So when Kayla emerges with a duffel bag packed with belongings, I leave my mother behind, still screeching and cursing about what I owe her. I leave her behind because I don't owe her shit except revenge, and she's not even worth that anymore.

CHAPTER 23

I watch her like I'm bingeing a fascinating new television show. She changes personality with her wardrobe. Today Kayla is wearing her traveling outfit: sleek black jean leggings and a stylishly slashed pink T-shirt. The girl is already hooked on shopping, but I've made it clear she'll be getting a job soon to cover some of those costs.

"A real job," I cautioned, and she smiled sweetly. Lord save me from the machinations of a child monster.

She's softened the twang of her accent as if she's a wealthy Dallas teenager who's accustomed to plane rides and airport smoothies, but I see her wide eyes. All the wonder of a five-year-old with none of the innocence.

"This is business class," I explain as we board the plane and find our seats.

"Not first?"

"First class is something you can discover on your own dime. I think these seats should be sufficiently comfortable for your narrow ass."

She shoots a squint toward the leather seats in front of us. "I thought they were going to be cool capsules anyway. Those just look like Grandpa's ugly recliner."

"You've seen too many commercials," I mutter, but she's already ignoring me to poke around on the in-flight entertainment system. I feel like a real mom now.

Just kidding. This is much easier to do without guilt or worry. As soon as we're in the air, I get out my laptop and get some work done on my new cases. I can't wait to be back in the office, kicking some ass. It's a new Rob-free era, and I'm ready to shine!

She maintains her air of boredom as we rise into the sky. When the flight attendant comes by, Kayla orders a Coke, then demands all three snacks when offered a choice. I feel tingles of affection when the woman grudgingly hands Kayla peanuts, pretzels, *and* a granola bar. Finally, someone I can actually relate to.

Ninety minutes later, I reach past Kayla to open the window shade. "Look down," I say.

"Huh. What's all that water? Flooding?"

"Land of Ten Thousand Lakes."

She looks at me blankly.

"That's what Minnesota is called. The Land of Ten Thousand Lakes. You'll like it."

"Whatever," she says, but I notice her sneaking looks out the window as we turn into the descent. It's new and different, and that will be enough to keep her interest for a little while. Then there will be a new house, a new school, new people. This should be easy.

"Do I really have to sleep on the couch?" she asks suddenly.

"Just for a few weeks. I'll find a new place."

"I could take your bed and you could stay with your boyfriend. I'll be fine."

"Sure, invite over anyone you want and trash the place."

"I'd be good," she promises with big eyes.

"Girl, please."

"I need privacy." Her voice rises a little. "I don't even know you! You could be taking me out of state to traffic me! I've seen *Dateline!*"

I notice the woman in the next seat stiffen and turn toward us, so I pitch my voice higher too. "I know you're scared, and this will be hard, but you'll get the treatment you need at the institution and they'll make sure you don't start any more fires, Kayla. We can't bring your parents back, but we can make sure you don't hurt anyone else."

Kayla stares at me. I stare back. Finally, she breaks into loud laughter and I join in. This girl.

"Don't try that again," I warn, and she gives me a thumbs-up. Teenagers like to test boundaries. Even I know that.

"I don't expect you to be normal," I say more quietly. "I'd be disappointed if you were. Believe it or not, we can be friends."

She snorts in scorn.

"I'm like you," I say with less patience now. "That's important."

"We'll see."

I take a deep breath and remind myself that I don't trust people either. It's the only smart way to get through life. "Yes," I say. "We'll see." I can be patient for a month or two. Probably. Maybe. She'll learn to trust me. And then we'll have each other.

We're off the plane and walking into the baggage claim area when I spot him. Luke.

He's holding two bouquets of flowers and a stupid balloon that says "Welcome Home!" What an idiot. He spots me, his worried mouth flashing into a happy grin, and I feel it. I *feel* it. A tiny bubble of pure joy that rises up unexpectedly in my chest.

I'm relieved he's here. I'm happy to see him. And it's not even about sex.

"Jane!" he calls out, as if I weren't looking straight at him. What an adorable dork.

Rushing toward us, he hands me a bouquet of gorgeous dark-red dahlias, and if that isn't the perfect flower for me, I don't know what is. Kayla, on the other hand, is handed a bouquet of brightly colored gerbera daisies, and I laugh in delight at the mismatch with her mean personality. She scowls down at her gift.

241

"Kayla, I'm Luke. It's so great to finally meet you."

"Yeah." When I narrow my eyes in warning, she tries again. "Great! Hi, Uncle Luke!"

His smile twitches the tiniest bit, but he nods. "How was the trip?"

I shift my flowers to the other hand and put my arm around Kayla. "It was Kayla's first plane ride."

"Exciting!" he says cheerily.

"Yeah," she responds. "Supercool."

I turn her slightly toward the baggage area. "Kayla, why don't you go wait for your bag. It's baggage claim three."

"Whatever you want, Auntie Jane." She smacks her gum and flip-flops off toward the crowd.

Turning back to Luke, I raise my eyebrows high. "A balloon and everything?"

"Don't make fun of me," he scolds, but he's grinning past his blush. "Never."

"It's so good to see you." And then he hugs me. A huge hug, pulling me tight into his arms, and for once I don't pull immediately away.

I like taking care of shit, and I'm good at it. I like being in complete control. But it doesn't hurt to know that someone could take care of me if I needed it, especially because I know I won't need it.

He loves me. And I want to keep him, so maybe I truly love him too. After all, other people can be selfish and mean and do terrible things, and that doesn't mean they can't feel love.

Am I so different?

"She's kind of a handful," I say into his chest.

"It's okay. You'll figure it out." Then he pulls back and looks down at me. "*We'll* figure it out. Together."

Together. I've never had that. Even when my best friend was alive, we both knew that any plans made could be broken up by the arrival of the right man, whether that was a cab ride home for a quick lay or a long-term relationship arriving to mess up a lease. But Luke says we'll figure it out together, and we will.

I was running from that when I left. But now I want it. I want it all.

I want to look at houses with him, pretending I'm the nervous wife and he's the strong husband. He'll try not to laugh when I go on and on about all the baking I'll do for our three kids. He'll blush when I whisper that we need extra space for our "adult playroom" just to watch the real estate agent's reaction. The game will be so much more fun with him than it would be alone.

I'll leave our sullen teenager at home, don't worry. She'll get the house I choose for her, and I don't need her selfish input.

Maybe it can all be fun. Maybe I can play my way through suburbia, carving out exactly the path I want to walk as I teach Kayla what she needs to learn. And maybe, just maybe, my sharp and shriveled heart will be enough.

CHAPTER 24

"Are you settled in?" I ask, standing in the doorway of Kayla's new bedroom in my new house.

"I think I'll survive," she says flatly.

It's our first night here, though we spent a little time hanging around the empty rooms this past week, planning out colors and furniture. She chose gray walls with purple accents, along with a matte-black four-poster bed that looks like it belongs in a modern high-rise apartment, especially with the white comforter and piles of accent pillows. I would've killed for a room like this at her age.

She's put one thing up on the wall: a poster of Harley Quinn from some Batman movie. Her few moving boxes are still piled in a corner near the closet. I assume she'll be living out of them for a while, because she hasn't touched them in the three hours she's been holed up in here.

It's a small house, not in the suburbs after all, but in a nice part of the city with a great high school. I stroll over to look out her window, but there's not much of a view this time of year. A fence shaded by the neighbor's evergreen, but the maple trees are bare.

Her bedroom is near the kitchen, toward the front of the house. Our master bedroom, added in a renovation to the tiny 1940s home, is at the back of the house, well away from her prying eyes and ears.

The house is mine, though Luke is here too. We decided I should be the one to buy, since I'm the one with a family to raise. I'm not charging Luke rent or anything. He's my boyfriend, after all. He considered renting out his condo in St. Paul, but in the end he sold it. I'm glad he did. I don't like the idea of him having an easy out. I want him here.

I did keep him in mind when choosing my home. He really likes this neighborhood, and his brother's house is only a five-minute drive away, so he can see his little niece anytime.

Don't worry. I've made it absolutely clear that Kayla is not to be asked to babysit. That kind of trouble is the last thing I need. It's been rough enough finally getting her settled into school. She accidentally tested into advanced math before she realized she should have thrown the test. Poor baby. She's smarter than she wants to be.

She's also really hating Spanish class, but the counselor insisted that a language is essential for those "on the college track." Kayla fought it, but there she is in Spanish class anyway, being actively resentful. The instructor is a man, so I'll have to keep an eye on things so it doesn't go off the rails. Otherwise she's in all the normal classes, though woodshop seems like it will turn out to be a mistake. I'd hate to see this girl around power tools.

Overall, the past month has been . . . dare I say nice? As if to support that characterization, my cat hops onto the windowsill in front of me and purrs, gazing out at the world beyond the glass along with me. She's in cat heaven with empty boxes everywhere, so I think she's enjoying the new family situation too.

I take a moment to scratch her chin before glancing back toward Kayla.

It *has* been nice. I'm sure of it. She plays along with my cozy relationship with Luke, sending me secret smiles when he's turned away. She doesn't give a damn about him, of course, but she's mostly polite or at least tolerant.

Luke, on the other hand, is over-the-top friendly with her, like a friend's dad from a sitcom. It's funny to watch. He's adorably eager and he's doing his best. So am I, honestly, though I don't have to try too hard. Kayla is fine. And she's smart. And I'm a sociopath. I just don't worry about much.

Work is going great, of course. I swooped back into town just in time to catch a few of Rob's biggest dropped balls, and I became a feel-good story around the office! The partners are impressed. I haven't even had to cut back my hours, because the new addition to my family is basically self-sufficient. This is the kind of parenting that management can believe in.

As of Friday, Kayla hasn't started any fights at school or stolen anything that I know of, but her phone is already buzzing with texts from boys. I understand the excitement. It's only smart for her to take advantage of being the new girl in town.

"I'm going over to Omar's later," she says. "We're going to study."

"Oh, for God's sake, Kayla. It's Saturday night. Cut the bull."

She stares for one full second before she breaks into a cold grin that makes me laugh. "Fine, we're going to Netflix and chill."

"Good Lord." I roll my eyes. "You got your Depo shot. Just make sure not to catch anything that will kill you."

"That's an excellent plan, Aunt Jane," she trills.

I drop onto her bed, setting her bouncing just a little. These foam mattresses aren't as fun as the old springy ones. "I've told you that you don't have to lie to me. Don't you believe me yet?"

Shrugging, she keeps scrolling through something on her phone. "You've been cool so far."

"I understand you," I try again. It's been over a month and we've only made a little progress. I need her to trust me or this won't be exciting at all. It will just be a normal "My teenager is an asshole" relationship, and who the hell wants that?

I nudge her bare foot, the nails now painted purple. "We don't have to keep things from each other that other people wouldn't get. I know how you feel inside. I've been keeping those thoughts secret my whole life because no one else thought like I did."

"Oh yeah?" She finally sets down her phone and meets my gaze. "Secrets like what?"

I should have anticipated this. Even normal humans expect tit for tat in trusting relationships, and Kayla and I are much more transactional than others. Now she's presented me with a problem, and she knows exactly what she's doing.

If I'm honest with her, she'll have leverage. If I don't make myself vulnerable, she won't give me anything at all. It makes perfect sense, of course, and that makes me want her trust even more, the little monster. I decide to give a little.

"I got a man fired from my office recently."

"Who?"

"A fellow lawyer."

"You got him fired on purpose?"

"Yes. He kept taking credit for my hard work. And then he lied about me to a client because he'd dropped the ball on something."

"How did you get him fired?"

"I logged into his work email and sent a sensitive document to the wrong people. They blamed him, of course, so he's gone now. And I'm in charge of his cases."

Her eyes crinkle into a real smile. "That's cool."

"It *is* cool, and he deserved it."

"Fuck him," she agrees.

"Thanks."

"So . . ." She pulls her knees to her chest and points her purple toes. "You believe in revenge."

"Absolutely."

"Have you ever killed someone?"

I pause and think. She's obviously still concerned that I'm grooming her for a *Dexter*-type situation, and luckily I can reassure her that I'm not. "No. I've never killed anyone."

"Because you think it's wrong."

"Not really. I've explained that I'm not good at morality, right?"

"Sure." She nods, but her mouth has gone flat again, closing up tight.

"Listen. I like my life the way it is, and I don't want to risk going to prison for fifty years. I don't think that killing is always wrong, but I am sure it will usually get you into trouble. Are you worried I'm going to kill you or something?"

"No."

"Do you think I brought you here to train you to become the perfect assassin and unleash you on the world?"

"No, but cool job."

"All right. Then if we're talking about morality and honesty . . . sure, I've wanted to kill someone before. I came close to it, actually. There was a man who really deserved to die, and I wanted to kill him, but I didn't. Because it didn't make sense for me. It wasn't smart."

"How were you going to kill him?"

"Knife, gun, whatever. I didn't care about the method. I had a couple of different opportunities, but I let them pass."

She cocks her head. "If you didn't kill him, what did you do to him instead?"

Aha. She does understand. I smile with pride at her perceptiveness. "What makes you think I didn't let him go unmolested?"

"Why would you?"

This is exactly the certainty I've always felt in life and no one else seems able to comprehend. He was bad to me, so he had to pay. What else could I have done?

I wiggle my eyebrows. "I used some recordings to ruin his life and his family's life. Sort of like you." I tickle her foot and she giggles. "See,

Kayla? We're alike, you and I. I can help you. Before you get yourself into trouble, or even after, just come to me and I won't judge you."

"You're sure?"

"I'm sure. So have fun with Omar and don't get into trouble. Okay?"

"Okay."

I pat her leg awkwardly and get up to leave, but her suddenly small voice stops me in my tracks.

"Did the police ever interview you about Little Dog?"

"No. I guess Nate didn't rat me out after all. I never got an inquiry about my contact with him. Why?"

She shrugs.

"Have they been in touch with you?" I ask.

"No. I just wanted to be sure."

Now I am frozen. The hairs on the back of my neck rise up. "Kayla? Why are you asking about Little Dog now?"

She shrugs, her fingers picking at some random thread on her new comforter. But I watch the corners of her mouth tighten, then turn up irresistibly. "Unlike you," she says softly, "I *have* killed someone, Aunt Jane."

"Oh?" I respond very carefully.

She can't resist meeting my eyes. She's too proud. "I heard him take that call with you. He thought I wasn't listening, but I was."

"Who?"

"Little Dog."

My heart pauses for the briefest moment, startling me with a sensation I've never felt before. "Little Dog?"

"Yeah. Then he made another call. He was planning to drop me off somewhere. Meet with that bald guy and turn me over. A few minutes later he tiptoes into my room to wake me up. 'Kayla, come on. We're supposed to meet your aunt in Enid.' You weren't going to meet me in Enid, were you, Aunt Jane?"

249

I shake my head. "No. No, I wasn't."

"So I got in the car with him, asked him to pull over so I could pee . . ."

"In Jenks."

"Yeah. We stopped in Jenks. I surprised him behind the car. You know what happened then. But he deserved it. You get it, right? He should never have tried to screw me over."

"That's true," I agree, keeping my voice low and even.

She smiles. Flips her hair back. "You're really not freaking out."

"No," I lie. "I'm glad you told me."

"Oh my God, I've been dying to tell someone."

"I bet."

"I took care of myself. I planned it so I wouldn't get caught. I even told him why I was doing it while he was curled up there crying like a baby. He couldn't just screw me over that way. An eye for an eye. That's even in the Bible. Fuck him."

I nod as she preens. She's flushed with the excitement of finally getting to boast.

"Thanks for being chill about it, Aunt Jane. I'll let you know when I'm going out."

"Okay. Thank you, Kayla."

As I take a step away, she beams at me. "You were right. I like it here."

"Good. I'm glad." I walk out, checking to make sure my cat has followed me before I close the door to Kayla's room.

The living room is only a few steps away. I join Luke on the couch, dropping down next to him to press my thigh against his. He set up the Wi-Fi first thing, and he's already watching something on Netflix while he takes a break from unpacking.

"Everything good?" he asks.

I take his hand and squeeze it. Then I hold on tight. "Everything's great. She seems fine."

"I think she's happy here," Luke says so softly, I think he's just saying it to himself.

My heart is calm now. My pulse steady. But my mind is churning with sharp spikes, turning over the past few weeks. I'm a sociopath. I don't have regrets and I don't have fear.

But there's now a killer in my pretty new house. And I invited her here.

ABOUT THE AUTHOR

 Victoria Helen Stone, formerly writing as *USA Today* bestselling novelist Victoria Dahl, is originally from the Midwest but now writes from an upstairs office high in the Wasatch Mountains of Utah. After a career in romance that included the American Library Association's prestigious Reading List Award, she turned toward the darker side of fiction and has written the critically acclaimed novels *Evelyn, After; Half Past;* and *False Step*. Her Amazon Charts bestselling thriller *Jane Doe* has been optioned by Sony Television. For more on the author and her work, visit www.VictoriaHelenStone.com.